CHINA
CONQUERS
TAIWAN

TED HALSTEAD

Copyright © 2023 by Ted Halstead

This is a work of fiction. Names, characters, businesses, places, events and incidents are either the products of the author's imagination or used in a fictitious manner. Any resemblance to actual persons, living or dead, or actual events is purely coincidental.

BOOKS BY TED HALSTEAD:

The Second Korean War (2018)
The Saudi-Iranian War (2019)
The End of America's War in Afghanistan (2020)
The End of Russia's War in Ukraine (2020)
The Russian Agents Box Set (2020) - A collection of the four books listed above
The Second Chinese Revolution (2021)
China Invades Taiwan (2021)
The Indo-Pakistani War (2022)

All books, including this one, are set in a fictional near future in which Vladimir Putin is no longer the Russian President. Some events described in these books have happened in the real world, and others have not.

To my wife Saadia, for her love and support over more than thirty years.

To my son Adam, for his love and the highest compliment an author can receive- "You wrote this?"

To my daughter Mariam, for her continued love and encouragement.

To my father Frank, for his love and for repeatedly prodding me to finally finish my first book.

To my mother Shirley, for her love and support.

To my granddaughter Fiona, for always making me smile.

All characters are listed in alphabetical order by nationality on the very last pages, because that's where I think the list is easiest to find for quick reference.

Chapter One

August 1st Building
Beijing, China

Army Commander Shi had deliberately arrived early at the August 1st building's secure conference room for senior officers. As planned, he had preceded the other two commanders for today's discussion of the invasion of Taiwan.

Shi had many problems with the invasion plans in front of him. He wanted a few extra minutes to go over them in his head before discussing them with his fellow commanders.

The Central Military Commission (CMC) was housed in the Ministry of National Defense compound, which everyone called the August 1st building. The date referenced the People's Liberation Army's founding during the 1927 Nanchang Uprising.

The August 1st building was the closest Chinese equivalent to the American Pentagon.

Shi was one of the few enlisted men who had risen through the ranks to become an officer. As a result, he was one of China's oldest generals.

And shortest. When Shi had joined the Army as a tank crewman, there had been a practical reason his height had been an advantage. In those early tanks, there hadn't been much room.

China had come a long way since then, Shi thought.

Air Force Commander Zhao strode in, greeted Shi, and sat without another word.

At a full two meters, Zhao stood out in nearly every gathering.

Zhao was also one of China's youngest generals. Shi found him overconfident to the point of arrogance.

Probably because China's days of overwhelming dependence on Russian equipment, or Chinese copies, were only a memory for Zhao.

Shi didn't admit even to himself that he envied Zhao's height. Besides, it wasn't as though Zhao had done anything to earn it. The China of Zhao's generation had been far more prosperous than Shi's, so his diet had been better. As simple as that.

Anyway, today's show belonged to Admiral Bai, an officer of Shi's generation. If the Navy failed to transport the invasion force to Taiwan, the war would be over before it began.

As though summoned by Shi's thoughts, Bai marched into the conference room and secured its door behind him, to Shi's approval.

Yes. This wasn't a discussion to be shared.

Ignoring Shi and Zhao, Bai walked up to the large-scale map of Taiwan that dominated the front of the room. And stared at it for several moments.

Bai then wheeled around to face Shi and Zhao and waved to the map.

"We have thought about reunification with Taiwan since before I joined the Navy. And we all know how long ago that was," Bai said with an ironic smile.

Shi and Zhao both laughed. Every word was true. Taiwan had been effectively independent since 1949. Nobody serving in China's military had been alive then, let alone on active duty.

"The invasion plans before you have been revised and polished for many years. But no matter how often you polish a turd, its smell remains the same. There is only one way to deal with it," Bai said.

Then Bai reached for his copy of the invasion plan summary, held it up, and tore it into pieces.

"This is the plan our enemy expects. It is not the one we will use," Bai said, his eyes glittering.

"What will you change?" Shi asked.

"We were going to start with a blockade. The advantages seemed obvious. Taiwan is an island dependent on imports by sea for everything from food to energy supplies. But there is a corollary that should have been equally obvious," Bai said. And looked expectantly at both Shi and Zhao.

Who looked at each other, both equally confused.

Bai shook his head. "We are surrounded by unfriendly countries, like Vietnam and the Philippines, or actively hostile ones, like India. Or allied with the Americans, like Japan and Australia. All would be happy to cooperate with an American-led blockade of China if we tried to enforce one on Taiwan."

"Surely that is too pessimistic," Zhao said with a frown. "Would even the Americans dare to sink our merchant ships to enforce such a blockade?"

"They wouldn't need to, and that's one of the many lessons we learned from the stupid Russian decision to invade Ukraine. Four days after they invaded, Turkey announced that only Russian ships already in a Black Sea port would be allowed to transit their country's waters. That meant Russia's Baltic and Pacific fleets were shut out of the war. Not a shot was fired to produce that result," Bai said.

Zhao wasn't convinced. "But there is only one way in and out of the Black Sea. Surely, no other country could effectively blockade us without using force!"

"It would be easy. All the Americans would have to say is that they could not 'guarantee the safety of any merchant ship' within, say, five hundred kilometers of what they'd call the 'Taiwan conflict.' Insurance companies would then drop coverage for any ship going to or coming from China. Our export volumes would plummet, and transport costs skyrocket. Any country that imports Chinese products would look for alternatives. Many countries with lower costs in Southeast Asia and the Indian subcontinent stand ready to provide them," Bai said.

"Fine," Zhao said. "I see the problem now. Is that the only change?"

Bai shook his head. "Just the first. We'd planned to start by taking the Matsu and Penghu Islands while offering the Taiwan regime a chance to negotiate surrender terms. Once again, the Ukraine conflict taught us that would be a mistake."

Now, Shi was the unhappy one. "We're just going to leave those islands sitting in our rear? Isn't that dangerous to our forces? And why not negotiate? Wouldn't we gain sympathy, at least from our friends abroad, for allowing Taiwan to avoid casualties among their civilian population?"

"We can't concern ourselves with world opinion. Most countries will condemn us anyway, just as they condemned the Russians for invading Ukraine. But few of them will lift a finger to help Taiwan, no matter what we do. And look at how long the fighting continued in Ukraine as the Russians nibbled at its southern and eastern edges! Everyone knew as long as the Russians failed to seize Kyiv, the war would drag on," Bai said.

Zhao's eyes widened. "You plan to aim straight for Taipei!"

"Well, that's fine in theory, but Taipei isn't a port," Shi said, waving at the map. "How will you land my troops and equipment? If you do it on a beach, it will take forever. Yes, Taiwan's Army is no match for my forces once I get them onshore. But it's certainly capable of striking a heavy blow against forces slowly unloaded piecemeal. And they can be expected to have a large force guarding their capital," Shi said.

Bai smiled. "The enemy has made a mistake. One that will cost them."

Then Bai used his finger to stab a point on the map of Taiwan's southern coast.

"This is Kaohsiung, by far Taiwan's largest port. And it's on the opposite side of Taiwan from the capital. But Taiwan has been building another port, slowly, over more than a decade. And that one is here," Bai said.

This time, Bai used a black marker to draw a large "X" on a point on the map.

Shi and Zhao could see at once that the point was near Taipei.

"This is Taipei Harbor, also known as the Port of Taipei," Bai said with satisfaction. "Only a tenth of Kaohsiung's cargo volume. But easily capable of handling ships of any size in our fleet. And with a highway that will take our forces to the center of Taipei in less than an hour."

"And no doubt just as well defended as Taipei itself," Shi said.

Zhao looked thoughtful. "We have new hypersonic missiles that could strike those defenders and evade missile defenses thanks to their speed and the ability to vary their course in flight. I now have enough J-20s to wipe Taiwan's F-16s from the sky and then carry out ground attacks."

Shi still looked skeptical. "But don't the Taiwanese have plenty of anti-aircraft missiles? How will you deal with those?"

"I have a plan," Zhao said. "But I must obtain the President's approval to implement it. I will see him soon to do so."

"A plan you won't share with us?" Shi growled.

"No," Zhao said. "I trust you and Admiral Bai. But neither of you has any role in implementing my plan. If it fails, your ships, troops, and vehicles will be unable to advance on Taiwan. It will only fail if the enemy learns of it in advance. No matter how careful they may be, every additional person I tell makes failure more likely."

Shi and Bai exchanged looks, and then both nodded.

But now it was Bai's turn to look unhappy. He turned to Zhao.

"You are right to be so concerned with operational security. The Americans will do everything they can to pierce it. For example, they persist in flying surveillance missions just off our coast, within so-called 'international airspace.' What will you do about that?"

"I will shoot them down," Zhao said.

A single short bark of laughter escaped both Shi and Bai.

"Will you now?" Bai asked with a smile. "And what will the President have to say about that?"

"The President has already approved," Zhao said.

A long silence filled the room while Shi and Bai looked at each other, unable to find the right words to express their deep concern.

Zhao shrugged and said, "Of course, we will deny all responsibility for the disappearance of the American reconnaissance plane. Those planes fly alone. The Americans will be unable to prove we did anything. Admiral Bai, I'm sure your bold new plan for ending the war at a stroke by seizing Taipei has a way to deal with Taiwan's naval defenses."

Bai nodded. "It does. First, our submarine fleet will strike before the enemy is even aware the invasion fleet has left port..."

Chapter Two

U.S. Air Force RC-135U
International Airspace
Off the Chinese Coast

Captain Mark Ross's eyes went reflexively over the cockpit displays. With particular attention to the one telling him the precise location of his U.S. Air Force RC-135U.

Yes, the RC-135U was in international airspace. By at least fifty-five kilometers. And ordinarily, the autopilot could be relied on to keep their reconnaissance aircraft precisely that distance from the People's Republic of China.

But one mistake was all it would take to give the Chinese the excuse they needed to send Ross and his crew to a watery grave.

Today's mission had a larger complement than usual on board. The two pilots, one navigator, and two airborne systems engineers were standard to keep the plane in the air. But today, there were twelve electronic warfare officers and eight mission area specialists instead of the usual ten and six.

There were more personnel because of increased mission taskings. After repeated incidents, RC-135U flights had been stood down for months. But Pacific Command's insatiable appetite for information about Chinese capabilities had only grown during that time.

So here they were. Just as defenseless as RC-135Us had been since their first mission in 1964.

Could F-22s or F-35s have escorted them? In theory, yes. Both were now based at Kadena AFB in Okinawa, right next to the two RC-135Us that were all the U.S. Air Force now had in its inventory. And plenty of tankers could have refueled the fighters while the RC-135U carried out its mission.

There were two reasons the RC-135U flew without a fighter escort.

First, cost. For an escort to be effective, at least two fighters had to be stationed with the RC-135U. The need to refuel meant at least four fighters would be needed.

And then there was the cost of operating the tanker. As well as whether the tanker should have its own fighter escort, which would increase costs again.

It was more important, though, that the Chinese would view fighters flying off their coast as an escalation. They already considered an unarmed reconnaissance flight provocative. Fighters that could carry not only air-to-air, but also air-to-ground missiles? Missiles that had the range to destroy ground targets inside China?

Also, China had long been capable of shooting down fighters off its coast without even sending up fighters. For example, the HQ-9B surface-to-air missile (SAM) had a range of over two hundred kilometers and a speed of over Mach 4. Plus, a one-hundred-eighty-kilogram warhead, so even a near miss would destroy its target.

And China had far more missiles than America had planes.

So, Ross was flying without a fighter escort.

First Lieutenant Bob Vinson dropped heavily back into the co-pilot's seat, shaking his head.

"Trouble finding the restroom?" Ross asked innocently.

That was the reason Vinson had given for leaving the plane's controls, but Ross knew that had only been part of it. It was Vinson's first

RC-135U flight, and he could hardly be blamed for a certain degree of curiosity.

"No, sir. I also took a look around," Vinson replied.

"Looked, not talked, right?" Ross asked, his eyes narrowing.

"Yes, sir," Vinson said with an emphatic nod. "I know they're all busy, and I kept my mouth shut."

"Good," Ross said. "Learn anything?"

"Well, sir, I already knew one of the Ravens' jobs is to watch out for threats to this aircraft. Just a glance at their displays, though, made it pretty obvious they have their hands full on that front," Vinson replied.

"Ravens" had been the Air Force term for electronic warfare officers since the job's creation decades ago.

Ross tapped one of the displays in front of him, which was currently dark.

"We've been tracked by Chinese radar since before we started gathering data on their electronic signals. This display won't light up unless one of two things happens. Either ground radar locks on to us tied to a SAM site, or a fighter jet is inbound. As you know from the pre-flight briefing, our options would be limited in both cases," Ross said.

"Yes, sir. Too bad all the crew and equipment we're carrying couldn't be jammed into a Blackbird, right, sir?" Vinson said with a smile.

Ross laughed at the image. The SR-71 Blackbird had only a tiny fraction of the room available on the RC-135U for electronic signals monitoring equipment. On the other hand, its ability to fly over twenty-four kilometers high and at a speed exceeding Mach 3 had kept it safe in even the most hostile airspace.

The RC-135U flew at about eight hundred kilometers per hour at around ten thousand meters, roughly the same as a typical commercial jetliner. Any fighter in China's inventory, or any SAM, could easily chase them down.

In fact, the RC-135U had only one defense. That it was doing nothing wrong.

The Blackbird had flown right over the old USSR with impunity. The RC-135U was sticking to what everyone, including the U.N., agreed was international airspace.

Everyone, that is, except the Chinese.

"What do you think the chances are that the Chinese will let us carry out our mission without interruption?" Vinson asked.

"Close to zero," Ross replied. "I'm sure our presence has already been reported up the chain of command. We haven't seen a response yet because orders from on high have to be drafted or confirmed and then sent down to action level. I don't think that will take long."

Vinson nodded. "What do you think they'll do, sir?"

"Probably just as in the briefing," Ross said with a shrug. "They'll send fighters to harass us like they did in 2022, and then we'll have a choice. Ignore them until they go away or return to base."

"How aggressive do you think they'll be, sir?" Vinson asked.

"Good chance they'll try what they did with us before. Flying way too close and risking collision. Or they could go a step further the way they did with the Australians in 2022. Add flares and chaff to flying way too close. We'll have to wait and see," Ross said.

"Yes, sir," Vinson said thoughtfully. "On the one hand, the Australians were on a recon patrol over the South China Sea, much further from the Chinese mainland than we are now. On the other, they were flying a P-8. It can carry armaments against land and sea targets, though it has zero self-defense capability against air attacks. I wonder if that's what set off the Chinese?"

"Who knows?" Ross replied absently, most of his attention on the displays before him. "I doubt any weapons were actually on board the P-8. Maybe the Chinese have decided they won't let anyone see what they're up to, like preparing to launch an attack on Taiwan."

Vinson nodded. "Speaking of seeing what we're doing, do we know whether that link from us to an RQ-180 drone and then on to a Japanese AWACS is working?"

"The Raven in charge of that daisy chain told me data is flowing.

He also told me we won't know how well it's working until they can review the data after the transfer. Said it would probably take weeks," Ross said.

"Yes, sir. Seems like a lot of trouble and expense just to get a data backup that may or may not work," Vinson said.

Ross shrugged. "You may be right. This is the first time it's been tried. It probably says something about how valuable Command considers this data. Besides, there are several scenarios where the data could be at risk. Equipment failure. Being forced down like that EP-3E in 2001 and having to destroy all the equipment ourselves."

Vinson nodded silently. He knew all about the Hainan Island incident in 2001. The Chinese had forced down an EP-3E reconnaissance plane after unsafe maneuvers by a Chinese J-8 fighter led to a midair collision, costing the Chinese pilot his life and damaging the EP-3E.

It took ten days before the Chinese released the 24-man crew. The EP-3E was returned months later in crates.

Vinson also knew as well as Ross did that the Chinese could shoot them down whenever they pleased. Neither would ever talk about that out loud.

Vinson had no sooner completed the thought than he heard Ross swearing under his breath. He had no trouble guessing the reason.

The threat display Ross had pointed to earlier was no longer dark. And Vinson had an identical display before him, so he could immediately see what had caused Ross's reaction.

Two Chinese J-16s on an intercept course.

The J-16s were far from the best planes the Chinese had available. Fourth generation and based on the J-11, which had been developed from the Russian Su-27.

But the J-16 could reach Mach 2 and had a range of three thousand kilometers.

Against the RC-135U, it wouldn't even have to waste a missile, Ross thought bitterly. Its 30mm cannon would be plenty.

The display helpfully showed how long it would take for the J-16s to intercept Ross's RC-135U at their current speed.

Not long.

But just a few minutes later, both of their threat displays ceased to show the two advancing J-16s. Instead, there was nothing but a random assortment of dots on their screens.

At the same moment, Ross and Vinson could hear a series of orders being given in the compartment behind them. But not clearly enough to listen to their content.

"Sir, what's happening?" Vinson asked.

Ross tapped on his threat display and said, "Now we know the Chinese have rolled out the J-16D model. It has jamming equipment mounted internally as well as external electronic warfare pods. Been around since at least 2015, but this is the first time we're getting a good look at it."

Vinson nodded. "So the Ravens are working to record the D model's capabilities."

"That's right," Ross replied. "They're also doing all they can to burn through the Chinese jamming and reestablish our link to that RQ-180 drone."

"Yes, sir. Is that to make sure the data is backed up?" Vinson asked.

Ross nodded. "That's one reason. The other is, unless the Ravens can defeat the Chinese jamming, those fighters could shoot us down, and nobody could prove what happened."

Chapter Three

Japanese Self-Defense Force AWACS
International Airspace
9,150 Meters Above the East China Sea

Haruto Takahashi was annoyed.

Not with the performance of the equipment or crew he supervised. Both were doing everything required by his mission orders.

But because, as usual, Haruto wanted to exceed those orders. So far, it wasn't working.

Haruto had pioneered the concept of integrating data from multiple sources on a single airborne platform. Ordinarily, an Airborne Warning and Control System (AWACS) would rely exclusively on its massive rotating radar to detect possible threats.

However, Haruto had been the first in the Japanese Self-Defense Force (JSDF) to spot the opportunity provided by their Boeing 767 airframe. It offered more room than the older Boeing 707 model used by the Americans until 2027. That's when they'd started taking delivery of the new E-7 AWACS, based on the Boeing 737 airframe.

But that conversion was still underway.

Haruto smiled to himself. Sometimes, it paid to be late to the party.

In 2023, Japan had begun implementing the most recent AWACS mission computing upgrade, or MCU. The MCU provided vastly updated software and onboard computers to process the data collected by AWACS' radar dome. Now complete, the MCU had cost Japan nearly a billion American dollars.

Additional computer and communications modules of Haruto's design and one extra crewman provided even more advanced capabilities. In previous missions, he had integrated data from other JSDF aircraft and drones into a single package.

Haruto had spent the past several years building on this accomplishment. In particular, he had improved the stability of the interface linking the different platforms. That meant each data source, such as a drone's visual image or radio intercept picked up by a JSDF reconnaissance aircraft, would display along with their AWACS radar data.

Just as important, if a single data source were interrupted, it wouldn't affect the display of the others.

Right now, the data source on his display was an RQ-180 stealth drone, a recent purchase from the Americans. Cruising at about eighteen thousand meters, it was now tasked with relaying the data feed from an American RC-135U. The RQ-180 had been heavily modified under Haruto's supervision to handle the data reception and transmission requirements.

Adding more data storage capacity on the AWACS had been easy as a technical matter. It had been as simple as removing hard drives that were several years old and replacing them with new ones that offered twice as much storage in the same space.

However, adding more data storage capacity on the AWACS had been a much greater challenge as an administrative matter. There was a schedule for replacing electronic components on board JSDF aircraft. As far as the bureaucrats at JSDF HQ in Tokyo were concerned, the ones already installed were just fine.

The JSDF had a budget. A certain Haruto Takahashi needed to understand that and adjust his expectations accordingly.

The hard drives were a laughably small and cheap component on the scale of the AWACS and the equipment it contained. On his far from princely JSDF salary, Haruto could have bought the hard drives he needed using his funds.

However, any equipment installed on the AWACS had to arrive via properly authorized government procurement channels. Haruto had to acknowledge glumly that there were good reasons for that policy.

Finally, Haruto had turned to Kaito Watanabe, his supervisor since the start of the AWACS modification project. Kaito knew little about the technical details of what Haruto was doing. But as the AWACS commander, he knew its original capabilities inside and out.

And Kaito had forgotten more about JSDF bureaucracy than Haruto would ever know.

Haruto had explained to Kaito that their mission to support the Americans in their attempt to transmit a data backup from their RC-135U would only succeed with the equipment he had requested.

"Mission success" was all Kaito needed to hear. He had climbed the JSDF bureaucracy until he reached a Colonel willing to listen rather than recite regulations.

The hard drives had reached Haruto with only a day to spare for their installation. Fortunately, it only took minutes to swap them out and less than an hour to test their performance.

And yes, the RC-135U's data feed had been copied flawlessly. So, as far as the mission orders were concerned, it had been a complete success.

But Haruto wanted more. The RQ-180 also had excellent high-resolution cameras. Haruto wanted to maintain visual surveillance on the RC-135U, but that simply hadn't worked so far.

Repeated Chinese harassment of any military aircraft that flew anywhere near China was well known. Even though those aircraft were flying in international airspace. The Chinese always denied flying too close and ejecting flares and chaff into the engines of foreign military aircraft.

But what if those actions were captured on high-quality video? Taken by a third-country aircraft, uninvolved with the incident?

That might be harder to deny.

And Haruto would have cheerfully bet a paycheck that the Chinese would turn up any minute to do just that.

Well, I won't have a video record whatever the Chinese are going to do, Haruto thought angrily.

Then Haruto realized he'd probably been too ambitious with "high quality" video. Yes, a nice, clear picture would be great. However, now he knew the data transfer requirements were too high.

A harsh, rasping buzz brought Haruto back to the present. He'd been on AWACS missions long enough to know what the sound meant.

Enemy fighters detected. Headed in their direction.

But were they the target?

A quick look at the nearest display gave Haruto the answer. No.

As expected, the fighters were headed straight for the American RC-135U.

While Haruto watched, the icons representing the fighters changed from generic "enemy aircraft" to "J-16."

Haruto grunted. Not the best the Chinese had, but more than enough to harass the RC-135U. In fact, wasn't there an electronic warfare version of…

Haruto hadn't even completed the thought when the AWACS radar display he'd been watching dissolved into static.

At the same moment, a loud chime from one of Haruto's consoles told him he had his own problems to deal with. It took little time to confirm his guess had been correct. The data feed from the RC-135U had been cut off.

The same jamming that had disrupted the AWACS's radar image of the J-16s.

Haruto wasn't surprised to hear Kaito's voice just behind him. After all, what alternatives did he have?

"So, Haruto, the Chinese have decided they don't want spectators for whatever they're about to do. Any tricks up your sleeve that might let us get a peek?" Kaito asked.

Haruto suppressed a sigh with difficulty. Mostly because he didn't want to give Kaito the satisfaction.

Kaito had done his AWACS training in America. As well as later refresher training. And kept in close contact with his American AWACS counterparts at the 961st Airborne Air Control Squadron at Kadena Air Base in Okinawa.

Haruto was sure Kaito had spent at least as much time learning American idioms as the finer points of AWACS operations.

"Tricks up your sleeve?"

Well, at least this expression wasn't as mystifying as some Kaito had used. Haruto had seen a total of one performance by a magician. So, this idiom was less opaque than "shoot the breeze."

With difficulty, Haruto returned his focus to the task at hand.

"I had been attempting to get a video feed of the RC-135U aircraft from the RQ-180 drone, but without success. It appears that the bandwidth necessary to store the RC-135U's electronic surveillance data left nothing available for video," Haruto said.

Kaito nodded. "But since our Chinese friends have cut off the RC-135U's data relay, why not stop recording static from their jamming and try again with video?"

Why not, indeed? Haruto started kicking himself for missing something obvious but then stopped.

Fix the problem first. There'd be plenty of time to beat himself up later.

Haruto's fingers flew over the keyboard as he terminated the electronic surveillance data link with the RC-135U. That done, he next intended to search for a frequency that wasn't subject to jamming by the two J-16s.

The RQ-180 drone's onboard software beat him to it. An image of the RC-135U, with the two J-16s following right behind, filled the closest display.

"Well done," Kaito said quietly. "Are all the radio frequencies in the area still being jammed?"

Haruto grimaced. "Yes, sir. I set that as the highest priority, but no go. The J-16s' jamming is directional and has cut off all signals broadcast by the RC-135U. Either data or voice transmission. The video feed works because the RQ-180 drone's optical sensors aren't affected by the jamming, and the drone found a clear frequency to transmit the video data. It's helped there by being further away from the jamming directed at the RC-135U and closer to us."

Kaito grunted. "I recall that this is supposed to be a stealth drone. Do you think the Chinese know that it's there?"

"No, sir," Haruto said immediately. "The J-16 is a fourth-generation fighter. It would have no trouble spotting an F-16 or F-15. But the RQ-180? At that distance? No chance."

"Well, so far, they don't look like they're pulling any flare or chaff tricks," Kaito said.

Haruto nodded. "Or pulling in front of the American plane and conducting unsafe maneuvers. Both J-16s are flying right behind it. In fact, it looks like they're starting to back off."

Kaito stared at the screen with an expression Haruto had never seen before.

"I know this plane's radio can't transmit a signal strong enough to make it through the Chinese jamming. Do you have anything that could do the job?" Kaito asked.

Haruto shook his head. "No, sir. Our drone isn't configured to transmit a radio signal. I doubt it would have enough power to burn through the Chinese jamming, even if it did. What do you want to tell the Americans, sir?"

Kaito leaned forward intently. "Not the Americans. I want to let those Chinese pilots know someone is watching them."

It took Haruto a moment to understand what Kaito was saying. They were using a stealth drone precisely to avoid letting the Chinese know they had any involvement with the American reconnaissance flight.

Never mind. Kaito was the AWACS commander. If he wanted the Chinese to know they were being observed, so be it.

"Sir, probably the fastest way to let the Chinese know they're under observation would be to fly the drone at high speed and a steep descent angle to ruin its stealth profile..."

Haruto's voice trailed off as first one, and then the other J-16 each fired one missile at the RC-135U.

"Too late," Kaito said sadly.

Both watched in horror as the missiles struck the American reconnaissance plane.

It never had a chance.

In seconds, the RC-135U was a cloud of flames, smoke, and debris headed down to the surface of the Pacific Ocean.

Along with over two dozen dead Americans.

After several moments of stunned silence, Haruto was the first to speak.

"Sir, that was no overeager Chinese pilot acting alone," Haruto said angrily. "Both J-16s fired on the American plane at almost the same instant,"

Kaito nodded. "You're right. Also, note that both planes backed away from the American aircraft before firing. That was to avoid any collateral damage from their attack. This was deliberate, cold-blooded murder."

"What do we do now, sir?" Haruto asked.

Kaito tapped at the display, which was starting to clear. "We used a stealth drone. And we're flying inside Japanese airspace near Yonaguni."

"Yes, sir," Haruto said automatically, not because he understood Kaito's point.

Haruto quickly thought over what he knew about Yonaguni. The closest Japanese island to Taiwan, just a bit over a hundred kilometers distant. On a clear day, the sharp-eyed claimed they could see Taiwan from Yonaguni. It had a recently extended runway, now capable of allowing an emergency landing for the AWACS.

No. Still not clear what Kaito was driving at.

Kaito was still staring at the display, which had finally cleared.

It was now empty.

"You see, the Chinese weren't aware of our recent AWACS software and hardware upgrade, which significantly increased the range of our radar," Kaito said.

Suddenly, Haruto understood. "The Chinese didn't think our radar could see the approach of their J-16s to the American reconnaissance plane."

"Exactly," Kaito replied. "And they certainly knew nothing about the stealth drone's presence or that its cameras could record their attack on a defenseless American aircraft."

Haruto scowled at the now clear display. "So the J-16s have already flown out of our radar range and within minutes will have landed. The Chinese must believe they can avoid blame for this crime. Even though the Americans will suspect the truth, the Chinese must believe that they will fail to act without proof."

Kaito nodded. "Agreed. It is certain that once we inform our superiors, they will pass on what we have learned to the Americans. That leaves just one question."

Haruto's eyes widened. "Yes, sir. What will the Americans do?"

Chapter Four

Kantei
Office of the Prime Minister
Tokyo, Japan

Prime Minister Kan frowned deeply as he reread the Japanese Self-Defense Force report on the downing of the American reconnaissance plane.

Not because of the facts of the attack itself. Yes, even though those were bad enough.

Because of what the report's authors had to say about China's immediate intentions.

Kan had decided to call on his predecessor for advice, former Prime Minister Yoshida. In theory, Yoshida had retired from the legislature and was no more than an elderly private citizen.

In reality, Kan knew that Yoshida was not content to spend his remaining days reading books and puttering around his garden.

Yoshida still had the respect of many in Japan's political elite. Though Kan doubted Yoshida wanted his old job back, he was certain Yoshida wanted his voice to be heard.

Kan had decided it was best to hear that voice directly rather than second-hand from other politicians or the press.

And besides, Kan admired Yoshida despite the many differences they had developed over the years. More than anything else, because Kan knew Yoshida put Japan's national interest ahead of his own.

Kan scowled again as he thought about the many rival politicians whose priorities he doubted.

Including a few that appeared to be receiving money from the Communist Chinese.

Though Kan didn't quite have the proof he needed to go public with those charges.

Yet.

An aide ushered Yoshida in and immediately withdrew.

Yoshida walked quickly and confidently toward Kan's desk.

Kan stood and smiled, walking around his desk to a nearby couch. "Welcome, my old friend," he said. "I appreciate your taking the time to give me your wise counsel."

Yoshida smiled, nodded, and sat on the couch Kan had indicated.

Though they were on opposite ends of the couch, Kan and Yoshida were now considerably closer than most Japanese adults found comfortable.

Clever, Yoshida thought. Kan is letting me know I might find myself closer to him than I also like politically.

Aloud, Yoshida said, "I read the JSDF report your aide provided with great interest. Too bad he couldn't leave it with me to review more carefully, but I understand the security requirements."

Kan nodded. "I know you do. That rule, for example, was enacted by a certain Prime Minister Yoshida."

They both shared a brief chuckle. It was true. Yoshida had always insisted on safeguarding sensitive information while Prime Minister.

"So, you will understand that only a few outside the JSDF have seen what I am about to show you," Kan said.

With that, Kan opened the lid of the secure laptop on the nearby coffee table and pressed his finger on its sensor.

The video recording the American reconnaissance plane's destruction was already cued to run.

After it was finished, both men were silent for several moments.

"I presume we have already shared this with the Americans?" Yoshida said.

Kan nodded. "Along with my personal regrets to President Hernandez for the loss of the crew."

Yoshida shook his head in disgust. "The Chinese have been publicly saying that they had nothing to do with the disappearance of the American plane. I know Hernandez. He won't let this pass without a response."

"Agreed," Kan said. "What do you think he will do?"

Yoshida sat silently for several moments. Finally, he sighed.

"Hernandez will understand that the Chinese are sending a message. We don't want you to see what we're doing. One thing in particular," Yoshida said.

"Preparations to invade Taiwan," Kan said flatly.

Yoshida nodded. "Just so. Hernandez will do something to show he is determined to ignore that message. How? That I don't know."

Kan tapped the laptop screen, frozen on the video's final image. The flaming debris that was all that remained of the American plane as it plummeted towards the ocean.

"And how do you recommend we respond to this savage act?" Kan asked.

This time, Yoshida didn't hesitate.

"Prepare for war," he said. "The Chinese may not have expected to be caught on video. But they knew the Americans would blame them for this."

Yoshida paused and lifted one finger. "And here is the other message. They don't care. China will seize Taiwan, whether the Americans like it or not. At a minimum, that means striking at least one target in Japan. The American base in Okinawa. It may mean striking other American bases in Japan as well."

Kan nodded. "I agree. I have considered issuing a warning once the Americans go public with news of China's role in the shootdown. If China attacks any part of Japan's territory, whether or not it is used as a foreign military base, we will consider it an act of war."

"Well, of course, it would be an act of war. Nobody would dispute that. But would such a warning deter the Chinese?" Yoshida asked.

Kan scowled. "Probably not."

"We must also remember that the Chinese have nuclear weapons, and we do not. As the only country to suffer a nuclear attack, it is no surprise that our public has never favored our traveling the nuclear path. But it means we must avoid giving the Chinese any pretext to use nuclear weapons against us. If we made a statement including the word 'war', we might be giving them just such an excuse," Yoshida said.

Kan was silent for a moment as he weighed Yoshida's words. Finally, he sighed. "You're right. The risk is too great. But I'm not willing to stand idly by while the Chinese move their forces within sight of our country."

"I'm not saying you should. But we can do much to impede the Chinese without overt conflict. Aggressively patrol our air and maritime borders. Step up our signals and intelligence collection. Much of our equipment, all the way up to our most advanced fighters, is the same used by the Americans. Offer to share parts and repair technicians. Tell the Americans all this, and then ask whether we can do anything else to help," Yoshida said.

"Agreed," Kan said at once. "I have already been thinking about all these measures. But I also plan to couple the offer with one request for assistance. Antiballistic missile defense. In particular, only about forty kilometers separate Tokyo from the naval facilities we and the Americans have at Yokosuka. It would seem prudent to rush more defensive capabilities to this area as soon as possible."

Yoshida smiled. "As Prime Minister, you and your top advisors will be safe in a bunker if the Chinese attack us with missiles. The other seven hundred members of our legislature will not. Asking the Americans for help with antiballistic missile defense is the one step where you are certain to face no political opposition. And it will help to drive home why we need to help the Americans, in turn, in case anyone wavers."

Chapter Five

The Oval Office, The White House
Washington, DC

President Hernandez closed the latest of many briefing folders on the latest crisis as General Robinson walked in.

Robinson was the Air Force Chief of Staff but had long since also served as Hernandez's unofficial National Security Advisor. Hernandez had tried several times to give him the title, but Robinson insisted he was more effective without it.

Seeing how much time the actual National Security Advisor had to spend dealing with Congress and the press, Hernandez reluctantly had to agree.

Foreign disputes were not why Hernandez had shifted from a successful business career to run for President. Infrastructure, education, immigration, and other domestic policy issues had all impacted his business. Finally, Hernandez had decided to stop complaining and do something about them.

Being sure he had the answers turned out to be different than being able to implement them. Hernandez couldn't even get his own party's united support. The other party? They said a united "no" even to bills they had supported up until the moment Hernandez proposed them. Just because Hernandez was the one offering them.

Still, Hernandez had made some limited domestic progress in his first term. But he knew that's not why he had been re-elected. No, that was because Hernandez had successfully managed one foreign crisis after another. Even though Hernandez saw each crisis as a distraction from what he wanted to accomplish as President. And now another one was here.

"Welcome, General. You saw Ambassador Fitzroy's presentation at the UN?" Hernandez said.

Robinson nodded. "It reminded me of the video of Ambassador Kirkpatrick's speech at the UN after the Russians shot down that Korean airliner in the 80s. Even though she only had audio tapes of the Soviet pilots' radio conversations to work with, it was still devastating. But the digital recording of the shootdown Fitzroy was able to show? I thought zooming in on the tail of one of the Chinese jets firing on our aircraft was especially well done. The red star left zero doubt about who was responsible."

"Yes, the Japanese did a remarkable job collecting that recording and getting it to us without delay. Good suggestion of yours that we have Fitzroy announce we'd just posted the original unedited recording on the Internet for anyone to see. Left the Chinese UN representative literally at a loss for words." Hernandez said.

"Speaking of the Japanese, sir, you've seen their offer of assistance?" Robinson asked.

"I did," Hernandez replied. "Very generous. I also saw their request for antiballistic missile protection. Are Patriot missiles available?"

"Sir, I've requested my Army counterpart answer that question. Given everything the Japanese are offering, I'm sure he'll do his best to give us a positive answer," Robinson said.

"The Army," Hernandez repeated, shaking his head. "General, the Air Force is responsible for our ballistic missiles, right?"

"Yes, sir," Robinson said with a smile. "But the Army has always had the mission of stopping incoming missiles and aircraft. Going back to the 1950s, when the first Nike Hercules missiles were deployed for air defense."

Hernandez grunted. "Fine. I suppose all the services have redeployment plans ready for an imminent Chinese invasion of Taiwan and are executing them?"

"Yes, sir. Your previous orders on that point were quite clear. It helps that we've seen this coming for some time. I'm not so sure that's true for our allies," Robinson replied.

"I have State working on that," Hernandez said. "Japan has already promised to do a lot. I plan to press them for more if we can come through with added antiballistic missile defense. I think the Europeans will sit this one out. Realistically, only Korea and Australia are possibilities."

"Agreed, sir," Robinson said. "We've worked with both countries for decades. Highly skilled and armed with equipment compatible with ours. They could make a real difference. Though with their current government, I think the Australians will limit their support to intelligence collection and logistics."

Hernandez nodded. "I'm hoping both countries understand that if China succeeds in seizing Taiwan by force, the question isn't whether China will come for them next. It's when."

Chapter Six

Zhongnanhai Compound
Beijing, China

President Gu looked out of his impressive office at the expansive Zhongnanhai Compound. It included much besides his office, such as the central headquarters for the Communist Party and the State Council. It also housed the Premier's office, the Central Committee's headquarters, and its highest-level coordinating institutions, such as the Standing Committee, Politburo, and Secretariat.

Usually, Gu found this concrete proof of the Party's domination of China's government calming.

Not today.

The voice of Gu's assistant floated from an unseen speaker. "Sir, General Zhao is here as you ordered."

"Have him wait five minutes. Then show him in," Gu said to an equally invisible microphone.

Gu's response to the Air Force Commander's presence went to his assistant's earpiece and wouldn't be heard by Zhao.

There were two reasons for the delay. One was to make the point that the Party called the shots, not the military. Another was that Gu wanted more time to consider what he would say to Zhao.

Precisely five minutes later, the doors to Gu's office swung open, and the unnaturally tall figure of General Zhao strode in.

Gu had taken a seat behind his imposing desk well in advance.

The General would be standing.

Zhao marched up to Gu's desk, snapped him a brisk salute, and said perfectly respectfully, "General Zhao, reporting as ordered, sir."

Then Zhao stood at attention, as protocol demanded.

Gu could find nothing to criticize in anything Zhao had said or done since entering his office.

But he was sure Zhao thought he and the other military leaders should be leading China. Not the Communist Party.

Gu had no proof of this. But he was working hard to get it.

For now, though, the conquest of Taiwan was about to start. And Gu had to make do with the tools he had.

"So, General, I presume you are aware that the attack by your fighters on the unarmed American reconnaissance plane was captured on video. Very high-quality video, I might add. That left no doubt we were responsible. I recall your saying that our electronic jamming would prevent the American plane from sending a distress signal. And that neither the Americans nor the Japanese would have any means to prove we shot down that American plane. So, your explanation, General?" Gu asked.

"First, Mr. President, all you have said is true. I have no excuse, but I do have a possible explanation. My technical experts believe the Americans must have deployed a drone with stealth features, rendering it undetected by our radar. There is no other way the digital images could have been captured without our knowledge," Zhao replied.

Gu looked at Zhao with astonishment. "General, you mean to tell me that all the powerful radars we have lined up on our coast and those on our two fighters were unable to detect this drone?"

"Yes, sir. I had trouble believing it, as well. But I agree with our experts. No other explanation makes sense. For example, no satellite could have captured images of an object moving at high speed at such a resolution. It must have been a stealth drone," Zhao said flatly.

"Well, no matter how the Americans did it, we look like fools in the world's eyes. As instructed, Ambassador Jian denied all the American charges at the United Nations. Even after the Americans displayed their video of the shootdown, Jian said the footage was fake. Then, the Americans said they had uploaded the original recording to the Internet so anyone could confirm its authenticity. Even our friends fell silent," Gu said bitterly.

"With respect, sir, the consequences of our actions are not all negative. Anyone tempted to side with the Americans once we begin military operations in Taiwan now knows we aren't afraid to use force. Even against the Americans, so why would we hesitate against the Japanese or Australians? Or anyone else who gets in our way?" Zhao asked.

Gu was about to tell Zhao he knew nothing about the realities of international politics, but then he paused.

Zhao had a point. Maybe it was time for China to take the gloves off. And let the world see its bare knuckles.

"Very well, General," Gu said. "Let's move on to your proposal to commence air operations against Taiwan. I thought we'd long since retired all our J-7 aircraft. And yet you propose to make them the spearhead of our operation. Won't that just result in the needless deaths of many of our airmen?"

Zhao's look of confusion and surprise was quickly suppressed, but not fast enough. For the first time since Gu had known the man, Zhao had appeared to be at a complete loss for words.

But Zhao quickly collected himself.

"Sir, I blame myself for a briefing paper that failed to clarify the operation. The J-7s will not be manned. We have converted them to heavily armed drones," Zhao said.

Now it was Gu's turn to be astonished. The truth was, as soon as Gu had seen "J-7" he'd stopped reading the operation proposal.

"Well, General, that makes more sense," Gu said. "Continue."

"Yes, sir. We included J-7s in large-scale exercises we did within Taiwan's so-called airspace in 2022. Much to their puzzlement," Zhao said with a smile. "Those J-7s were our first operational drones created from retired fighter aircraft. We determined that they could be controlled successfully by our nearby fighters, serving as uncrewed wingmen. Since then, we have made further improvements. Now, we can control J-7 drones remotely from great distances. The relatively short span between our coast and Taiwan will be no problem."

"Fine, General, but do we have enough to make a dent in Taiwan's defenses?" Gu asked.

Yes, that detail had probably been covered in the proposal Gu had stopped reading. But so what?

To his credit, Zhao nodded as though the question was perfectly reasonable. Well, the man had reached the rank of Air Force Commander. Some skills were to be expected.

"We believe so, sir. Missiles will destroy many or even most of the J-7 drones before they can launch their payloads. Fired either from Taiwan's ground sites or by their fighters. However, even then, their destruction will have a purpose," Zhao said.

Really? "Explain, General," Gu said.

"Our satellites will be trained on every square centimeter of Taiwan. Any buried anti-aircraft missile facility that fires will be pinpointed. Any hidden airstrip launching fighters will be discovered. And with nearly four hundred J-7 drones attacking simultaneously, I am confident that at least some will get through and cause significant damage. Finally, we estimate that at least a thousand Taiwanese missiles will be launched at the incoming J-7 drones. That's quite a few missiles they won't have to use against our manned aircraft when we send those next," Zhao said with satisfaction.

Gu nodded. Yes. There was a reason this man was Air Force Commander.

"Good, General," Gu said. "Much clearer than the briefing paper. Your operation is approved. Let me know once all preparations are complete."

Chapter Seven

USS America
Sasebo, Japan

Captain Mercer looked over the readiness report with approval. As the U.S. Navy's only forward-deployed amphibious assault ship, *America* should, in theory, be able to head to sea at any time.

The reality was a bit more complicated.

With a crew of twelve hundred and nearly two thousand Marines onboard, food was always an issue. Storage space was finite. And no sooner was fresh food delivered than it started to spoil.

Some of the more than three thousand men on board *America* were always on leave. Or carrying out some task on base that took them off the ship.

Mercer had canceled all leave. Leaving the ship for any reason now required his approval.

So far, no one had asked.

America's air assets all needed regular maintenance. That was especially critical for their twelve MV-22B Osprey tilt-rotor transports, which would carry out *America*'s primary mission.

Delivering two thousand Marines to their objective.

Starting from the first test flight in 1991, fourteen Ospreys had been lost, causing a total of fifty-four fatalities. Fortunately, most of those crashes had been before improvements led to the Osprey finally being declared operational in 2007.

Mercer still considered Osprey maintenance a top *America* priority.

Six F-35B Lightning attack aircraft based on *America* would protect the Ospreys on their way in. All were the Short Take-Off and Vertical Landing (STOVL) version, and unlike the Harriers they replaced, they were capable of supersonic flight.

Seven AH-1Z Viper attack helicopters would provide close air support for the Marines once they had landed.

Four CH-53K heavy transport helicopters would carry out resupply. Finally, there were two MH-60S Seahawk helicopters for air-sea rescue and medical evacuation.

The ratio of maintenance time to time in the air varied for each aircraft but was roughly three to four hours. Crews had been working hard for weeks to ensure that as much of that time as possible had already been spent on base in Sasebo rather than later at sea.

Fuel was simpler. Though they didn't have it as easy as nuclear-powered aircraft carriers, filling their tanks with enough JP-5 for *America*'s gas turbine engines was no challenge. As a bonus, JP-5 was the same fuel used by *America*'s helicopters and Ospreys.

Though the commonality ended there. F-35Bs needed JP-8.

Taiwan was only about twelve hundred kilometers away. And Mercer was sure they would make at least one stop before they were sent there.

Commander Tyler tapped Mercer's ready room door, which was partly open as usual.

Without even looking, Mercer said, "Enter."

He knew who it would be. Tyler was his Executive Officer, whose job was to ensure that when Mercer gave an order, it was carried out.

Tyler walked in and grinned, nodding toward the report in front of Mercer. "Well, Captain, you were right," he said.

Then, he handed a printout to Mercer. "New orders, sir."

Mercer looked them over quickly. They were short and to the point.

"So, we're to leave for Okinawa as soon as possible and inform PACOM once we're underway. That'll be this afternoon, right?" Mercer asked. In a tone that made it clear there was only one correct answer.

Yes.

"Yes, sir," Tyler said.

Mercer nodded. It was the answer he'd expected, not just because of the readiness report. The Navy and Marines sent their best to the front lines. For years, they'd all known a war with China over Taiwan wasn't a question of if but when.

Since China had just been caught on video shooting down an unarmed American reconnaissance aircraft, they clearly had an answer.

Now.

"There's not a word in these orders about Taiwan. But we'll be eight hundred kilometers closer once we arrive in Okinawa. A coincidence?" Mercer asked.

Tyler smiled. Leading, sometimes obvious, questions were Mercer's way of explaining what he wanted.

In a way, Tyler thought the questions showed Mercer respected his abilities.

As long as Tyler continued to give him the right answers, anyway.

"I don't think so, sir. I've already given orders that we're to be prepared to refuel on arrival in Okinawa and top up our provisions," Tyler said.

Mercer nodded. He'd read the adage "an army marches on its stomach" attributed to both Napoleon and Frederick the Great. Either way, he was determined that the Marines on board his ship would board their Ospreys in the best shape possible.

Because Mercer had no idea what conditions would be like for the Marines when they arrived off the coast of Taiwan. But he was sure of one thing.

Fine dining wouldn't be part of the picture.

Chapter Eight

August 1st Building
Beijing, China

Lieutenant Xu looked up at the front of the building as dubiously as the first time he had seen it. The building that was China's equivalent to the American Pentagon.

Back then, Xu had been a Sergeant and had no idea who was waiting for him. Or with what mission.

Now, thanks to his wife Qian's prodding, things were different. Xu had gone through officer candidate training and been among the few selected for assignment to Special Forces.

Then Xu guessed that somebody at the top of China's Army had decided the country needed more Special Forces. Because the number of units with that designation had grown in a very short time.

So quickly, anyone already in a unit found himself either commanding it or transferred out to take charge of a new detachment. And trying to bring their unit to Special Forces standards in what seemed like the blink of an eye.

Xu had done his best. But he knew how hard he had been forced to work to earn his spot in the unit. And how long it had taken.

There simply hadn't been time to hold the new men to the same standard.

Well, they were just going to have to make do. Because Xu knew Colonel Chang would have ordered him to his office for just one reason.

To give him and his men a new mission.

Why in person? Xu didn't know for sure but suspected the reason was their shared history.

Xu had met Chang while commanding the outpost on the Indian border where Xu had been posted as a sniper. Xu had thought Chang's interest in history a bit eccentric for a Chinese Army officer but regarded him as capable and genuinely interested in the welfare of his men.

In fact, Chang had visited Xu twice while Xu had been recovering from injuries. The first time at the outpost's clinic when Xu had been wounded by mines placed covertly by a new Indian drone. The next was when the Indians used missiles fired from larger drones to kill everyone in the outpost but Xu, who had been in the concrete base armory at the time. Chang had only escaped because he had been called to Beijing for consultations.

That time, Xu had also been visited in hospital by the now-deceased President Lin. He had decorated Xu for killing an Indian sniper with a Barrett rifle captured by Chinese commandos who had raided an Indian outpost on their side of the border. That raid had led to the Indian attack that killed everyone present at the Chinese outpost but Xu, so he had accepted the decoration with decidedly mixed feelings.

Lin's award presentation had been televised, so Xu had become something of a celebrity. It was not a role he'd enjoyed. Xu had been told to appear several times at various events and pose with others for photos and did as he was ordered. But Xu wanted nothing more than to return to being an ordinary Army sniper. Nothing more, nothing less.

Xu had been concerned that all the publicity had made his face too well known for an assignment in Special Forces. After all, they were the units most likely to be deployed abroad.

But no. The intervening years had helped in two ways. First, in these days of social media fame was more fleeting than it had ever been. Second, Xu was no longer a youngster who barely needed to shave.

Indeed, the face in the mirror that looked back at Xu every morning as he shaved had changed quite a bit since his time at the Indian border.

It also helped that Xu had been granted a dispensation from regular military grooming standards like all Special Forces soldiers. This was to ensure Xu and the other men in his unit could blend in if deployed outside China.

Nothing was more likely to attract unwelcome official attention upon arrival in a foreign country than a military haircut.

That cut both ways, though. Xu wasn't looking forward to the officers' reaction at the August 1st Building reception desk. Special Forces still made up such a tiny fraction of China's military that most officers didn't know much about them, including their different authorized grooming standards.

Xu had already had to explain himself at length at several other Beijing military offices. Fortunately, thanks to his wife's foresight, today he had come prepared with written orders.

Steeling himself, Xu marched stiffly to the reception desk and reached into his pocket for his orders. Before he could even open his mouth, though, the corporal at the desk raised one finger.

Xu correctly understood this to mean he should stand silently.

"Yes, Colonel, he is here," the corporal said into the telephone now pressed against his ear.

"Yes, sir. At once, sir," the corporal said, hanging up the phone.

Jerking his head towards Xu, the corporal wheeled around and began to walk briskly into the nearest corridor.

Xu had to hustle to keep up.

Though Xu had been in the same building to see Chang before, he quickly became concerned. This time, it was a much longer trip.

And before, he had been deposited in a small, nearly deserted office suite. Not this time.

Instead, what Xu could see of the suite was enormous. At least double the size of the offices occupied by his base commander, a General. And packed with officers and enlisted men, all scurrying about on tasks of some sort.

Xu had barely had time to focus on the bedlam before him when a different corporal was at his side.

"Lieutenant Xu?" the corporal asked.

Xu nodded.

"Follow me," the corporal said.

This time, the trip was much shorter. After passing through three doorways, the corporal came to attention and announced, "Lieutenant Xu, Colonel."

Chang had been examining a map of Taiwan but now turned around, a broad smile on his face.

Xu immediately noticed that Chang was now wearing Special Forces insignia.

"Lieutenant Xu! Congratulations on your promotion! So good to see you! Please, sit!" Chang said, gesturing to the chair in front of his desk.

"Thank you, sir," Xu said. He noticed that the corporal had not only left but closed the door behind him. Noise from the outer offices was still audible, but compared to the din before, it almost qualified as silence.

"Things are much busier here than during your last visit. I have convinced my superiors that we must expand our use of Special Forces to succeed in Taiwan," Chang said.

"So you are the officer behind their quick growth. Sir, I wish I and the other unit commanders had more time to prepare the men," Xu said.

Chang nodded impatiently. "Yes, yes. Well, parts of that training are irrelevant to the conflict ahead. Parachute landings, for example. Completely impractical for an island with dense radar coverage. Instead, you will all enter Taiwan like you did on your last mission."

Xu's eyebrows flew upwards. "You mean, arrive on regular commercial flights? But don't you think their security services will spot us?"

"Maybe. But I doubt it. We still have some time before the invasion fleet sets sail. There will be only one or two of you on each flight. None of you will be carrying anything remotely suspicious. And no regular military computer system has a word about this operation," Chang said.

"Tiger only?" Xu asked.

"Tiger only," Chang repeated with an emphatic nod.

"Tiger" was a new network built around three concepts. Only high-security equipment was connected to it. The network was a closed loop, with zero connection to the Internet. And its use was restricted to Special Forces personnel.

No exceptions.

Hard experience had taught that even the so-called "secure" regular military networks were too vulnerable to compromise. In particular because they had so many users and administrators.

"Are the equipment and supplies my men will need already available in Taiwan, Colonel?" Xu asked.

"Yes," Chang replied. "They have been split into storage at several locations so that a single discovery would not end your mission. You will have to approach each with caution."

Xu nodded but said nothing. It was obvious that if any stored weapons were discovered, the Taiwan authorities would set up surveillance to seize anyone who appeared to retrieve them.

"Let's see if you can guess your mission objective. What would you say is the greatest hazard faced by our liberation fleet?" Chang asked.

There it was again, Xu thought. The sort of question no Chinese officer would ordinarily ask a subordinate. The kind that had given Chang a reputation for being a bit odd.

But Xu realized it was actually a test. Was he able to appreciate the true importance of the mission objective? And do whatever was necessary to achieve it?

Fortunately, Xu had thought about the question before this meeting with Chang.

"Land-based anti-ship missiles," Xu replied after only a moment's hesitation.

Chang smiled. "Excellent. Why land-based in particular?"

"Well, sir, sea and air-based missile launch platforms are often moving and inherently less accurate. They are also relatively easy to detect. Land-based missiles can be buried deep underground, making them harder to find and difficult to destroy even if their exact location is known," Xu said.

"I'm glad you've given this matter some thought, Lieutenant. We have intelligence on the location of these missiles from numerous sources. Your team will go to one of the locations where we have the highest confidence," Chang said.

Xu nodded. "The enemy will doubtless have decoy sites. If our target turns out to be one of these, do we have a secondary objective?"

"Yes," Chang replied. "But due to how we have been forced to structure your assault, it's unlikely your unit will be able to break contact with the enemy and survive intact to reach it."

Xu let the silence that followed stretch for as long as Chang needed to explain himself. He already knew this would be a risky mission.

Now Xu would find out whether it was merely dangerous or suicidal.

"I will give you the good news first. The target has no static guard force. Such a guard force would betray the launch site's location to aerial surveillance. Due to concerns about civilian casualties, there is no minefield surrounding the target," Chang said.

Xu began to feel more optimistic. Having to navigate a minefield was not a prospect any soldier relished.

"There is only one access road to the launch site, blocked by a gate about a kilometer away. Its use is authorized only for maintenance workers and the target's quick reaction force. However, your unit will advance on the launch site through the woods on the opposite side," Chang continued.

Right, Xu thought. An asset this valuable would hardly be left defenseless.

"Now, the bad news. The enemy's quick reaction force comprises highly trained, well-armed soldiers. We expect the QRF to have about double the number of troops in your unit. They will be summoned by an extensive network of concealed sensors, as found at all of Taiwan's missile launch sites. Motion, infrared, optical. Maybe others we don't know about. Evading them would be impossible. Jamming them would alert the enemy to an assault as surely as spotting you and your men," Chang said.

To his surprise, Xu relaxed. He had feared that the mission planners had overlooked this point, no matter how obvious it seemed. It was good to see that his faith in Chang hadn't been misplaced.

"Once your men are in place near the target, we will launch two HN-3A cruise missiles. One will deploy submunitions designed to blanket the target area and should eliminate all the enemy sensors," Chang said.

Xu fought to keep a dubious look off his face but doubted he'd been successful.

He was right. Chang grinned and said, "Sorry. Force of habit from briefing my superiors. All they want to hear is good news. I must remember you're that rare asset in our Army, a soldier who's seen combat. You're right, of course. The explosions will tell the enemy an attack is underway. And one or more sensors may survive and show your advance on the target in detail. At the same time, the QRF will be hurrying to stop you. But that's why the second HN-3A missile is coming in right after the first."

"Mines," Xu said softly.

Chang nodded. "Just so. They will be distributed between the only access road and the missile site. Since you will be coming from the woods on the other side of the target, you should be safe from the new minefield."

Xu hesitated, and Chang immediately shook his head. "Ask your questions. That's why you're here. I know better than to charge one of our most decorated soldiers with defeatism."

"Thank you, sir. Just how accurate are these cruise missiles?" Xu asked.

"Well, since you'll be near the receiving end, that's a fair question. Missile accuracy is defined as circular error probable, or CEP. The HN-3A is one of our latest missiles, first deployed in 2007, and one of the most accurate with a CEP of five meters," Chang said.

"Five meters," Xu repeated. "That's very good."

"Well, first, I must explain that CEP is defined as the radius of a circle whose perimeter includes the landing points of fifty percent of the rounds," Chang said.

Xu was silent for a moment. Then he said slowly, "So, if the missile deploys twenty mines, ten can be expected to land within the five-meter CEP. The others will probably be further from the target center."

"Correct," Chang replied. "So, keep your unit well back from the initial strike and the new minefield."

Xu now understood why no secondary objective had been assigned to his unit. Between bomblets and mines that landed outside the CEP and fire from the enemy QRF, his unit was expected to have few survivors.

If any.

"Sir, how much time will we have until the QRF arrives at the launch site?" Xu asked.

"A good question," Chang replied. "I wish I could give you an equally good answer. Enough time to plant your charges where they will be effective against buried missiles? Maybe not without the mines to slow the QRF's arrival. However, the mines should buy you the extra time you'll need. Only fools would rush forward once they trip the first mine and realize what we've done."

Xu nodded but in fact wasn't so sure. Brave men might realize how critical time was in preventing his unit from achieving its objective.

How much courage did the enemy have? The political officer in Xu's unit had said that Taiwan's soldiers were soft and unlikely to sacrifice themselves for their capitalist overlords.

Xu had decided it was best to assume the enemy was just as brave as they were and plan accordingly. He had passed that word quietly to all the other men in the unit.

Except, of course, the political officer.

Fortunately, everyone else in the unit shared Xu's opinion of that particular officer.

"Sir, I requested two QJY-201 light machine guns be added to the weapons prepositioned for my unit. Do you happen to know whether that request was approved?" Xu asked.

"Initially, no. Your soldiers can only carry so much, and adding the two machine guns meant subtracting elsewhere," Chang said.

Xu nodded his understanding. They would carry communications equipment, weapons, explosives, and medical supplies. That meant...

"I secured an exception and approved your request. But you will now be carrying minimal medical supplies. Any badly wounded men must be abandoned in the hope that the enemy will provide care after capture. From what we know of the enemy, I believe that is likely. Also, the weight saved doesn't equal what's added. Your soldiers will all have to make do," Chang said.

"Yes, sir. They're good men who won't grumble once they know the reason for the extra load," Xu replied.

"Excellent," Chang said. "You'll be given the documents you and your men will need for travel to your objective on your way out. Good luck, Lieutenant," Chang said, smiling broadly.

"Thank you, sir," Xu replied and left, his head swimming with all the details that needed to be addressed before he and his men boarded their flights.

After Xu left, Chang again looked over the large map of Taiwan that dominated his office. Had he gone too far this time, he wondered.

Colonels didn't normally take the time to give orders in person to Lieutenants. In this case, though, it had been necessary.

Because Chang had erased all traces of the orders for Xu's unit from the Tiger network once he had confirmed the supplies and equipment for the mission had been prepositioned. And the tickets for travel to Taiwan had been purchased.

Why? Because Chang knew Chinese military communications had been compromised before. Yes, the creation of the Tiger network was supposed to have taken care of that problem.

Maybe it had. But Chang was the only one who knew how remarkable it was that Xu was still alive. And he had an irrational belief that as long as Xu stayed that way, they could win this war.

Chang, still facing the map, shook his head at his foolishness. What did he think Xu was, a good luck charm?

Whether he was right about Xu's importance, Chang thought one thing was sure.

He'd done everything he could to ensure Xu's success. A success that might keep some of China's invasion fleet afloat.

Chapter Nine

FSB Headquarters
Moscow, Russia

Boris Kharlov did his best to suppress a frown as he entered the Director's office. Not because of who he saw sitting nervously on the familiar large leather sofa.

There were several reasons for that. Circumstances beyond her control had forced Vidya Kapoor to defect to Russia. Before that, she had been the highest-ranking agent deployed abroad of India's intelligence agency, the Research and Analysis Wing.

R&AW might not have the resources or history of agencies like the FSB or CIA. But it had grown rapidly in recent years, as India's leaders recognized the threats posed by Pakistan and China couldn't be met solely through military means.

So, their team had found that "India's best" turned out to be quite good on their last mission.

Their team leader, Alina, had found that out the hard way on their first encounter. Her attack on Vidya from behind had turned out to be overconfident despite Kharlov's assistance as a frontal distraction.

And Kharlov knew his appearance couldn't help attracting attention. Not only was he considerably larger than the average Russian, Kharlov was probably more fit now than when he had served years ago with Russian Special Forces, Spetsnaz.

But the distraction hadn't been enough. Vidya had somehow guessed an attack was coming from behind and became the only person Kharlov had ever seen put Alina on her back.

Well, not for long. Alina had succeeded in first rendering Vidya unconscious and then drugging her. All without Kharlov lifting a finger to help.

Vidya gaining the upper hand for even a moment impressed Kharlov, particularly because Alina was the only agent he feared.

Not because Alina represented a present danger. On the contrary, she had spent months overseeing Kharlov's recovery from injuries he'd sustained during their last mission.

Over the past several years, Kharlov had spent more time in bed with Alina than all the women he'd known before her put together.

But as far as Kharlov knew, sex and mutual respect were where their relationship ended. Neither had ever spoken a word about what feelings, if any, one had for the other.

Alina could still best him in one-to-one unarmed combat. At first, Kharlov had found this inexplicable, given his greater size and strength.

Now he knew better.

Just as Kharlov knew that if the Director ever decided he had become a liability to the FSB, Alina was the agent he'd send to deal with the problem. Whatever their history, Kharlov had no doubt she would carry out her orders.

As Alina had done for many years before they met.

So, the woman on the couch had managed to best Alina, even for a matter of moments? Yes, Kharlov was impressed.

Other men might have been more interested in Vidya's silky waist-length dark hair and a face that needed no makeup to be attractive.

The contrast with Alina's blond hair and icy blue eyes could hardly have been starker. But though a part of Kharlov acknowledged Vidya's beauty, it came with no hint of attraction.

Kharlov sighed to himself. Yes. He was in love with Alina.

So, where was she? When Kharlov had been summoned to the Director's office, he'd expected to find her here.

For that matter, where was the rest of the team?

Vidya, though, seemed pleased by his arrival.

"It's good to see you, Kharlov. I heard that you were badly injured after I was sent to Moscow. You seem, if anything, even more fit than when I last saw you in Pakistan," Vidya said.

"I've been cleared to return to duty," Kharlov replied. "I have Alina to thank for my recovery. Just when I thought I could do no more, she knew how far to push for that last bit of effort. Without going too far and aggravating my injuries before they could fully heal."

"Interesting," Vidya said thoughtfully. "A side of Alina I wouldn't have expected. I'm glad it led to such positive results."

Kharlov just smiled and nodded. Alina had nearly eliminated Vidya as a security risk during their last mission. Kharlov still wasn't sure he understood Alina's reasons for changing her mind.

Still, it helped explain Vidya's surprise. And speaking of surprise...

"Has anyone told you where the rest of the team is?" Kharlov asked.

Vidya shook her head. "I've heard nothing. The team members I didn't meet in Pakistan all contacted me while I was in training. Mikhail Vasilyev and Neda Rhahbar even had me to their home for dinner."

Kharlov's eyebrows flew upward. "Really! I'm sure that must have been an interesting evening."

Vidya laughed. "It was, actually. Neda had been an exchange student in Pakistan, so we had quite a few experiences in common. Her Iranian perspective was illuminating for me. Though I knew better, it's still easy to think of all Muslim cultures as the same. Shia versus Sunni might seem in some ways to be much closer than Hindu versus

Islam. But sometimes it seems animosity among sects can be even greater than between religions."

Kharlov nodded but said nothing. His mother had attempted to raise him in her Russian Orthodox faith but had failed. Largely because, as a child, Kharlov had refused to believe that a supposedly all-powerful God would allow his father to beat his mother so badly.

Or allow the many other horrors Kharlov had witnessed first as a soldier in Chechnya, and then as a warlord in eastern Ukraine.

Kharlov was spared having to ask further questions by the Director's arrival.

FSB Director Smyslov's entry to a room never passed unnoticed. Even larger than Kharlov, Smyslov's full, bushy beard, and craggy eyebrows immediately made everyone think of the stereotype of the Russian bear.

Today, Smyslov seemed determined to copy another of its attributes. The Russian bear was famously ill-tempered.

"So, you are wondering when the rest of the team will join you on this mission. Well, not today. And maybe not ever, depending on your performance," Smyslov growled.

Neither Kharlov nor Vidya could think of a suitable response and simply nodded.

Smyslov handed each of them a slim folder. Once they had opened it, Kharlov and Vidya could see each contained a single sheet of paper.

"The President has directed that these mission orders be handed to you by me personally for security reasons. For the same reasons, you will return the folders to me once read. This will be your only opportunity to ask questions, so use this meeting with me well," Smyslov said.

The scowl accompanying the words reminded them that the Director's time was valuable.

It took only moments for them to read the single page.

A glance at Vidya was all it took for Kharlov to understand that she expected him to take the lead.

Since she was just out of training, Kharlov thought that showed she possessed at least some common sense.

"Director, these orders do not mention any assets we may call upon to help us enter or leave China. Once we cross the border, is all subsequent travel by foot, or is there some detail I've missed?" Kharlov asked.

Smyslov's scowl deepened. "I pointed out to the mission planner that the distances you must travel while avoiding detection may be impractical on foot. Particularly since you will need to carry equipment and supplies. Unfortunately, the target location and time frame gave us no choice in the matter."

"Sir, nothing in these orders explains why reaching the target must be done so quickly. With even a little more time, there may be options worth exploring. Is there any flexibility to the mission deadline?" Kharlov asked.

Now Smyslov's scowl faded, and he looked more thoughtful. "A reasonable question," he said and sat quietly for several seconds.

Then Smyslov shook his head decisively. "No. Some of your team are already in Taiwan, and the others follow tomorrow. It's not a big island. But we have to give the team members time to reach their targets once the information you obtain allows us to identify them. And what we've learned of China's invasion timetable suggests you may be too late, even if you reach the objective by the mission deadline."

"Understood, sir," Kharlov said. "But I am confused by the statement in the orders that we're to 'avoid capture at all costs' since that is true in every mission. Is there a meaning I have missed?"

"It's one I said should be spelled out, but I was overruled," Smyslov said.

Kharlov fought to keep his reaction off his face but knew he'd failed. Only one person could overrule the Director.

Smyslov gave Kharlov a thin smile. "Yes, the President didn't want it spelled out and said I was not to raise it verbally. But since you've asked a direct question, I will answer it. You may have assumed that if captured, there would be some hope for your exchange. After all, it's been done before."

Vidya glanced at Kharlov and then followed him in nodding. Yes, that was no secret. Captured spies had been exchanged many times over the years. Russia was famous for nearly always getting better than it gave, as in the 2010 exchange with the Americans of four persons for ten FSB agents.

"This time, you should understand no trade will be possible. Any connection between you and Russia will be denied," Smyslov said.

Then he turned to Vidya. "To be blunt, that is one reason an agent fresh out of training is being sent on such an important mission. You are not Russian in appearance. However, your computer skills and Chinese language ability are also important to the success of this mission, so don't think you're viewed as expendable because you're foreign-born. On the contrary, on Alina's recommendation and with my approval, the President has conferred upon you this singular honor."

Smyslov extracted another slim folder from a desk drawer and handed it to Vidya.

"This folder, you may keep," Smyslov said.

Vidya looked at the naturalization certificate it contained and showed it to Kharlov. Then she looked up at Smyslov.

"Thank you, Director," Vidya said.

"You are most welcome," Smyslov said. "Now, I must explain another reason for haste. We have just learned that the Chinese have positioned military assets near our border, supposedly to deter smuggling. However, the number and type of these assets have us worried they could be used in an invasion. We'd thought the Chinese would wait until operations in Taiwan were complete before attacking us as well. Now we believe they might see the world's coming focus on Taiwan as a perfect opportunity to strike us."

"But, Director, surely we still outmatch the Chinese in nuclear weapons. We could threaten them with a first strike that would eliminate most of their arsenal and still have enough to pose a credible deterrent. Or am I missing something?" Kharlov asked.

Smyslov shook his head. "There is a story that goes back two thousand years ago to the Greeks. It is known in Russia and nearly every other country as some variation of 'The Boy Who Cried Wolf.' I assume you know it?"

Kharlov briefly looked confused, but understanding quickly dawned. "The President's predecessor. He often threatened to use nuclear weapons against the Western powers assisting Ukraine."

"Correct," Smyslov said with disgust. "And in the end, did absolutely nothing. So, would we make the same threat once Chinese forces cross our border? Of course. Would we say that there is a difference between an invasion of Russian territory and the conflict in Ukraine? Absolutely. But would that be enough to deter the Chinese? The President thinks it might not."

"So our best hope of avoiding a Chinese invasion of our territory is to ensure their attack on Taiwan fails. I suppose overt assistance to Taiwan is still out of the question," Kharlov said.

Now, Vidya could no longer restrain herself. "I'm sorry, but why? Surely nothing is more important than preventing a foreign invasion!"

Smyslov nodded. "No one could fault you for that conclusion. However, our dependence on revenue from petrochemical exports to China has become nearly total. It was already serious before the conflict in Ukraine but was accelerated by that mistake."

"I see," Vidya said slowly. "But haven't many countries dropped their sanctions against Russia by now?"

"Yes, some have," Smyslov said. "But many other countries realized that their economies were too dependent on Russian oil and gas and took steps to address that once we cut off their supplies. And not only by lining up new sources. Also, by increasing investment in renewable energy, which grew worldwide to over one trillion American dollars by 2022. That investment has continued to accelerate since then."

"Worries about climate change and pollution," Vidya said as she nodded in agreement. "Those have driven Indian growth in solar power development for years."

"Or so the politicians say. In fact, as usual, it's all about money," Smyslov growled. "The Americans haven't built a new coal-fired power plant of any size in over a decade. They are in the process of retiring a quarter of their current coal-fired capacity. This happened even under a previous President who proclaimed his love of coal. Why? Because renewables are a cheaper source of electric power production."

Kharlov frowned. "But if we can do nothing visible to the Chinese, how can we make a difference in the upcoming conflict?"

"The truth is, we can do little. But even that little may help tip the balance. And that is where you two come in. Your mission target is a set of servers that are part of the so-called 'Tiger network.' They store messages relating to all current Chinese special operations plans, including those for the upcoming invasion of Taiwan. You will access the facility where the servers are stored and download those messages," Smyslov said.

Kharlov nodded. All that was covered in the mission brief.

"Our orders say we are to transmit all the information we obtain to Moscow once we have safely exited China. You said that the rest of the team will be waiting in Taiwan for you to review that data. That the plan is to identify possible targets where they could intervene. But why not provide the information to the Taiwan authorities for their action instead?" Kharlov asked.

Smyslov looked annoyed and started to reply.

And then stopped and paused for several seconds.

Shaking his head, Smyslov said, "I keep having to remind myself that you and the rest of your team are not ordinary agents. We place you in the highest-priority missions with a limited chance of success, where circumstances often force improvisation. So, your question deserves an answer."

Then Smyslov paused again, clearly weighing how much to say.

"My recommendation to the President was exactly what you suggested. He rejected it, pointing out that any information coming to the Taiwan authorities from an unverified source would likely be discounted. Or worse, seen as disinformation, intended to draw resources away from the real targets," Smyslov said.

"A reasonable point," Kharlov said, nodding. "Chinese special forces won't be able to attack every high-value target in Taiwan before the invasion. Disinformation is a perfectly credible tactic, especially since it costs nothing."

"Agreed. And the President made one other point. No matter how we tried to conceal the source of the information, there would always be the risk that it could be traced back to us. With our dependence on Chinese petrochemical purchases, that is a chance we dare not take. Especially with Chinese troops massed on our border. We may be wrong, and they are there only as an option. One that will certainly be exercised if the Chinese discover we've fed critical intelligence to the Taiwan authorities."

"So that is the reason the information will instead be passed to other members of our team in Taiwan. Who will act directly to stop the Chinese special forces units," Kharlov said.

"Correct," Smyslov replied. "And given what we know of the Chinese invasion timetable, there is no time to lose. You will depart for the Chinese border this evening, and the rest of the team will go to Taiwan tomorrow."

Vidya looked increasingly confused as Smyslov spoke, so now he turned to her.

"Something about all this makes no sense to you?" Smyslov asked gently.

"Well, yes, Director," Vidya said. "I understand that the Chinese must not find out Russia attempted to prevent the success of its invasion of Taiwan. But if team members are captured or killed in China or Taiwan, isn't the risk of discovery the same? Or worse..."

Vidya's voice trailed off as she tried to fathom the expressions on Smyslov's and Kharlov's faces.

Vidya was stunned by what happened next.

Both men roared with laughter. And kept laughing until tears were streaming down their cheeks.

What have I gotten myself into, Vidya wondered, dazed.

Finally, Smyslov and Kharlov were able to collect themselves.

"My dear," Smyslov said, "I personally authorized you to read the unredacted files of this team's past missions. You have done so?"

"Yes, Director. Every page," Vidya replied.

"Good. Your impressions?" Smyslov asked.

"Initially, I was surprised at your decision to share this information with a new team member. But by the time I had finished, I understood. There can be few teams anywhere that have accomplished so much against such long odds. I will have to work hard to match that standard, but I am ready," Vidya said.

"Well said," Smyslov said approvingly. "But now remember, the President had my job before he became Russia's leader. What lesson do you imagine he took from these missions?"

Vidya sat quietly for a moment and then looked up with a mixture of wonder and alarm. "He doesn't believe our team can fail."

Smyslov shrugged. "Close. Better to say he prays it will not. Though he is no more a believer in the Russian Orthodox god of our forefathers than I am, the President is a man of faith. In Russia's destiny? In his own? I'm not sure even he knows. But this much is certain. We have no better options."

Chapter Ten

Tactical Mobile Over-the-Horizon Radar
Angaur Island
Republic of Palau

Tom Burke, arms folded, looked over the Tactical Mobile Over-the-Horizon Radar receiving station and smiled. TACMOR was initially planned in 2018, but the first construction contract wasn't awarded until 2022. Slated for completion in 2026, that date had slipped.

And maybe that wasn't surprising. Doing anything on time in Palau was a challenge. First a German possession and later taken by the Japanese, Palau had been seized by American forces during WWII. A U.S. trust territory until 1994, it was now independent.

The Republic of Palau consisted of over five hundred islands, most uninhabited. Fewer than twenty thousand people lived in the entire country.

Much of Palau's budget was still supported by American aid under a Compact of Free Association (COFA). Under COFA, citizens of Palau were also free to live and work in the U.S. without visas.

In exchange, the U.S. military had exclusive basing rights in Palau and freedom to operate throughout its territory.

About a thousand kilometers west of Guam, Palau had been chosen as the first post-Cold War TACMOR site because it was within range of the waters off China's coast. Including the Taiwan Strait.

"Good morning, boss! Still having trouble believing it's finished?"

Sam Holt, Burke's deputy, had been a godsend when he'd finally arrived. Sure, he had a few faults.

Self-expression wasn't one of them.

Burke's smile didn't falter because Holt was right. And Holt deserved just as much credit as Burke for getting TACMOR operational.

"Yes," Burke said. "Heard from Babeldaob this morning?"

Holt nodded. "Transmitting at full power, no issues. The link is stable. You'd almost think the people running this place knew what they're doing."

Burke laughed because it was true. After all the years of frustration, it was more than pleasant to hear everything was up and working.

Babeldaob was Palau's largest island, and its transmitter was over a hundred kilometers away from where they stood on Angaur Island, home to TACMOR's receiving station. Babeldaob had Palau's only international airport, and moving in materials for transmitter construction had been straightforward.

Not at Angaur. Its airstrip had been a gravel relic first bulldozed from the jungle by U.S. forces in WWII. As part of the TACMOR installation, it had been upgraded in 2020 to allow use by C-130s.

Before TACMOR's construction, only a hundred or so people lived on Angaur. However, all the activity around TACMOR had attracted the attention of some far more numerous residents.

Palau was part of the Pacific Ocean region called Micronesia, which had about two thousand islands. Among them were four other independent countries: Kiribati, the Marshall Islands, the Federated States of Micronesia, and Nauru. Plus two U.S. possessions, Guam and the Northern Mariana Islands.

Angaur was the only island out of those two thousand to be blessed with feral macaques, a type of monkey inhabiting many countries in

Asia. They were descended from macaques imported over a century ago during German occupation.

Nobody had told Burke this before his arrival. However, the macaques had wasted no time in introducing themselves.

Burke had consulted with residents about the best way to deal with the macaques. After they stopped laughing, they all had the same advice.

Don't feed them.

Oh, and scare them off as much as you can. They carry disease.

Burke had checked, and sure enough, all of the macaques on the island were carriers of the Herpes B virus, which was harmless to them. But potentially fatal to humans.

Two macaques were staring at Burke and Holt right now from the safety of a nearby tree. However, the macaques made no move toward them.

Burke had instructed all staff and construction workers to refrain from feeding the macaques for months. And to yell and wave off any that approached.

Anyone who failed to follow these instructions would be fired for cause.

It had taken three firings before everyone involved with TACMOR understood that Burke was serious. But humans and macaques finally received the message, and one of the project's main impediments had been overcome.

"The techs are happy?" Burke asked.

Holt nodded. Neither of them knew anything about interpreting the data collected by TACMOR.

The project's total expense needed to obtain that data wasn't classified. But it was buried in so many different line items few knew its actual cost.

Burke and Holt were two of those few.

As high as that number was, though, several TACMOR technicians had commented about the even higher expense of the alternative.

Manned and uncrewed surveillance flights, supplemented by shipboard observation when possible.

All of that was both expensive and risky. As the shootdown of the RC-135 had just demonstrated.

Even more important was that with TACMOR operational, the U.S. military had a 24/7 data source available on a region they believed likely to constitute its next battleground. Against a near-peer enemy.

Sure, TACMOR didn't provide a picture granular enough to use for targeting missiles. But that wasn't its purpose.

Instead, TACMOR guaranteed China wouldn't be able to launch a military force of any significant size without the U.S. knowing about it almost immediately.

If no problems appeared with TACMOR's operation over the next few months, Burke could declare it a success and move on to his next project. He'd already recommended Holt as his successor.

Risk. Burke's gaze traveled to a nearby U.S. Army Patriot missile defense system. The Air Force had known from the start that TACMOR would be an inviting Chinese target in the event of war.

To their credit, the U.S. military had wasted no time testing the Patriot system's capabilities in Palau. In 2022, an F-35B Lightning had provided targeting data to a Patriot battery set up temporarily on Palau, long before TACMOR had become operational.

The drone substituting for an incoming enemy cruise missile had been flying at an altitude of three kilometers and been successfully destroyed thirty kilometers away from Palau.

There had been other tests since. All had been successful.

But Burke wondered how realistic they had been. For example, as far as he knew, no F-35Bs were stationed anywhere near Palau.

And how many missiles did the Chinese have to spare for TACMOR? More than one or two, Burke guessed.

He'd read about the hypersonic missiles the Chinese were developing. Could a Patriot battery destroy those as well?

Firmly pushing those thoughts down, Burke turned to more present problems. Ones he could do something about.

"Is the rec center expansion on track?" Burke asked.

Holt nodded. "Opening should still happen next week. Boss, I was skeptical. But once you got the funds, it all came together faster than I'd thought. Just knowing it's coming has already helped."

Burke nodded. Angaur was one of the most isolated postings the U.S. military had to offer. There was only a local economy to speak of if you liked to fish or collect coconuts.

Military support facilities like commissaries, post exchanges, and recreation centers were usually funded primarily from the money collected from their customers. Allowances were made for remote, small installations like Angaur. But Burke had been forced to use his contacts to cut through the red tape that would have typically prevented the rec center expansion he'd recommended in time to do any good.

Nearly a billion dollars had been spent on making TACMOR a reality. But it was so much scrap metal without alert, willing people to operate the equipment and computers needed to collect and interpret its data.

The same was true for the Patriot batteries defending TACMOR on both Angaur and Babeldaob, which came under an entirely different budget.

Burke nodded to himself. He was satisfied he'd done all he could to be sure TACMOR and its people were ready.

The Chinese had sent an unmistakable message by shooting down an American reconnaissance aircraft.

We don't want you to see what we're doing.

Striking TACMOR would be a logical next step.

Well, Burke thought, even if the Chinese manage to destroy us, we'll surely know one thing.

The Chinese are moving on Taiwan.

Chapter Eleven

USS Reno
Joint Region Marianas
Guam

Submarines had been based in Guam since its recapture from the Japanese in 1944. But "Joint Region Marianas" had only existed since 2009, when several U.S. military bases were put under a single combined headquarters. Those included the Navy, Marine, Coast Guard, and Air Force bases on Guam and all U.S. military operations in the Northern Marianas Islands, Palau, and the rest of Micronesia.

The *Los Angeles* class attack submarines of Submarine Squadron 15 on Guam had been replaced over the past year by *Virginia* class subs. The *USS Reno* was the most recent. With its arrival, Submarine Squadron 15 was now composed entirely of *Virginia* class subs.

Captain Dobbins hadn't been surprised to receive the orders sending them to the waters south of Taiwan. He didn't need the latest classified intelligence reports to know that the Chinese would invade Taiwan. A newspaper was good enough for that.

Dobbins smiled wryly to himself. A newspaper. He was probably the only one on board who still had a paper subscription. While he was on deployment, his wife Emily was the only one able to read it.

But he was adaptable enough also to have a digital subscription, which was handy when he spent a long time away from home delivery. Like now.

Well, Dobbins thought, it's not wasted. Emily likes the feel of paper in her hands just as much as I do.

Yes, I'm lucky that Emily has put up with being a Navy wife as long as she has.

If everything goes according to plan, my next and final assignment will be near our home in San Diego. And then I'll retire.

Dobbin's thoughts were interrupted by the voice of his executive officer, Lieutenant Commander Miller.

"Sir, we're ready to get underway. All departments report 100%," Miller said.

Well, that made a nice change, Dobbins thought. He'd been warned that every sub had issues on its first deployment after construction. Yes, those should all have been addressed before the sub was declared operational.

But a *Virginia* class submarine was one of the most complex pieces of equipment on the planet.

Problem-free?

Not likely.

Some issues had been addressed between sailing from the Newport News, Virginia shipyard to San Diego. Even more were fixed when *Reno* arrived at Pearl Harbor, the primary maintenance facility for submarines in the Middle Pacific.

But the ship wasn't all that was new. Many of the crew were on their first tour of submarine duty. Some of their issues were reasonably easy to fix, especially simple lack of knowledge. Miller had done an excellent job there.

Being cut off from the world for weeks or even months at a time? For the new young crewmembers, that was harder to fix.

Of course, isolation had always been an issue to some degree. It was a much more severe issue for the new crewmen used to being "connected" via the Internet during every waking moment.

Combined with the many other career options in a robust American economy, Dobbins had heard these were challenging days for Navy recruiters.

Especially ones trying to find recruits for the submarine service.

Well, it helped that *Reno* was the latest and best the Navy had to offer. The crew might still need some work. But every berth had been filled.

Dobbins brought his attention back to Miller. "Good, XO," Dobbins said. "Let's get underway."

"Yes, sir," Miller replied and hurried off to give the orders that would see them on their way to the waters near Taiwan. Minutes later, they were submerged and on their way.

Dobbins frowned as he looked at the map display. About three days.

It would take a lot less time than that to get to what Dobbins considered a comfortable depth.

Then Dobbins smiled to himself. The Challenger Deep was only a few hundred kilometers away. Over ten thousand meters deep.

Much farther, of course, than *Reno* was designed to go. Not to mention in the direction opposite from Taiwan.

Dobbins had always envied the scientists who got to explore such depths, naturally, in specialized vehicles. He'd always believed that a higher priority should be placed on examining the vast amount of Earth's underwater surface that needed to be better mapped.

"Captain, sonar is detecting opening torpedo tubes," Miller said. In a voice that struggled to remain calm.

"Fire two torpedoes down that bearing. Deploy countermeasures. Evasive course at top speed. Designate contact *Sierra One*," Dobbins said.

He didn't know how precise a fix sonar had on the enemy submarine. But that didn't matter. Right now, the priority was to get that sub busy with something other than firing on *Reno*.

Like avoiding *Reno*'s torpedoes.

"Two torpedoes fired at us by *Sierra One*. And Captain, two more torpedoes fired at us from another bearing."

Miller delivered that news in an admirably calm voice.

Dobbins did his best to follow Miller's example as he repeated the orders he'd given in response to the first attack.

Knowing that it wouldn't matter. Somehow, two enemy submarines had managed to reach firing range undetected. And fire four torpedoes first.

They'd had all the time they needed to line up precise shots. *Reno*'s hastily fired torpedoes would only hit an enemy as a wild stroke of luck.

How had the enemy subs managed it?

It was Dobbins' last thought before the first enemy torpedo hit.

And then another.

Reno's countermeasures defeated two enemy torpedoes. But it didn't matter.

Reno sank like a stone before it could let anyone know its fate.

Chapter Twelve

Apartment Building
Moscow, Russia

Vidya was nervous. "Why are we making this detour? Won't we miss our flight?"

Kharlov shrugged. "We have time, though not much. This shouldn't take long."

Then he knocked on the apartment door.

Alina's expression when she opened it was anything but welcoming.

"Aren't you two supposed to be on your way to the airport?" she asked.

"Yes," Kharlov replied. "But we need to discuss something quickly before we go."

Alina's scowl only deepened, but a quick jerk of her head allowed them in.

Despite her nervousness, Vidya immediately saw that Kharlov moved around Alina's apartment like someone who knew it well.

And the reason for that must be...

Vidya tried as hard as she could to suppress her realization. And as she sat next to Kharlov to avoid looking at Alina.

Proof her efforts had failed came immediately. As Alina's face drew close to hers, Vidya could feel her breath.

And smell it. I wonder if the spearmint is from toothpaste or mouthwash, Vidya thought numbly.

"You will tell no one," Alina hissed as her eyes drilled into Vidya's.

Vidya nodded and said nothing.

Alina drew back, apparently satisfied.

"Explain," Alina snapped, now staring at Kharlov.

Kharlov laid out his plan in a few sentences, then sat waiting for Alina's response.

It didn't come right away.

A few moments later, Alina shook her head with resignation.

"The reason you didn't make this proposal to the Director?" Alina asked.

"It only occurred to me on the ride here," Kharlov replied.

Alina looked at Kharlov intently and then nodded, apparently satisfied.

"And this man who worked for you in Ukraine, who happens to be in Myanmar and available to arrange transport to the Chinese border and beyond. You are certain he can be trusted?" Alina asked.

"He works for Rosoboronexport. We both know he had to get a security clearance for that job. Though not one high enough for what I will ask him to do. More importantly, I trusted him and all of my men with my life daily. You know my file," Kharlov said.

Alina pursed her mouth and nodded.

Vidya was sure parts of that file didn't meet with Alina's approval.

But it seemed Alina was satisfied that Kharlov believed the man was reliable.

"You think this man's assistance will improve the chances of mission success? Sufficiently to risk security by including him?" Alina asked.

"Without his help, the mission will fail. We simply don't have enough time to reach the objective on foot," Kharlov replied.

Vidya could hear the sincerity in Kharlov's voice and found herself holding her breath.

Vidya had no idea who this man was who Kharlov planned to include in their mission. But now she hoped Alina would agree.

"Very well. Approved," Alina said.

Then Alina fixed Kharlov with an icy stare that made Vidya cringe. Now what?

"Did you consider making this change without my approval?" Alina asked.

Kharlov shook his head. "Not for a moment. I've learned my lesson. Besides, it would have been poor thanks for all the hard work you've put into my recovery. That's a debt I still have to repay."

Alina's blue eyes softened. "Good. Remember, the debt can only be repaid if you succeed in your mission and return from it alive."

"On your way," Alina added roughly and quickly left through a door that Vidya guessed led to a bedroom.

Moments later, they were back on their way to the airport.

In a way, Vidya realized she found the entire strange encounter with Alina comforting.

First, she trusted Kharlov's judgment. If he thought this old comrade would be helpful, she believed him.

More important, Vidya was a great believer in motivation. Everyone wanted to survive. But often, more was needed.

No, Vidya had seen what had passed between Alina and Kharlov.

Vidya had no illusions about her chances of surviving this mission without Kharlov.

She felt much better knowing her companion had the oldest motivation of all to return home alive.

Chapter Thirteen

Zhongnanhai Compound
Beijing, China

President Gu looked up as his assistant entered, with Admiral Bai at his side.

Ignoring his assistant, who exited and closed the door behind him, Gu exclaimed, "Admiral, so good to see you! Please, have a seat, and let's take some tea."

Making the Air Force Commander wait had been to send a message. So was this reception.

Gu welcomed success and would treat anyone who brought it accordingly.

Gu waited until they were both seated on either side of a long low table, and it had been set with a tea service before he spoke again.

"I've read your report and am impressed that your plan succeeded so well. Can we do it again?" Gu asked.

Bai frowned and shook his head. "As I said when I first sought your authorization for this plan, such an ambush could only work once. We don't know how often the American sub is supposed to contact its headquarters. But I'm sure the Americans will soon know something is wrong. If we try an ambush again, it could well be our subs that are surprised and fall victim."

"A pity," Gu sighed. But he saw Bai's point and paused.

"Very well," Gu said finally. "Do you still propose to carry out the next step you outlined in your original proposal? It seems a pity to eliminate the agent we recruited at the American headquarters in Hawaii. Isn't he our only one?"

"Yes," Bai replied. "But the Americans aren't stupid. They will realize the only way we could have eliminated one of their subs so soon after it departed Guam is if we knew the exact time and course of its departure. That means we had someone with access to the sub's orders. They will investigate and then find the money we paid the traitor. No matter what pains we took to conceal it."

"I suppose you're right," Gu said. "Once caught, the man would certainly tell all he knows. But didn't we use a Russian recruiter?"

"Correct, Mr. President. A former FSB agent. He has since had an unfortunate accident. The payment to our agent at Pearl Harbor was also routed through Russia. But all those steps may not be enough to fool the Americans," Bai said.

Gu frowned. "Why not? The Russians were never America's friends. And after all the help the Americans gave Ukraine, the Russians rightly blame them for the heavy losses they took in that war. Plus, didn't your original briefing papers point out the Russians have done this before, with an entire family of spies?"

Despite himself, Bai was impressed. He hadn't expected Gu to read that far into the brief, let alone retain such details. John Walker Jr. was a United States Navy chief warrant officer who had spied for the Soviet Union for nearly two decades until his arrest in 1985. Walker had helped the USSR access almost a million U.S. Navy classified messages. He had also recruited his brother and son, who obtained even more Navy secrets.

As a result, the Soviet Navy made substantial technical advances in many areas. Even worse, they knew precisely where every American submarine was located for those two decades.

Yes, Bai thought. Gu was right that the Americans would not dismiss the Russians as suspects out of hand. But...

"It is true, sir, that the Americans must consider Russian involvement a serious possibility. However, the Russians are only a shadow of their former selves. The FSB is not feared and respected as the KGB once was. Suspicion will eventually fall on us. But we will gain a useful delay," Bai said.

Gu shrugged. "Very well, I'm convinced. Eliminate the agent as you originally planned. I'm sure we must expect to sacrifice many assets before we can finally reclaim Taiwan."

Chapter Fourteen

Type 003 Aircraft Carrier Fujian
Somewhere Near the Taiwan Strait

Lieutenant Tan Sichun's pulse quickened as she saw who was rapidly approaching her J-15B fighter. The squadron commander!

It didn't help that Tan's pulse had already been racing. A carrier landing in rough seas was guaranteed to accomplish that, no matter how many times you'd done it.

And this had been Tan's first time. Sure, she'd done plenty of practice landings, first on a simulator at the Naval Aviation University in Yantai. Where she had answered the Navy's call in 2023, specifically asking for women with a university background in science and technology to train to become carrier aircraft pilots.

Then, on a land runway, the exact dimensions as what she'd have to deal with on *Fujian*.

Next, repeated landings on *Fujian* during calm weather. When Tan had learned very quickly that nothing truly prepared you for landing on a surface that moved up and down like a bucking horse.

Tan had come through all those tests with flying colors. She smiled as she thought of how apt the English expression was in her case.

That wasn't only Tan's opinion. Even many of the other pilots, all men, were starting to show her grudging respect.

Had Tan done something wrong with this landing? It couldn't have been too bad because Tan was still breathing, and there were no warning lights on her console. Was there some damage to her plane that the J-15B's sensors hadn't revealed?

Well, nothing for it but to see what the Commander wanted. Tan was ready to deal with whatever was ahead as long as he wasn't going to ground her.

The canopy opened, and the familiar smell of salt air and burning aviation fuel hit Tan's nose.

The smell that told Tan she was home.

A crewman was already leaning a ladder against Tan's jet, and she quickly clambered down it.

It wouldn't do to keep the Commander waiting.

Commander Ge was just steps away. He gestured silently for Tan to walk with him.

Usually, Ge's walking pace was quite brisk. Not today.

Tan realized that whatever Ge had to say, he wanted it to be out of the hearing of her fellow pilots.

The noise level on the flight deck guaranteed privacy.

"Lieutenant, your last landing was outstanding. I couldn't have done better myself," Ge said.

Tan was startled and momentarily at a loss for words. Praise? After months of drilling under Ge, it was the last thing she'd expected.

Yes, Tan had seen proud men wilt under the lash of Ge's scorn. And invective that included quite a bit of vocabulary she'd never heard.

Thankfully, none of it had been directed at her so far.

Finally, Tan managed to say, "Thank you, sir."

Ge grunted. "Every pilot on this carrier is competent, or I'd have ensured they never boarded. But you're more than that. You're a natural aviator, and that's something you're born with that goes beyond your training. So, I'm making you a flight leader."

Tan could hardly believe her ears. A flight leader? Her?

That meant she would command all the planes assigned to a particular mission from *Fujian*. And since *Fujian* carried forty combat jets as well as other reconnaissance and support aircraft, that meant…

Ge said, "I am, of course, selecting multiple flight leaders. All the jets on this carrier will never be committed to a single mission. You might be put in charge of just a few. But it could be one or two dozen. You know the challenge that lies ahead."

Reunification with Taiwan. Yes, even the cooks knew that.

Aloud, Tan said, "Yes, sir. I will work hard to meet this great responsibility."

"See that you do," Ge said gruffly, but then, to Tan's astonishment, added a small smile.

It was the first Tan had ever seen on his face.

"You know some of the other pilots will never be happy that a woman is leading them," Ge said and looked at Tan closely.

Tan was suddenly sure that the wrong response could see the flight leader title being taken away as quickly as it had been offered.

Still, she spoke immediately.

"Sir, that is their problem, not mine. My only concern is to perform as flight leader as well as I can. When I succeed, I believe even the skeptics will be convinced," Tan said.

"When I succeed, Lieutenant?" Ge repeated, raising his eyebrows.

"Yes, sir," Tan said. "We have the world's best planes, ships, and pilots. Our cause is just. Nothing can stand in our way."

Ge nodded thoughtfully. "Good, Lieutenant. I'm glad you're approaching this challenge with the proper attitude. Now, get cleaned up, eat something, and see the Duty Lieutenant in the briefing room. He'll have the materials you need to study for your new role. You may find some surprises."

"Yes, sir," Tan replied and then hurried off to follow Ge's orders.

Some surprises? Tan thought she knew what at least one might be.

Like all Chinese military pilots, Tan had been drilled endlessly on the need to stay in constant contact with her flight controller. On or near land, at an airbase. At sea, onboard the carrier.

But Tan had heard a rumor. That new instructions had gone out to flight leaders. Saying if circumstances changed too quickly for them to report and receive new orders, flight leaders were to act on their initiative.

One example Tan had thought about many times was being ordered to engage and destroy Taiwan's fighter jets to clear the way for the invasion fleet. But while flying toward the enemy fighters, spotting cruise missiles headed toward the fleet from a different bearing.

So, stick with the mission and hope the fleet's defenses could knock down the cruise missiles on their own? Or change course toward the missiles and hope to destroy them in time to return to the mission?

Before the enemy fighters launched their own missiles at the fleet.

Maybe someone back at headquarters had realized that in combat, there would be times when they had to trust their leaders in the field.

Tan shook her head, chiding herself. This speculation was pointless.

She would know the answer soon enough.

Chapter Fifteen

East Sea Fleet Headquarters
Ningbo, China

Senior Captain Ding knew his choice to base the liberation fleet at Ningbo had been criticized. However, as the lead invasion planner, Ding still believed Ningbo was the best choice.

Ningbo was the world's busiest port by cargo tonnage and the third busiest container port. That meant the facilities were present to handle the largest fleet assembled since WWII.

Ningbo might not be China's closest port to Taiwan. But the logistics were far easier to manage at Ningbo due to the port's sheer size. The extra distance also meant the fleet could assemble out of range of Taiwan's anti-ship missiles and organize its defenses without the threat of attack.

Ningbo's commercial port was adjacent to a large existing Navy base, which also served as headquarters for the East Sea Fleet. All commercial ships destined for Ningbo had been rerouted to other ports. The berths and other port facilities had all been closed to the public, and temporary barriers manned by military police had turned the entire port of Ningbo into a Navy base. The transition had been easy since part of the port had already been a Navy base.

Ding boarded the small craft waiting to take him to the ship that would serve a key role in today's operation. *Lhasa,* one of the new Type 055 *Renhai* cruisers. And one of the most potent warships China possessed.

Fitting, Ding mused, that *Lhasa* would house the task force commander. Who he would advise as Admiral Bai's representative.

Lhasa had been the capital of the independent nation of Tibet until 1951. After the defeat of Tibetan forces the previous year by the People's Liberation Army, it became the Chinese Tibet Autonomous Region.

Now, *Lhasa* would lead the way to incorporating another wayward province into the People's Republic of China.

Taiwan.

The first vessels Ding passed on his way to *Lhasa* were in the rear. And they were the least glamorous vessels, though perhaps the most important of all. Three *Fuchi*-class replenishment ships, each carrying 10,500 tons of fuel oil and gasoline, 250 tons of fresh water, and 680 tons of cargo and ammunition. Just after them came a single Type 919 hospital ship, the third to be built since 2020.

Next, Ding passed the twenty-nine Type 072 landing ships. They carried far fewer helicopters than the Type 075 but would take more total soldiers altogether.

There were differences between the original Type 072s, Type 072As, Type 072IIs, and Type 072IIIs. On average, though, each ship could carry two hundred fifty troops, ten amphibious armored vehicles, and four *Yuyi* class air-cushion medium landing craft. Most also had a single helicopter.

Eight Type 071 amphibious transport docks each carried eight hundred troops, ten amphibious armored vehicles, four *Yuyi* class air-cushion medium landing craft, and four helicopters.

Many of these ships had always been based at Ningbo. Over the past few months, others had been transferred from the South Seas Fleet, headquartered at Zhanjiang. Yet more had come from the North Seas Fleet, with headquarters at Qingdao. Some ships had just arrived over the past week.

The three Type 075 landing helicopter docks came next. The nine hundred troops and thirty assault helicopters each carried were supplemented by ten amphibious armored vehicles and four *Yuyi* class air-cushion medium landing craft.

Together, they amounted to the world's largest amphibious assault capability. Greater, even, than that possessed by America's Navy.

Next, three Type 055 *Renhai* cruisers. Including *Lhasa*.

Far ahead, Ding could see *Luyang* and *Sovremenny*-class destroyers. *Jiangkai*, *Jiangwei*, and *Jianghu*-class frigates.

The destroyers, frigates, and cruisers were well out front. Their job was to protect the ships carrying troops, armored vehicles, helicopters, and supplies.

Ding also knew that over two dozen Chinese submarines patrolled the waters between Taiwan and the mainland. Looking for any enemy submarine or ship that dared to venture from its base to threaten the invasion fleet. Including any American submarine foolish enough to stick its nose where it didn't belong.

Ding's review was interrupted by their arrival at *Lhasa*. A long, spindly structure hung from the cruiser's side was to be his means of boarding. Ding hoisted himself onto the metal steps and began the long climb to the deck.

The structure swayed in time as each passing wave rocked the ship. Ding was forced to concentrate as he placed each hand and foot upward.

It's fortunate I've worked hard every day to keep myself in shape, Ding thought.

Even so, Ding's breath was coming fast and shallow as he reached the top of the boarding ladder and climbed down the last few steps to the deck.

A lieutenant was waiting and saluted Ding.

"Sir, I've been ordered to escort you to Captain Song," the lieutenant said.

Ding just nodded. Better to save every remaining bit of energy for this next encounter.

Especially since more ladders were ahead.

It wasn't long before Ding found himself standing before Captain Song on the bridge.

Song said, "Everyone, listen up! This is Senior Captain Ding, aide to Admiral Bai. He speaks with the Admiral's authority and is here to advise me as task force commander. If he gives you an order, obey it. If he asks you a question, answer it. Do you all understand these orders?"

The chorus of "Yes, sirs!" that followed from the bridge crew was almost loud enough to hurt Ding's ears.

Ding did not doubt that Song meant every word and that the bridge crew would follow his instructions to the letter.

Ding was just as sure that every move he made and every word out of his mouth would be reported to Song within minutes.

As it should be, Ding thought.

Song looked directly at Ding, who thought the man had aged since his last photo. However, Song was like Ding in believing in physical fitness. If anything, Song was in even better shape.

Ding was relieved to see it. There were plenty of admirals and captains at headquarters who, while not precisely fat, had let themselves get soft.

Hard and fit was needed for the tense and busy days ahead. Ding thought to himself that, once again, Admiral Bai had proved his judgment was excellent in such matters.

"Welcome aboard *Lhasa*, Senior Captain. How would you like to proceed?" Song asked.

"Admiral Bai is very concerned about the threat posed to this task force by anti-ship missiles, Captain. Perhaps you could show me your defenses against that threat," Ding replied.

Song nodded and gestured for his executive officer to take charge while he was away from the bridge.

Song understood, of course, that the real purpose of this tour would be to let them speak freely away from the ears of the bridge crew.

Once they were on deck, Song pointed to the closest of two Type 726-series launchers.

"These launchers can fire two types of missile countermeasures. Flares to confuse infrared seekers and small decoys with active radiofrequency jammers. As you can see, we have one each on the port and starboard side," Song said.

Without waiting for a reply, Song pointed at the closest of two 30 mm H/PJ-11 guns.

"These 11-barrel Gatling guns have a rate of fire of about 10,000 rounds per minute. As Close-In Weapon Systems, they are intended to take out any missile that gets past our flares and decoys. Again, we have one each on the port and starboard side," Song said.

Ding nodded. "Similar systems are present on most of the other ships in this fleet. Do you believe they will be sufficient?"

Song shook his head. "Certainly not. Some missiles will inevitably pass through our defenses. The only question is how many and how much damage they will cause. The answer will depend on several factors. How many missiles are fired. How able they are to avoid our countermeasures. The size of their explosive warheads, and the speed of the missiles on impact."

"Good," Ding said. "I'm glad to see you've given this problem some thought. What have you done to address it?"

As if on cue, sirens sounded on the nearest *Renhai* class cruiser. They were immediately followed by a swarm of activity that reminded Ding of the last time he had accidentally kicked over an anthill.

"We finished our most recent damage control drill about an hour before your arrival. Every ship in this fleet is on a rotating schedule of such drills. While we await the order to set sail for Taiwan, I'm making sure that every sailor knows what is expected of him when missiles hit," Song said.

"Excellent, Captain," Ding said. "A single anti-ship missile can damage a ship but not sink it. Even multiple hits can be survived if the crew secures the affected compartments and keeps fires from getting out of control."

Song nodded. "Exactly the areas we are focusing on in these drills. You may tell Admiral Bai that we know we will take hits."

Then Song paused and looked Ding right in the eye.

"But no matter what, we will land our troops and tanks on Taiwan."

Chapter Sixteen

Presidential Office Building
Taipei, Taiwan

President Cheng scowled as National Security Bureau Director-General Yan walked into his office. Not at Yan. He was the most competent man Cheng had on his staff.

As usual, Cheng had to force back his impulse to tell Yan to eat something. Short, pale, and rail-thin, Yan always appeared to have forgotten to eat his last two or three meals.

Cheng kept his mouth shut because he knew he looked like he might have eaten Yan's missing meals. He wasn't quite obese. His wife saw to that. But Cheng knew his stress response was overeating. He couldn't blame Yan for the reverse.

No, Cheng's scowl wasn't for Yan. Instead, it was for the situation Yan had come to discuss.

The Republic of China (ROC) had been founded in 1928, led by Chiang Kai-shek as Director-General of the Kuomintang (KMT). When the KMT lost control of mainland China to the Communists, they fled offshore to Taiwan in 1949. In the meantime, the Communists on the mainland declared the People's Republic of China (PRC).

The PRC and the ROC agreed on just one thing. There was only one China. Naturally, each believed they should control all of it.

For decades, each had done nothing to alter the fact that the ROC was an independent country in every way that mattered. It looked like that might be about to change.

Though the ROC included some other islands, well over ninety percent of its population lived in Taiwan. So, instead of the "Republic of China," nearly everyone called it simply "Taiwan."

By many measures, Taiwan was more successful than the PRC. It ranked fifteenth richest globally with a gross domestic product (GDP) per capita of over 25,000 American dollars, higher than Portugal's. The PRC's GDP per capita was still under $9,000, less than Mexico's.

After the ravages of COVID-19, PRC unemployment shot up to 15%, though the government did its best to conceal that fact. Taiwan had been more successful at COVID containment thanks to imported Western vaccines that worked well, unlike the PRC's version. So, Taiwan's unemployment rate was 4%.

Ironically, income inequality was more severe in the Communist PRC than in capitalist Taiwan. The share of PRC national income earned by the top 10% increased from 27% in 1978 to 41% in 2018. At the same time, the portion made by the bottom 50% dropped from 27% to 15%. The section of Taiwan's national income earned by the top 10% increased from 24% in 1978 to 36% in 2018. Simultaneously, the share made by the bottom 50% dropped from 30% to 23%.

The average residential Internet speed in the PRC was 7.6 megabits per second, ranking it number fifty-five in the world. Behind Sri Lanka.

Taiwan's average residential Internet speed was 85 megabits per second, ranking it number one in the world.

But most of Taiwan's citizens considered its freedom their greatest asset. The British news magazine *The Economist* ranked every country's freedom annually using a wide range of criteria. Taiwan ranked number 11 and had the top title of "full democracy." The

United States ranked number 25 and had the next best title of "flawed democracy." The PRC ranked number 151 and was bluntly labeled "authoritarian."

Cheng sighed and rubbed his forehead with one hand while he irritably waved Yan to a seat in front of his desk with the other. Well, one comparison wasn't in Taiwan's favor. They had a population of 24 million. The PRC had nearly one and a half billion people.

And the world's largest armed forces to match.

Only the difficulty of mounting an amphibious invasion had kept the PRC at bay this long. However, the PRC had been busy building and buying ships and planes. And everything else it would need to incorporate Taiwan as another PRC province.

Whether Taiwan's 24 million people liked it or not.

"So, the PRC plans to invade. The latest on our preparations?" Cheng asked.

Cheng and Yan had known each other for many years. That, plus a mutual agreement that Taiwan's situation was at best desperate, had long since led them to dispense with pleasantries.

There was no time for them.

"All our forces training in America have been recalled. They should be back by the end of this week," Yan said.

"Good," Cheng said. "About two thousand men, right?"

Yan nodded and added with a rare smile, "And women, sir."

Cheng nodded back but said nothing. Women had served in Taiwan's military since its founding, but nearly always in non-combat roles such as intelligence and medical care.

In 2023, women had been allowed to volunteer for reserve force training that included combat specialties. That decision followed the announcement that compulsory military service for men would be extended from four months to a year starting in 2024.

Both decisions reflected the need for more personnel in all branches of Taiwan's military. The problem was simple. With low unemployment, civilian jobs offered better pay and less hardship.

The only reason to serve amounted to patriotism. How committed were Taiwan's citizens to its freedom?

In 2021, Afghanistan's citizens had given one answer to that question.

In 2022, Ukraine's citizens had given another.

Now, it was Taiwan's turn to answer that question. How much was their freedom worth?

Taiwan's active duty force, with only 169,000 personnel, appeared entirely unready to face a Chinese invasion. However, that force had never been designed to stand alone.

Instead, the primary purpose of universal male conscription was to train a reserve force of 1.6 million.

"How are preparations to mobilize the reserves?" Cheng asked.

Yan shrugged. "Weapons and supplies are confirmed sufficient for full mobilization. Orders have been drafted, and transportation readied. As planned, reservists will be deployed near their current residence to the maximum extent. Of course, that will not always be possible."

"Obviously," Cheng said. "I suppose we won't know how many reservists will fail to report until we issue activation orders."

"No, sir," Yan replied thoughtfully. "But I am optimistic. We've always known that a small percentage of our citizens harbor Communist sympathies. Others fear the dangers and hardships of military service. Most of our people know enough about the mainland not to welcome a Communist takeover. As long as our citizens believe we have a chance to resist, I think most reservists will answer their orders to mobilize."

"That's the key question," Cheng said. "Will we stand alone, or will anyone give us real help? Any hint that the American trainers are getting ready to leave?"

"The short answer is no," Yan replied. "I think that it's worth recalling how quickly training numbers on both sides have increased. In 2023, the American trainers stationed here went up from a few dozen to two hundred, and more every year since. There are now about a thousand. We only had a few hundred personnel being trained in America each year, but in 2023, that increased to five hundred. That number has also gone up each year."

"There were American trainers in Ukraine in 2022. When Russian tanks crossed the border, where were they? Already gone. And when the Americans left Afghanistan in 2021, how much notice did they give the Afghan government?" Cheng asked. Not really expecting an answer.

But Yan had one. "American trainers may have left Ukraine. But look at how much support in money and weapons they provided once the Ukrainians proved they had the will to fight against the Russian invaders. And how much American leadership counted for similar help coming from their allies. As for Afghanistan, their people had two decades of American assistance to prepare to stand on their own against the Taliban. How is it America's fault that the Taliban's success in 2021 was so easy?"

"Fine," Cheng sighed. "You're right. Since 2021, the Americans have repeatedly said they would help us against the PRC and backed words with actions. We have to hope that will continue. Now, what about Japan?"

"We've heard nothing directly. Our sources say that the Americans are discussing a coordinated military effort with the Japanese. I think we will hear nothing definitive from either country until they agree on how their forces will cooperate in the battles to come. Or indeed, if Japan will do nothing but allow the Americans to use their bases and defend their own borders," Yan replied.

Cheng nodded glumly. "Yes, my expectations there are not high. Japanese defense spending indeed grew by twenty-five percent in 2023. And that growth continued, so in 2027, they met their target of spending two percent of their gross domestic product on defense. That was a sharp increase from their historic limitation of only one percent. Thanks to Japanese economic growth, it meant their military spending much more than doubled. Still, Japan's focus is on self-defense. Not protecting their neighbors."

"Well, sir, the news is better than we expected from Korea and the Philippines," Yan said. "Both countries have just announced they will allow American forces to operate from bases in their countries in our support. The Philippines, in particular, made two coastal bases in Cagayan province available."

"That is good to hear," Cheng said, brightening. "Those bases are less than four hundred kilometers from us. And the Americans have been using them since 2023, so they're ready for operations."

"Yes, sir. I think the mainlanders will find conquering us won't be as simple or easy as they'd hoped," Yan said.

Chapter Seventeen

SpaceLink Pacific Mission Command Center
Vandenberg Air Force Base, California

Eli Wade had his fingers in many pies. Solar roofs, electric cars, tunnels for transportation. But his most important project had always been space. Because that is where he believed the future was calling.

Wade looked through the glass wall of the conference room, beyond which was the floor containing dozens of SpaceLink employees. All were working on the latest SpaceLink V2 launch.

"So, after today, will we finish replacing all V1 and V1.5 satellites with the V2 version?" Wade asked.

SpaceLink project manager Mark Rooter nodded. "Absolutely. The argon-fueled thruster they carry will save us even more money than the switch from xenon to krypton."

Wade scowled, and at first, Rooter was startled. Wade always liked saving money.

But the scowl had nothing to do with that.

"The V2 thrusters will be more powerful, right? I specified that, remember," Wade said.

"Yes, sir, boss. I guess you've been reading the news about Taiwan, right?" Rooter replied.

Wade's scowl deepened. "That's exactly right. It's the downside of taking military money. SpaceLink is great for backup military communications, and we've proved it can work even with fighter aircraft. But it makes us a big fat target for the Chinese."

Rooter nodded. "And the Chinese haven't been shy about saying so, all the way back in 2022."

Now, Wade wasn't scowling anymore. Instead, he looked worried.

"I remember. Someone at the Beijing Institute of Tracking and Telecommunications wrote that China should develop hard and soft kill methods for destroying our satellites. Including the use of Chinese satellites equipped with ion thrusters. And since then, they've followed through with their plan to deploy just as many low-Earth communications satellites as SpaceLink."

"That's right, boss. Then, in 2023, someone at the People's Liberation Army's Space Engineering University in Beijing gave more details. China's satellites would be launched under a network codenamed GW, owned by the newly established China Satellite Network Group Co. GW's explicit purpose was to compete with, track, and, if necessary, destroy our satellites," Rooter said and then hesitated.

Wade smiled and said, "Out with it, Mark. What else is bothering you?"

"Well, sir, it's those researchers at the University of Texas. The ones who started using our synchronization sequences in 2022. The signals beamed down by our satellites to help receivers coordinate with them. To develop a backup GPS," Rooter said.

Now Wade's scowl was back. "I remember. I said no when they asked us to coordinate with them on the project. Are you saying that wasn't the end of it?"

"No, boss, it wasn't," Rooter replied. Then, seeing Wade's expression quickly added, "I mean, it was for us but not them. Without any help from us, they kept up their research and developed a backup GPS accurate to within thirty meters."

Wade relaxed. "Well, nobody will be able to use that for military purposes. Especially targeting."

"Yes, sir. But other researchers at Ohio State University picked up on the idea and applied machine learning to the project. I read their paper. It was pretty impressive," Rooter said.

Wade's expression told Rooter to get to the point.

"Well, the OSU team was able to get accuracy to ten meters," Rooter said.

Now Wade looked thoughtful. "Ten meters. OK, it's still not good enough for targeting. But useful for navigation, especially if your only alternative is a compass or breaking out a sextant."

"Right, boss. But our satellites were already a Chinese target. If they've been reading the same university research papers I have, I bet they've moved further up on China's priority list. So, what should we do about it?" Rooter asked.

Wade said nothing for several moments. Then, he shook his head and said, "I've got to give this more thought. I'll have a decision for you this afternoon."

Then he looked through the glass wall of the conference room again to the dozens of SpaceLink employees working on that day's launch of dozens of V2 satellites.

"Nobody leaves after the launch this morning," Wade said. "Whatever I decide, they'll have more work to do."

Chapter Eighteen

Kadena Air Base
Okinawa, Japan

Lieutenant Colonel Dave Fitzpatrick's new assignment as commander of the F-35s that made up the 44th Fighter Squadron wasn't his first posting to Japan. That had been at the northern end of the Japanese island of Honshu, where Misawa Air Base had been called "the tip of the spear." The focus there had been on two potential attackers, Russia and China.

Or, God forbid, both at once.

Fitzpatrick had been deployed on many assignments since his first at Osan Air Base in Korea. Iraq, Afghanistan, Syria – Fitzpatrick had flown combat missions in all of them.

Now that he was at Kadena, Fitzpatrick was two thousand kilometers south of his old posting at Misawa. But one thing was the same.

China was still the main threat.

And that's what he would discuss today with his counterpart for the F-22s that made up the 67th Fighter Squadron, Lieutenant Colonel Frank Drake.

Drake was standing just outside the headquarters building and saluted as Fitzpatrick approached. They were the same rank, but Drake was a "by the book" officer. Since Drake knew he had been promoted more recently than Fitzpatrick, anytime he saw Fitzpatrick, he saluted him. There was nothing wrong with that.

But at first, Drake's prickly personality and love of regulations had rubbed Fitzpatrick the wrong way at Misawa, where they had both been squadron commanders. Enough that he had seriously considered accepting an assignment that would have cut his tour at Misawa short.

In the end, though, he'd come to terms with Drake's style. It helped that Drake knew his business, both as a pilot and as a squadron commander. It helped even more that once they'd come to know each other better, it turned out that Drake had a sense of humor.

For example, Drake's father and grandfather had both been pilots. One night, over beers at the officer's club, Drake told Fitzpatrick a story about his grandfather, a B-52 pilot named Dave.

On his last tour, the Vietnam War was still underway. But Dave was assigned to Seymour Johnson Air Base in North Carolina, then under the Strategic Air Command. A large sign next to the gate proclaimed that fact and SAC's motto, "Peace is Our Profession."

One day, as Dave drove up to the gate, he noticed a team working quickly to remove the sign. Just as they finished, he caught the addition someone had made with spray paint to "Peace is Our Profession."

"War's Just A Hobby."

Well, war was coming, Fitzpatrick thought. Time to do whatever we can to win it.

Once they entered the headquarters building's secure briefing room, Fitzpatrick gestured for Drake to have a seat. Drake looked pointedly around the large room with plenty of other seats.

Fitzpatrick smiled. "It will be just us today. You'll see why in a minute."

Drake shrugged and sat while Fitzpatrick cued the first PowerPoint slide on the projector.

"I told you before I left Misawa that my next assignment would be working on the Variable In-flight Simulation Test Aircraft at Edwards Air Base. Which just happened to be an F-16 back then," Fitzpatrick said, nodding to the red, white, and blue F-16 shown on the slide.

Drake nodded. "The VISTA X-62A. But I heard that the F-16s got traded in for F-35s. And I'm guessing that's why you transitioned from the F-16 to the F-35, right?"

"That's my next slide," Fitzpatrick replied, showing an F-35 painted in the same red, white, and blue colors, then paused.

"We were testing two artificial intelligence programs, which we always called AI for short. The first was from the Air Force Research Laboratory, Autonomous Air Combat Operations or AACO, which focused on combat with a single adversary beyond visual range. The second was from the Defense Advanced Research Projects Agency called Air Combat Evolution, or ACE, designed for dogfight-style maneuvers with a closer, visible enemy."

Drake grunted. "I hope you made progress beyond a single enemy fighter because the Chinese sure won't come at us one at a time."

"We did, but it wasn't easy. The more planes, the more variables, and the more strain on hardware and software," Fitzpatrick said.

"Right," Drake said slowly. "But since we're talking about this, I guess you think you succeeded. What does that look like?"

Fitzpatrick didn't answer but went to the next slide. It showed an F-15EX, F-22, and F-35 flying side by side. Their paint was the standard Air Force gray.

"We now have the latest versions of AACO and ACE ready for all these fighters. Technicians are installing the modules on our planes as we speak. With luck, we'll have time to train our pilots in their use before the shooting starts," Fitzpatrick said.

"Really? From what we've heard in our latest intel briefings, that could be a matter of days," Drake said.

"Yes," Fitzpatrick said firmly. "The point of this program is to make combat easier, not harder. Take one likely scenario: a mixed group of Chinese fighters advancing on Taiwan. Say, J-11s, J-16s and J-20s. Each has a different top speed and represents varying threats. Which should be targeted first? Which of our planes should target each enemy plane? With which missile?"

Drake looked at Fitzpatrick skeptically. "You're saying the AI will make all these choices for us?"

"No, not at all," Fitzpatrick replied. "The AI only suggests. It makes no decisions and launches no missiles. But what we've tried to do is distill thousands of hours of combat experience into this software. I've spent hundreds of hours in the air with it when it was flying the plane. Including simulated combat missions."

"You're a braver man than me," Drake said, shaking his head. "But you're standing before me, so I guess it works. Do you mean that if, for example, a pilot was wounded, the AI could fly him back to base?"

"That's exactly what I mean," Fitzpatrick said. "I'm not going to tell you this AI is perfect. We could get poor performance, especially if we have bad intel on Chinese fighter capabilities. We won't know anything for sure until the war starts."

Drake shrugged. "Well, that's like any other war throughout history. Sounds like it could give us an edge, though. Lord knows that with the number of fighters China can field, we'll need every advantage we can get."

"Well, we'll have one more ace up our sleeve that'll be an unpleasant surprise to the Chinese. MALDs," Fitzpatrick said.

"I saw some in action during an exercise a few years back. Miniature Air-Launched Decoys. I saw one that mimicked the radar signature of an F-35. Another was a MALD-J designed to jam enemy radar. But they've been around for years. What makes these special?" Drake asked.

"First, quantity. We'd purchased one thousand MALDs by 2014. Since then, we've bought another 1,500. So, getting our hands on hundreds here at Kadena hasn't been a problem," Fitzpatrick said.

Drake frowned and lifted his hand. "Before you go on, they're air-launched, right? Will that be another job for your F-35s?"

Fitzpatrick shook his head. "No. We could, of course, but we'll be loaded up with anti-aircraft missiles. B-52s will do the job in large batches, escorted by Japanese F-35s."

"That makes sense," Drake said, nodding. "MALDs have a range of nearly a thousand kilometers, so the B-52s will be able to launch from within Japanese airspace."

"Right," Fitzpatrick said. "Now, the second recent development for MALDs is the data we collected from the Ukrainians."

Drake grunted. "I read that we sent some MALDs to the Ukrainians starting in 2023. Good to see we're getting some return from that investment."

"We sure have," Fitzpatrick said. "Chinese radar and quite a few of their fighter aircraft were originally based on Russian designs. So, the guys in research think they've been able to tweak the MALDs being sent to us to make them even more effective against the Chinese."

Drake slowly nodded. "Well, I still think we'll have a real fight on our hands."

Then Drake paused and smiled.

"But I've got to admit I like our chances a lot more than I did when I walked in here."

Chapter Nineteen

Grishkov Residence
Moscow, Russia

"It's time to start rounding up our guests," Arisha said pointedly to Anatoly Grishkov.

Grishkov had been married to Arisha for nearly two decades. It was long enough to know there was only one correct response.

"Yes, dear," Grishkov said.

It was a short trip to the study where Mikhail Vasilyev was playing chess with Boris Kharlov.

"Time for dinner," Grishkov said.

Vasilyev shrugged and waved at the board in front of him. "A pity. Mate was coming in a few moves."

Kharlov's eyebrows flew upwards. "Yes, just so. I'm glad you recognize the hopelessness of your position."

Vasilyev laughed. "Of my position! Come, Anatoly, settle this for us. You may not be a master, but you're more than good enough to see that my victory is inevitable."

"No, thank you," Grishkov said firmly. "My assignment was to get you both to the dinner table. I have more guests to corral after I'm done with you two. And my boss won't accept failure."

Vasilyev and Kharlov traded glances.

Kharlov smiled and said, "A smart soldier knows when to follow orders without delay. Besides, I can smell Arisha's cooking from here. You don't have to tell me twice."

Grishkov's next stop was the living room, where all the other guests had congregated. Neda Rhahbar, Vasilyev's wife, was deep in conversation with Vidya Kapoor. Alina and Evgeny were watching a news program on TV.

Grishkov turned to Alina and Evgeny first. "Sorry to interrupt your viewing, but dinner is ready."

Alina snorted with contempt, nodding toward the TV. "No apology is necessary. My security clearance gives me access to enough information to know that nearly every word from the bleached blonde on the screen is wrong. Or a deliberate lie. The only entertaining part is trying to guess which."

Evgeny smiled. "I'm old enough to remember reading *Pravda* as a child during Soviet days. Even then, I remember thinking any newspaper that needed to call itself 'truth' should be read with caution."

Fortunately, part of the training for an FSB agent was always maintaining awareness of their immediate surroundings. Grishkov didn't need to say anything to Neda and Vidya.

Moments later, they were all seated at the dinner table, loaded with an impressive assortment of Russian delicacies. Steam rose from all of them except the salads.

Vidya smiled and said, "Arisha, I'd thought we Indians set the standard for treating guests. Just from what I can see and smell, I'm happy to admit I was wrong."

Arisha nodded brusquely, but Grishkov could see she was pleased. "Thank you," she said. "But that's enough talking. You must eat before this food grows cold and all my work goes to waste."

Talking ceased and resumed only occasionally as a guest complimented Arisha on the quality of her cooking.

Grishkov was even more pleased at this than Arisha. As he had hoped, his guests were happy with the meal. That should make his news, Grishkov thought, easier to swallow.

Seeing that all the guests had finished eating, Arisha moved to stand to begin clearing the table. But a look from Grishkov reminded her to stay seated.

Usually, it took much more than a look to stop Arisha, Grishkov thought wryly. But this time was different.

After all, the entire evening had been her idea.

Grishkov cleared his throat, and all eyes turned toward him.

"First, let me again welcome all of you to our home. You are all important to us, and most of you have saved my life at one time or another," Grishkov said.

"The reverse is just as true!" Neda exclaimed, and everyone laughed.

"Yes, well," Grishkov hurriedly continued, "several of you are already aware that Sasha and Misha are away at university. None of you, though, have heard that they are both studying in France."

Vasilyev and Kharlov exchanged knowing glances but said nothing. Ever since the "special military operation" in Ukraine, parents with sense and money sent their sons to study abroad as soon as possible.

As Grishkov's partner, though, Vasilyev was willing to bet that it had been Arisha's idea in this case.

"After this mission, the Director has agreed that I may retire from Federal government service and that we may move to France to be closer to our children," Grishkov said.

A stunned silence greeted his announcement.

The silence stretched on for what seemed a great deal of time but was actually just a few moments.

Grishkov added, "Arisha is flying out to look for a home near Paris in a few days. The Director was good enough to recommend a trustworthy company to move our belongings so she won't return.

So, this was the last time I could be sure we'd all be able to get together."

Kharlov said, "We will miss you. It is fortunate your children are in France. If you get bored with retirement, I'm sure a little contract work would be available from French intelligence."

Arisha's reaction was immediate and vocal.

Neda and Vidya looked at each other since they were the only ones in the room who didn't understand what Arisha had said.

Both had learned Russian curses, both directly and indirectly, and had thought they were fluent.

But not fluent enough.

Grishkov quickly said, "I have no intention of working for the French or anyone else. When we are not visiting our children, I plan to spend my time traveling with Arisha. I may have gone on voyages before outside Russia, but I would like to experience what it's like without someone shooting at me."

Everyone but Arisha laughed, and Vasilyev said, "I think you'll find Western Europe more agreeable than Iran or Afghanistan."

Arisha sniffed and said, "There, I agree with you. I've read how the women in those countries are treated."

Kharlov looked at Arisha and said, "Please forgive my poor attempt at humor. I am well aware that Anatoly has earned his retirement many times over. I wish you both many years of peace and enjoyment."

Arisha's immediate response was a glare and opening her mouth for what everyone, including Kharlov, was sure to be another stream of invective.

But then she closed it and shook her head.

"You saved my Anatoly's life in Ukraine at no small risk to your own. For that reason, you are forgiven," Arisha said sternly.

Then she smiled, and everyone fought back a sigh of relief. "In fact, if you behave yourself, you may have tea and dessert. Come, let us prepare."

Neda, Vidya, and Alina knew without needing to ask that this meant they were to join Arisha in clearing the table and then bringing tea and dessert.

All three were FSB agents, like all the men around the table. But none resented helping Arisha while the men remained seated. Because they knew Arisha believed strongly in Russian traditional values, and this was her home.

Of course, if any of the female FSB agents had held such a gathering at their homes, matters would have been organized differently.

As they loaded plates into the dishwasher, Arisha turned to Neda and said, "I'm glad your husband will be going with Anatoly. It's the only reason I agreed to let him go on another one of these adventures. Mikhail, at least, has the same common sense as his father."

Mikhail's father had deliberately sacrificed himself to keep Grishkov alive on their second mission together. Though he had never told Arisha the highly classified details, she knew her husband held a near superstitious belief that Mikhail would keep him from harm.

Neda smiled. "I'm just as glad that Anatoly will be with Mikhail. They usually keep husbands and wives apart on missions, and I suppose I understand their reasons. But if I can't watch out for Mikhail, I'm glad Anatoly will."

Arisha frowned and shook her head. "He hasn't said a word to me, but I know he will be involved in this foolishness over Taiwan. The Chinese are hungry, and Taiwan is too near and sweet to pass up. Mark my words, it won't be enough for them. They'll try to bite off a piece of us next."

Neda, Alina, and Vidya all looked at each other, trying to think of a response.

Arisha laughed and said, "I wish I had a picture of your expressions! Don't worry, I know you can't say anything. Just make sure you all stay safe, and bring my Anatoly back to me!"

Chapter Twenty

Taoyuan International Airport
Taiwan

Lieutenant Xu waited in line for his turn at the immigration counter, clutching his passport and immigration form. He had been worried that the threat of war would sharply reduce traffic to Taiwan and that he would stand out as a Chinese visitor.

Nothing could have been further from the truth. Taoyuan was now the world's tenth busiest airport and judging from the crush of people around him, nobody believed war was imminent.

Xu thought back to 2022. When Ukrainian politicians were publicly agreeing with Russian government assurances that mass troop movements on their border were merely exercises. Tourists had still been arriving in Kyiv back then, too.

A quick look told Xu that far from standing out, Chinese citizens appeared to be the majority of visitors. Yes, some appeared to be Japanese, and a handful of Westerners. And some visitors who were Chinese in appearance might be from countries like Malaysia and Singapore. Or even the United States.

However, Xu was one of many in line clutching their passport. The red cover with a gold seal on top and lettering below of a Chinese passport was easy to spot, even from a distance. Xu could see plenty of them.

So, there would be nothing surprising about Xu's tourist visit to Taiwan. Even when the news talked about the threat of war constantly.

Now, Xu thought gloomily, all I have to worry about is how much they'll focus on Chinese men of military age.

At least his hair wouldn't give him away. Thanks to the dispensation given to Chinese special forces because of situations like this, Xu's hair was longer than it had been since his teenage years.

Finally, Xu's turn at the immigration desk arrived. The man there gestured silently for Xu's passport and immigration form. Then he put the passport in a reader and looked at a screen.

"Purpose of visit?" the man asked.

"I'm going to see as much as I can in my short time. I'm also going to do some shopping for my family. I've heard the prices here are excellent!" Xu said enthusiastically.

"Length of stay?" the man asked, in a tone Xu was delighted to hear sounded bored.

"Just a week," Xu said. "That's all the time I could get off from my job."

The man stamped Xu's passport and returned it, nodding toward the baggage claim and customs area. Xu murmured his thanks and hurried off.

Xu stood at the baggage carousel, where his suitcase had yet to arrive. He looked at his passport and saw with relief that he'd been granted the standard thirty-day stay for Chinese citizens. He'd said a week because that's what he'd been told to say, but Xu had been worried he'd get no more than that.

It turned out that the people organizing this mission knew what they were doing, Xu thought. A small detail, but still comforting.

No sooner had the thought formed than Xu's suitcase slid onto the baggage conveyor belt. Moments later, Xu was on a sleek modern train to downtown Taipei. The trip took only half an hour.

Xu hadn't expected to stay in a luxury hotel in Taipei. That was fortunate because the one reserved for him perfectly matched his cover identity as a middle-class tourist trying to stretch his budget.

All that mattered to Xu was that he had a private bathroom and clean room. He doubted he would be staying long.

It was more than adequate for a Chinese soldier like Xu, who had spent years in either tents or spartan barracks.

Tomorrow at noon, Xu was supposed to receive the secure cell phone he would need to receive instructions to rendezvous with the rest of his team. And their target location.

Until then, his orders were to avoid attracting attention and behave like a tourist.

Xu's preference would have been staying in his room, where he had thought "attracting attention" would be impossible. His briefer in Beijing had quickly vetoed that idea, pointing out that nobody from China visited Taipei to stay in a hotel room.

Hotel staff would think, at best, that Xu might be ill. At worst, they might wonder if he was laying low for some other reason.

So, as soon as Xu deposited his suitcase, which had nothing but his clothes, he was out the door to act like a tourist.

Xu's hotel was steps away from Metro Taipei, the city's subway system. With one hundred thirty-one stations, Xu wasn't surprised that one of them led directly to his destination.

The Taipei 101 building. The tallest skyscraper in the world when it was built, it had since been surpassed by the Shanghai Tower and several others. It was still an impressive structure that Xu had always wanted to visit.

It took only minutes for the subway train to deposit Xu at the station serving the Taipei 101 building. Even more quickly, Xu had reached the line for tickets to the observation deck.

Ticket secured, Xu walked to the elevator that would take him to the 89th floor. He saw a sign saying the trip would take thirty-seven seconds and shook his head. That would require a speed of about a thousand meters per minute since the building was the first to exceed half a kilometer in height.

That was ridiculous.

As the elevator doors slid closed, Xu set the chronometer on his digital watch and noticed another man nearby doing the same. They smiled at each other, with an unspoken message passing between them.

You can't believe everything you read.

Xu's chronometer hit the thirty-seven-second mark as the doors opened on the 89th-floor observation deck.

The other man smiled at him again. This time, it was rueful. Xu was sure his answering smile looked just as embarrassed.

Xu had been posted to China's mountainous border with India and was no stranger to heights. However, he had never been to the Shanghai Tower or any other skyscraper in China. His duties had never given him the time.

Here, at nearly four hundred meters up, Xu could enjoy a 360-degree view of Taipei's entire cityscape. It was indeed impressive.

Once Xu had taken it in, though, he moved on to a feature that interested him even more. Taiwan was in a known earthquake zone, and the island was also subject to frequent typhoons. He had read about how the building was kept safe from both threats and was eager to see it in person.

It was only steps away. The world's largest tuned mass damper, with a weight of six hundred sixty metric tons and a diameter of nearly six meters. Xu knew it was designed to counteract forces causing the building to move automatically.

Xu read a sign saying that the damper was suspended from the 92nd to the 87th floor and that its most significant movement had been about a meter. That had been to counteract the winds from Typhoon

Soudelor in 2015, which had exceeded two hundred kilometers per hour.

The sign also claimed that the damper could counteract an earthquake of any known magnitude. Xu had read, though, that so far, it had only had to deal with an earthquake measuring 6.8 on the Richter scale.

A voice in Xu's head asked how well it would withstand multiple strikes by Chinese ballistic missiles.

Xu had never been told that the Taipei 101 building would be a target in the upcoming invasion.

But his superiors might see its destruction as a blow to enemy morale, Xu thought.

Xu disagreed. He thought targeting this building, which had no military purpose and would undoubtedly cause thousands of civilian casualties, would only stiffen Taiwan's resolve to resist assimilation by his country.

At least, Xu thought, that's how I'd react. I hope our leaders will agree with me.

In the end, it didn't matter, Xu concluded with a shrug.

He might only know his own small part in the coming offensive. But Xu was confident that there was no way this island could stand against the might of the world's largest country.

Which finally had a military to match.

Chapter Twenty-One

Yangon International Airport
Yangon, Myanmar

Vidya Kapoor looked around the arrival terminal with barely concealed surprise. In a low voice, she said to Boris Kharlov, "I expected something like a regional airport in India, or maybe worse. This isn't half bad, though."

Kharlov nodded towards nearby shops selling Versace and Calvin Klein products. "You're right. I read that this terminal was opened in 2016, but my expectations were also quite low. Myanmar's reputation took quite a beating with the most recent military coup in 2021. A reputation that hadn't been great even back when the country was still called Burma. I suppose the generals decided keeping up the international terminal was a cheap way to give visitors a positive first impression."

Vidya grimaced and said, "Well, let's see how they do with delivering our bags intact. I'm still ready to be disappointed."

"I've read that looking down on all things Burmese is an Indian tradition that even predates British India days. Any chance that has affected your outlook?" Kharlov asked with a smile.

Vidya flushed and, for a moment, said nothing. Then, slowly and reluctantly, she nodded. "Maybe so. Honestly, I haven't thought through anything I just said. Maybe the most dangerous prejudices are the ones you're not even conscious you have."

Bags secured, they reached the exit doors to the terminal which slid open, revealing a large black Mercedes sedan idling directly in front of them.

Kharlov smiled at Vidya's reaction. "Rosoboronexport, the sole entity authorized to deal with Russian arms exports, has resources. This car is just a small illustration of that point."

Kharlov opened the back door for Vidya while the driver hurried to load their baggage.

Once they were both seated, the driver put the sedan in gear while passing back a slim leather wallet. It contained his identification.

Kharlov nodded, showed it to Vidya, and passed it back.

"As you see, Sergei works for Rosoboronexport. Years ago, he worked for me. You may speak freely before him," Kharlov said.

Vidya nodded her understanding.

Kharlov turned to Sergei. "I hope our equipment arrived on schedule?"

Sergei nodded. "In the trunk, ready to go."

Kharlov smiled. "Excellent," he said and then turned back to Vidya.

"To continue our earlier discussion, underestimating local opposition could be dangerous. Myanmar's intelligence agency was up and operating against the Japanese when this was British Burma almost a century ago. They've worked hand in glove with the military, which helps explain why generals have been in charge of Myanmar's government most of the years since independence."

"That brings me to my main worry about this mission," Vidya said with a frown. "I understand from the briefing papers that when we arrive in Mandalay, two look-alikes will take our place for the next several days. But we are supposed to demonstrate Russian weapons the military here is interested in buying, correct?"

Kharlov nodded.

"Well, if Myanmar intelligence is so capable, surely high-quality images of us will be shared with whoever will be at the demonstration. Won't our doubles then be exposed as fakes?" Vidya asked.

"They would be if we weren't back to show the weapons' operation by then. The doubles will be restricted to the compound we've rented in Mandalay, so only glimpses from a distance will be possible. The delay between arrival and presentation is standard to allow recovery from the flights and setup preparation time. As long as we're back in time, there should be no problem," Kharlov said.

Vidya nodded. "Well, it's fortunate that the target isn't too far from the border. And that I happen to be familiar with it."

Kharlov's eyebrow climbed as he asked, "You just happen to know more about it than the information in our briefing papers? What is your source?"

"A low-ranking Chinese soldier we persuaded to defect when I worked for Indian intelligence. He had previously been assigned to guard the target location," Vidya said.

"How can you be sure the man wasn't planted to feed you disinformation?" Kharlov asked.

"Always a possibility," Vidya acknowledged. "But we thought it unlikely. One of our local agents came across him in Macau, where he was on leave and doing very poorly at one of the casinos. Persuading him to sell what he knew was quite easy."

Kharlov grunted. "If his superiors had found out he was addicted to gambling, a soldier would have faced court-martial at best. But whatever he told you is probably no longer valid. Surely, the Chinese would change security arrangements once his disappearance was discovered."

"Perhaps," Vidya replied. "But we used the car registered to the man to stage a single-car accident. The body we placed inside was burned beyond recognition. Fortunately, the defector's ID papers survived in the car's glove compartment."

A sudden look of understanding crossed Kharlov's face. "I'm sure you were debriefed thoroughly when you first arrived in Moscow. In particular, about any missions you had undertaken for Indian intelligence. Was this operation among those you discussed?"

Vidya smiled. "I think you have uncovered the answer to this so-called coincidence. The Director was certainly given this information. And probably decided not to include it in the briefing for security reasons. After all, why repeat what an operative assigned to the mission already knew first-hand?"

"Good," Kharlov said. "That all makes sense. How long ago did this happen?"

"About a year ago," Vidya replied. "The good news is that the facility housing the servers was built just months before, so I doubt they would have been eager to change its security arrangements. Especially based on nothing more than a guard dying in a car crash, which are quite common in China."

Kharlov's response was interrupted by their sedan suddenly slowing. A quick look ahead was enough to understand the reason.

A military checkpoint.

"Sergei, how common are checkpoints on this road?" Kharlov asked.

"Very," Sergei responded glumly. "I have driven to Mandalay many times during my tour here. The only surprise is that it took this long for one to appear."

Kharlov nodded his understanding. "So, they are mobile. Given this country's endless state of near civil war, I suppose that's a tactical necessity."

"Well, yes," Sergei said. "The military here learned decades ago that any fixed position, no matter how well fortified, was nothing more than a big fat target. They may not be as nimble as the insurgents, but they've learned the hard way to keep moving."

"Just how likely is it that we'll run into these insurgents once we leave Mandalay?" Kharlov asked.

Since traffic had slowed to a crawl as they approached the checkpoint, Sergei could answer by taking his right hand from the wheel and rocking it back and forth.

"On the one hand, I picked the best route possible from Mandalay to your target location just over the Chinese border. It's a major highway with a significant government presence," Sergei said and then stopped.

"And on the other?" Kharlov asked.

Sergei smiled. "I was thinking about how to put that. All the insurgent groups operate primarily in the border areas. They will try to avoid direct engagements with government forces. But I'd say your chances of encountering them are about fifty-fifty."

Kharlov winced. "I had no idea security here was so poor. Our chances of surviving such an encounter?"

"You will be hidden in the next transport I have arranged for you to board in Mandalay. As long as you remain undiscovered, your chances will be quite good. Insurgents are generally not interested in killing for its own sake since that draws a heavier government response. Instead, they usually accept 'contributions' from a driver or sometimes rob him and the vehicle's contents," Sergei said.

"And if we are discovered?" Kharlov asked quietly.

"Kidnapped at best," Sergei replied. "Shot out of hand at worst. Either way, you will certainly be unable to complete your mission on time."

"Understood," Kharlov said.

Vidya's only comment was to raise an eyebrow.

They drove the rest of the way to Mandalay in silence.

Chapter Twenty-Two

SpaceLink Pacific Mission Command Center
Vandenberg Air Force Base, California

Eli Wade was back in the same glass-walled conference room where, just a few days before, he had ordered the development of a backup GPS capability using SpaceLink satellites.

SpaceLink project manager Mark Rooter looked up nervously from the stack of paper before him. Several of the folders from the stack were open in front of him.

Rooter didn't look exactly ready.

"Need a little more time, Mark?" Wade asked sympathetically. After all, it was Wade's decision to refuse approval for the project years ago that had made it necessary to do it in a hurry now.

Rooter shook his head. "No, boss. Just checking a few details before I give you the status update you wanted."

"Good," Wade said. "Then let's get to it."

"The bottom line is, we think we're ready to go. At least, we are at our end," Rooter said.

Wade nodded. "Excellent. I honestly thought this would take us more time."

"Well, normally, it would have. But you remember the universities that have been working on this project for years. They did most of the heavy lifting for us. Once we plugged our much more accurate satellite positioning data into their programs..." Rooter shrugged.

"Got it. But that still leaves the customer end of this project. I'm sure what we've got will work as a backup to navigate ships and planes. But only the military can say whether it will be good enough for targeting weapons. And I'm sure there's work to do on their end to accept our data as a valid input, right?" Wade asked.

"Exactly right, boss. But they've got some really capable people working on the GPS program. If they get the word to make this work, and we are close to a shooting war with China, I'll bet it will happen quickly. Of course, there's just one person who could give this the priority it needs," Rooter said.

Wade grunted. "Hernandez. He was already going to be my first call after this meeting. If I can't get him, then his buddy Robinson. If anyone will want a backup GPS, it's an Air Force general."

"Yes, sir," Rooter said and then looked like he would say something else.

But didn't.

Wade, of course, noticed.

"Isn't this where you remind me that someone ought to be paying us for all this hard work?" Wade asked with a smile.

Rooter smiled back, relieved he didn't have to raise the topic.

"Yes, boss. I know there's no time for the normal contracting procedures. But shouldn't we at least get an agreement in principle that the government will give us compensation for our efforts? Especially since it really has cost us money," Rooter said, waving in the general direction of the dozens of staff visible through the conference room's glass wall.

Wade nodded. "Normally, I'd agree. Two things, though. I know Hernandez and Robinson. I sure have disagreed with some of their decisions. But they're both fair-minded and reasonable. One way or another, we'll get paid. But even if we weren't, I'd do this anyway."

At first, Rooter looked surprised, but then he slowly nodded as well.

"You think we will be in a shooting war with the Chinese. And that they're going to knock down our GPS satellites," Rooter said.

"I do. And while we're on that subject, we've got both our Victus Nox rockets ready, right?" Wade asked.

Rooter nodded. Victus Nox, Latin for "conquer the night," was the name Space Force had chosen for a program to deploy a satellite to orbit as rapidly as possible.

Wade was still unhappy that another company had been picked for the first demonstration launch in 2023. Even though his had won the contract for the next two.

The 2023 Victus Nox launch had happened twenty-seven hours after the go order from Space Force. Wade was determined to beat that record.

"Just one thing, sir. When I saw how things were going between China and Taiwan, I decided to prep another rocket, just in case. So we've got three ready to go, not two. I was able to move some things around in the launch budget for the extra expense. I'm pretty confident Space Force will pay the regular price for the third launch," Rooter said.

"Great work," Wade said. "I just hope our military can use all we're doing in time to make a difference."

Chapter Twenty-Three

Mandalay, Myanmar

Boris Kharlov woke with a start as the sedan abruptly stopped. Sergei had parked it inside a cavernous cargo handling facility.

Kharlov noticed at once that their Mercedes was the only sedan present. Trucks of every size imaginable occupied most of the building. Cargo waiting to be loaded accounted for almost all of the remaining space.

A moment later, Kharlov felt Vidya Kapoor's eyes on him. Glancing in her direction, he saw Vidya was smiling.

"I'm glad you were able to get some rest," Vidya said. "Good to know you don't snore. Could be awkward in the field."

Kharlov didn't know what to say to that, so he turned to Sergei.

"How long until our transport arrives?" Kharlov asked.

Sergei nodded toward a man Kharlov could now see had emerged from a nearby truck.

"Right now. You did say 'as quickly as possible,' yes?" Sergei replied.

Kharlov nodded, but Vidya frowned.

"I need a few minutes to freshen up before we go. I hope there's somewhere suitable nearby," Vidya said.

"There is, right over there," Sergei said, pointing. "But first let me introduce you to your next driver. We've used him many times before, always with good results."

When Sergei finished speaking, the man was standing near their sedan. He was thin and relatively short.

Kharlov thought that though he was no expert on Asian ethnicities, the man looked more Chinese than Burmese.

Vidya and Kharlov exited the sedan while Sergei walked toward the man, who stood silently.

"Good to see you again, Lishi!" Sergei said in English. "I have the passengers here, and they'll be ready to go in just a few minutes."

Lishi nodded. "Good. Any cargo with the passengers?"

Sergei pointed to the sedan's trunk. "Yes, but nothing that should be too difficult to fit. I see you have the usual truck."

"Yes," Lishi said. "Have you told the passengers how they will travel?"

"No," Sergei said. "I thought it would be easier for you to show them. Let me help you move their cargo while they get ready for the next stage of their journey."

Kharlov and Vidya looked at each other, wondering what "easier to show them" might mean.

Both decided that rather than asking questions, their time would be best spent in whatever facilities were available before leaving Mandalay.

When they returned, Kharlov and Vidya were just in time to see the last of their equipment packs being transferred to Lishi's truck.

Sergei stuck out his hand, which Kharlov and Vidya both shook.

"I will now leave you in Lishi's capable hands. Good luck," Sergei said. Moments later, he was gone.

Lishi gestured towards the back of the truck. "Let me show you where you will be sitting, and then you can tell me if some or all of your belongings will accompany you. Or if we can leave them where they are stored now."

Then Lishi clambered onto the truck with Kharlov and Vidya close behind.

Once they had all walked to the interior side closest to the cab, Lishi tapped the metal wall.

It didn't sound hollow.

"Wait here and touch nothing," Lishi said, walked briskly to the truck's end, and jumped down. Then, they could hear him running to the truck's cab.

A few moments later, Kharlov and Vidya could hear a faint "snick," and a hairline crack appeared in the metal wall before them.

When Lishi jumped back in the truck this time, he closed the cargo doors behind him but didn't secure them. As soon as the doors closed, overhead lights snapped on.

Pointing first to the hairline crack and then to Kharlov, Lishi said, "Go ahead, open it."

Kharlov could fit his fingernails into the gap, and pulled. A section of the wall swung soundlessly towards him. A narrow space stood revealed, with two plastic seats bolted into the wall adjacent to the cab.

Kharlov gestured towards two metal cylinders next to one of the seats. "I'm guessing oxygen cylinders? Does this mean the space is airtight?"

Lishi shook his head. "I doubt it. But I did as well as I could to make it so, to keep both sound and smell inside the space. So without oxygen, breathing over time would become difficult."

"So if you're worried about smell, you think the truck will be searched with dogs," Kharlov said flatly.

"I know it will," Lishi replied. "I have crossed the Chinese border many times. No one in this space has ever been detected. Still, whenever the truck slows or stops, you must be careful to cease all speech and movement. And take only shallow, quiet breaths. A dog's hearing is also very sensitive."

"How long do you think the trip will take?" Vidya asked, frowning as she looked at the hard plastic seats.

Lishi smiled. "Many hours. But you will not have to hide in this space unless the truck slows or stops. I will stop twice for fuel and once for you to relieve yourselves. I suggest you avoid eating and drinking during the trip."

Then Lishi paused and pointed at a pile of canvas sheeting on the truck bed. "For obvious reasons, there are no seats in this area. But you can fashion a soft place to sit by bunching up a canvas sheet. Now, please place any belongings you don't wish to be inspected by Chinese border guards in the hidden space. Be sure to leave enough room for you to sit."

Kharlov and Vidya looked at each other. Equipment for tapping into a server? Women's clothing? Clothing fitting a man nearly double Lishi's size?

Somehow, everything they had would have to fit in with them.

Minutes later, though, they signaled Lishi that they were ready to go. Moments after that, the truck got underway.

Progress was slow until they exited Mandalay and reached the highway, but then they picked up speed. As Lishi had promised, there were only a few stops where they had to hide, and they lasted only a short time.

Meanwhile, Vidya had decided to make use of the time.

"The Director gave me your file to read at my request. I had to read it in his office suite, and I was searched by his assistant to ensure I had no device capable of copying or photographing the file. To my surprise, it was not redacted," Vidya said.

Kharlov nodded. "And why do you suppose that was so?"

Vidya looked up, startled. "I expected you to object, not to ask questions. Though that is one I'll admit didn't occur to me."

After a pause, Vidya said slowly, "Giving me your unredacted file was a way to show I had the Director's trust. Even though I'm from a foreign intelligence service."

"Well, yes. But it also contained numerous object lessons the Director wanted you to learn," Kharlov said.

Vidya thought that over. "I suppose one lesson was to obey orders, even if disobeying them might risk mission failure. I saw the reprimand you received for using unauthorized explosives during the mission in America."

"That's right," Kharlov said. "We came very close to being captured by the Americans. The fact that Russian agents were operating in the United States, especially carrying out acts of sabotage, was not something our President wished discovered."

"The section covering your operations against human trafficking when you were a warlord in eastern Ukraine before the Russian invasion initially puzzled me. You told the FSB you did those raids to hurt your rivals, who were your competitors in smuggling weapons and other contraband. But that made no sense," Vidya said.

"No? Why is that?" Kharlov asked with a small smile.

"Because you could have struck them more easily at a time and place of your choosing. And not spent any time on liberating trafficked women and children or seeing them safely out of Ukraine," Vidya replied.

"So what is your explanation?" Kharlov asked.

"I think it's because of your alcoholic father and the violence he directed against you, your mother, and..."

Kharlov raised his right hand and said, "Enough."

Vidya stopped speaking.

"The truth is, I didn't do a lot of careful thinking back then. I didn't like women and children being sold into slavery. I had the men and weapons to do something about it. The reasons I gave the FSB were true as well. The men we killed were also smuggling weapons and other goods and were my competitors. Maybe the lesson you should learn is that motives can be complicated, and many things can be true at once," Kharlov said.

Vidya nodded. "After reading your file, I also realized you want to become Director."

Kharlov threw back his head and laughed. "What convinced you of that? The reprimand from the Director?"

Vidya wasn't smiling. "No. The risks you undertook to succeed in that mission, and many others. Your level of motivation and the risks you've run far exceed those of an ordinary FSB agent."

"Well, you think so because you haven't seen the files of our other team members. Theirs are just as impressive. And Alina's even more so. She was also in the FSB long before me," Kharlov replied.

Vidya shook her head impatiently. "No woman has ever headed the KGB or FSB. For that matter, women are very thin at the top of the Russian government, and that was true in Soviet days as well. As for the rest of the team, Vasilyev has a foreign wife. Even though Neda is now a Russian citizen, she'll always be considered Iranian."

"OK, fine," Kharlov said. "Grishkov has said he plans to retire, so maybe there is no other candidate for Director within our team. But there are thousands of FSB agents. Having just started your career, you cannot possibly know what they may have accomplished."

"Maybe not," Vidya replied. "But throughout my training, I heard the whispers from my colleagues. And even the instructors. Our team is legendary. Few others have managed a single success to rival ours. None have one after another over a span of years."

Kharlov grunted. "Maybe so. But that's not because any of us are superhuman. After our first successes, the President kept giving our team the most difficult and high-priority missions. The Director saw to it that we received the support we needed, once even against the President's direct orders. And we have been very lucky."

"Not always," Vidya said. "I read the mission report where Vasilyev's father was killed."

"Yes. That happened before I joined the team." Kharlov replied. "But it doesn't change my point. Grishkov was very fortunate to survive and only did so because the senior Vasilyev sacrificed himself."

"And, of course, Tukmakov died during your last mission. And you barely survived yourself," Vidya said.

"Well, that's all true," Kharlov said irritably. "How does any of that make me a candidate for Director?"

"Because everyone knows you've risked everything repeatedly to accomplish the mission and succeeded despite the odds. That's how the Director and his predecessor, now the President, reached the position. I think we both know the President would never pick someone without the same qualification," Vidya said.

"I'll give you credit for imagination if nothing else," Kharlov replied. "But I think you'll agree with me on one thing."

"What's that?" Vidya asked, arching one eyebrow.

"For any of your imaginings to come true, first, we must accomplish this mission. As well as return safely to Russia," Kharlov said.

Vidya smiled and nodded and said nothing more.

Finally, they approached what Lishi had said would be their last stop before crossing the Chinese border.

But before they reached that stop, the truck slowed suddenly as it emerged from a curve in the highway. Kharlov and Vidya wasted no time hiding from whoever was ahead.

The truck's lean as it went around the curve had let them guess that Lishi couldn't see whatever was ahead until it was too late. But now they could only imagine what was making the truck slow and stop.

Their guess was quickly confirmed by a voice loud enough to reach them, even in the space Lishi had done his best to seal off.

A roadblock. And based on their short distance from the border and the man's aggressive tone, manned by insurgents.

Brief pauses, which they guessed were caused by Lishi's responses, were met by louder and louder demands.

Finally, a single gunshot rang out.

Kharlov and Vidya exchanged alarmed glances. They each had a handgun. Neither had any illusions about their chances against the number of armed men who would be at an insurgent roadblock.

Lishi had told them that the truck's contents would be removed if the worst happened. And then the truck itself might be stolen. Or moved off the road and abandoned.

Or moved nearby and burned as a warning to anyone resisting the rebels' demands.

Kharlov and Vidya had already discussed these scenarios and decided their best chance was to wait quietly and hope the truck was abandoned.

And that if they smelled smoke, they would emerge from hiding, guns blazing.

At worst, it would be a faster death.

Moments later, the truck lurched back into motion.

Kharlov and Vidya looked at each other and knew they had the same question.

Who was at the wheel?

A few minutes later, they got their answer.

The truck slowed and pulled off the highway. Moments later, there was tapping against the wall of their space in the recognition pattern Lishi had told them just before departure.

Then the wall opened. Sure enough, it was Lishi.

Kharlov and Vidya both lowered their pistols.

After all, Lishi could have been forced to reveal the recognition pattern.

"Sorry about that," Lishi said. "Never had someone fire in the air before to try to scare me. I think this was his first roadblock. Anyway, we finally agreed on my 'contribution' to their cause. I hope that will be the last excitement before I drop you off in China."

Kharlov winced. Never tempt fate with hope, he thought.

But to Lishi, he just nodded.

And in fact, Lishi's hope proved to be justified. Lishi had said he'd often crossed the Chinese border without incident. He'd promised that the search of the truck and examination of his papers would take only minutes.

That all turned out to be true. About an hour after darkness fell, Lishi pulled the truck onto a secondary road with little traffic and then eased it to the curb.

Right on time.

The tapped recognition pattern from Lishi told Kharlov and Vidya it was time to go.

As they emerged from the truck with their gear, Kharlov and Vidya could see no headlights in either direction.

But that could change at any time.

Apparently, Lishi had seen them exit because the truck rumbled to life and pulled back on the road. In moments it was gone.

A few meters ahead, a rutted dirt road turned off to the right. It went in the same direction as their target.

Of course, they would not walk on this road since a vehicle's headlights could reveal them with little warning. Fortunately, neither the terrain nor the vegetation nearby hindered their steady progress.

Back in Moscow, Kharlov had looked at a map and calculated that they should easily reach their target within a few hours.

That was critical since they had to accomplish their mission and escape in darkness.

And Lishi had warned them that he would not linger at the rendezvous point for the return trip.

Kharlov glanced back at Vidya. Could she keep up the pace?

Well, she was right where her training said she should be. Far enough away that they were separate targets that could not both be eliminated by a single grenade or mine. But close enough to warn each other of impending danger.

Kharlov smiled. Vidya wasn't the only one who had asked the Director for a teammate's file. All her instructors rated Vidya as highly capable, both intellectually and physically.

Most importantly, that assessment was shared by the senior trainer. Evgeny.

Kharlov thought they would soon see whether that judgment had been correct.

Chapter Twenty-Four

Chinese Special Forces Server Facility
Yunnan Province, China

Kharlov and Vidya were both wearing their infrared goggles. Otherwise, they might have never spotted the target facility, illuminated solely with IR light.

Their briefing had said there were two reasons for this. The first was that the standard security measure, brilliant illumination with visible light, would have made the facility easy to detect by American reconnaissance satellites.

The second was more of a surprise. GRU, Russian military intelligence, believed that Chinese special forces command wished to keep the location of all such facilities secret from the regular Chinese military.

Whatever they might wish, Kharlov had trouble believing they would be successful.

But the desire for secrecy also explained the small guard presence. During the first two shifts, there were two guards each.

The third midnight to dawn shift, though, had only a single guard. Kharlov and Vidya were observing him now under cover of the area's abundant vegetation.

Like them, the guard was wearing IR goggles. He walked slowly along the paved parking lot that occupied several hundred square meters in front of the facility.

So far, the guard appeared to be the opposite of alert.

Kharlov and Vidya took nothing for granted, though. They remained crouching, waiting for their best chance.

It took almost an hour, but that chance finally came. The guard stopped pacing, took a slow look around, and slumped against one of the many trees bordering the parking lot.

Then, the guard tapped his digital watch several times. Kharlov and Vidya glanced at each other.

No doubt, setting an alarm.

Minutes later, the guard was still. At maximum magnification, their IR goggles showed the man's chest rhythmically rising and falling.

Yes, the guard appeared to be asleep. But he could wake at any moment.

They had a way to deal with that. Vidya brought the weapon to her shoulder and took careful aim through its scope.

Fortunately for the guard, this mission required he be left alive. It was imperative that Chinese military leadership not realize their communications facility had been compromised. If they did, their special forces troops could be issued new orders.

So the weapon Vidya was aiming fired a special liquid charge at low velocity, not a bullet. It was encased in a membrane tough enough to withstand ejection and transit to the target. But clear and designed to dissolve on contact with the target, releasing its contents.

Those contents were a powerful sedative that made the target unconscious for at least two hours. It was compounded from substances already present in the human body, making it undetectable in subsequent screening.

Capable of penetrating clothing, the sedative was even more effective when coming into direct contact with skin.

That's why Vidya was aiming for the guard's exposed neck.

Success!

Vidya saw the guard's head droop in a pose that signaled a shift from sleeping to unconscious.

But nothing could be taken for granted.

Vidya had already changed from the boots she'd worn to reach the facility to soft-soled shoes designed to leave no footprints behind. Of course, they required a user with training. Ideally, one who weighed less than, say, Kharlov.

They had already decided when planning the mission that Kharlov would remain outside to watch for any unexpected visitors.

Once she reached the guard, Vidya could see at a glance that he was still breathing. A quick brush from one gloved hand removed a few undissolved strands of the sedative charge's casing from the guard's neck, which floated away in the breeze.

Vidya didn't bother altering the alarm on the guard's watch. She could see they would be ready to leave long before it would sound.

And no alarm would be enough to rouse the guard from his unconscious state.

Vidya frowned as she walked up to the facility's entry keypad. If the defector's description of its type had been inaccurate, or if it had been recently replaced with a more secure model, their mission might be over right here.

But no. It was exactly as Vidya had expected. Russian intelligence had long experience getting its operatives into places they weren't supposed to be. The keypad yielded to the electronic device Vidya had attached with little effort.

No alarm sounded, and the building's only door slid open.

So far, so good.

The building was small, with only three rooms. One contained electrical and support equipment. Another had a restroom.

The third and largest housed the servers that were the whole purpose of the facility. It was the only room with an additional keypad.

It was as easy to defeat as the one outside.

The ranked servers' familiar humming, blinking lights, and the air's slight tang of ozone told Vidya she was in the right place.

She quickly spotted a workstation hooked to one of the servers. Ordinarily used to diagnose hardware problems and upload software updates, it should serve just as well to download recent messages transferred through the facility.

Here, though, is where the defector's knowledge ended. As a guard, he knew nothing of server operations.

Were there security cameras in the server room?

Not that Vidya could see. Not much reassurance.

But the guard had said there were no cameras outside, and Vidya had seen none.

Vidya remembered the Indian intelligence assessment that these facilities existed because Chinese special forces didn't trust regular military communications channels. Maybe they saw security cameras as a separate vulnerability.

Data transmissions of message traffic required little bandwidth and could be easily overlooked. Security cameras had to send high-bandwidth communications of the collected images to a remote location. They could be detected much more easily.

Vidya shook her head to clear it of such pointless thoughts. She couldn't see any cameras. There was no time to do a more thorough search.

She would have to hope for the best.

The workstation had a USB port. Now, to determine whether the software she had designed based on her knowledge of Chinese military communications would work.

Or whether she would find herself trying to write code under less-than-ideal conditions.

The software was designed to extract any file recognized as a message format found on any server that could be accessed from the workstation. It would bypass any password or security access restriction if it performed as designed.

Vidya attached her portable hard drive to the workstation and held her breath. Would the software now being automatically uploaded work?

The drive had a small LCD screen with only one function. It recorded data successfully transferred as a percentage of the drive's five-terabyte capacity.

Within seconds, the display read ".001%" and continued to climb. About five minutes later, the display read, "transfer complete." The software had finished transferring any data it could identify as a message file.

Time to go.

After securing the drive, Vidya eased the server door shut.

Moments later, Vidya carefully closed the facility door behind her as well.

Still no alarms. At least, none she could hear.

The guard was still unconscious where Vidya had left him. Kharlov was nowhere in sight.

Good. He wasn't supposed to be visible.

Vidya was sure Kharlov was nearby, watching the guard and alert for any unexpected company.

Now for the last step. The guard couldn't be left to wake on his own. It might only happen once his replacement arrived.

Vidya withdrew the syringe containing the stimulant that would eventually rouse the guard and frowned. The syringe had a dose sufficient for a guard on the large side by Chinese standards.

But a bit too much for this man, Vidya decided. Carefully, she squeezed out a small amount on the ground next to the tree and tapped the syringe on its side.

No air bubbles she could see.

Vidya carefully lifted the hair on the back of the guard's neck. Then, with skill honed by long practice, Vidya slid a 27-gauge butterfly needle into a vein and injected the stimulant.

Vidya could see no immediate change in the guard's breathing or posture.

Good. He was supposed to gradually transition to sleep and then wake within the next hour.

But no two people were alike. Some remained asleep longer.

Some were awake within minutes.

Kharlov appeared at Vidya's side as she changed back into her boots while still keeping an eye on the guard.

Vidya knew Kharlov had served with Russian special forces before he joined the FSB.

She was still impressed that a man his size could move so quietly.

Kharlov said nothing.

Good. That meant there was nothing to report.

Time to disappear into the vegetation and hope they could reach their rendezvous with Lishi in time.

While hoping the guard didn't realize something had happened when he woke. And raise an alarm that might even see the border closed.

Vidya shook her head to chase these thoughts away. They only invited bad luck.

Kharlov looked back at her and grinned but said nothing.

Just as if he could read her thoughts.

But everything went smoothly. They arrived at the rendezvous without incident, and Lishi was right on time.

A few minutes ahead of schedule, they were at the border. The guards on both sides of the border gave the empty truck only a cursory search.

Less than an hour later, Lishi pulled the truck onto a secondary road. Ten minutes after that, they were bouncing down a dirt track.

Mercifully, only for a short time.

All the equipment they needed to transmit the data they had collected with such effort was with them.

Except a portable power source. And a satellite dish.

Those had been secreted inside the unimpressive shack Lishi's truck now approached.

If the FSB agent sent for the task from Rangoon had done his job.

He had. Vidya sent the data via satellite to Moscow Center minutes after their arrival.

Encrypted, of course, in case anyone from the Chinese side of the border happened to notice the transmission.

Vidya and Kharlov climbed back into the truck for the rest of the return ride to Mandalay.

"So, I suppose you have no idea what we just sent to Moscow," Kharlov said.

Vidya nodded. "That's right. All I know for sure is that the software successfully located message traffic and downloaded it to my portable hard drive. But the messages could have been cookie recipes for all I know."

Kharlov grunted. "I think we both know better. The real question is whether any of the traffic will provide actionable intelligence. Especially, enough detail to give our comrades in Taiwan the upper hand in the struggle ahead."

"Yes," Vidya replied. "I wish there was time to join them."

Kharlov shook his head. "You read the same briefings I did. The Chinese Navy and Air Force will get to Taiwan before we could."

Chapter Twenty-Five

Taipei, Taiwan

Mikhail Vasilyev sighed as he rubbed his eyes, weary from hours of reviewing information on their laptop screen.

Anatoly Grishkov, sitting next to him doing the same thing, smiled and stretched.

At least, there was plenty of room to do so. Their cover as businessmen had called for a hotel that was decent by local standards.

Thanks to the many hammer blows that had hit the Russian economy since the foolish invasion of Ukraine, it would have been called luxurious back home.

"Come, come!" Grishkov exclaimed. "All the way here, you complained that we'd be too late to catch the show. Or we wouldn't get the information we needed to make a difference. And yet, here we are in time. With excellent briefing materials, even detailed photos, courtesy of Chinese spies!"

Vasilyev had to smile, too. "Yes, you're right. The target is clearly the port of Taipei, and someone working there must have taken the photos. We know the Chinese soldiers who are supposed to seize the port will be hidden onboard cargo containers. We even have the container numbers. But there are a few details we still need."

Grishkov nodded. "Yes. The name and arrival date of the ship that will bring the containers. And the time the soldiers will emerge from those containers. Unless they're fools, I expect that will happen at night. But the timing will be tricky for them."

"Clearly," Vasilyev replied. "Too late, and everyone in Taiwan will know a Chinese invasion fleet is underway and will be on the highest possible alert. Too early, a small Chinese special operations force will be overwhelmed by regular Taiwan Army troops before the invasion fleet arrives."

"There is another factor," Grishkov said with a frown. "Once Chinese troops report that they have seized the port, their Air Force could be called on to attack any Taiwanese troop transports or armored vehicles sent to retake it. This port is within easy range of even land-based enemy aircraft, let alone ones from China's carriers."

"They could," Vasilyev said. "But Taiwan has its own fighters and plenty of surface-to-air missiles. Still, I think you're right. To keep the port until the arrival of the invasion fleet, the Chinese would be willing to take heavy losses in the air."

"Very well," Grishkov said. "Moscow Center has promised to try to answer our questions about the ship that will bring the containers. And to use our local assets to preposition weapons at the port for our use when the time is right. But I still have one question for you."

Vasilyev nodded. "Why don't we just pass on what Kharlov and Vidya learned to the local authorities?"

"Exactly!" Grishkov said. "Now, I understand nobody here has any reason to trust Russia. After all, we've sold weapons, including our best fighter jets, to China for many years. But if we gave Taiwan the raw data, surely they'd be convinced."

"Maybe so," Vasilyev replied. "But maybe they'd think it just a clever forgery designed to draw their forces away from the real target. However, there is a more important danger. We have concrete intelligence that Chinese agents have infiltrated Taiwan's military and security agencies at the highest levels."

"Yes, I remember seeing that in the briefing papers," Grishkov said glumly. "So if one of those agents reported back to Beijing that Russia was providing intelligence from their special forces to Taiwan…"

"Then the orders could be changed. And the Chinese might suddenly become less interested in purchasing Russian oil and gas," Vasilyev said.

"Very well," Grishkov sighed. "I suppose I will have to earn that French chateau the hard way."

Vasilyev laughed. "Well, I have every incentive to help you succeed in reaching that goal! Neda has already started planning for us to visit you and Arisha as soon as you're settled. Just one thing to do first."

Grishkov laughed, too. "Try not to get shot."

Chapter Twenty-Six

Alishan Forest Railway
Taiwan

Alina had to remember not to frown in order to fit in. The tourists packing this train were all smiling, laughing, and having a great time.

And why not? First, the train itself was impressive. Imported by Taiwan's Japanese colonial authority from America in 1912, it had recently been restored to its original coal-burning working condition.

Next, the rail line was even older, having been built to facilitate the export of Taiwanese cypress logs. Those trees, now endangered, had long since been replaced by tourists on the trains traveling on that rail line.

A rare exception had been made to use two types of Taiwanese cypress in the railroad cars' restoration. The scent of cypress permeated every bit of the train.

Even in her current mood, Alina had to acknowledge that the scent was pleasant. Though dressing like a tourist per mission orders annoyed her so much, it spoiled the experience.

Sandals? Really?

A typhoon had damaged one section of rail but had since been repaired. So, the line was once again its original nearly one-hundred-kilometer length.

And along that length, it climbed from thirty meters to well over two thousand meters, making it the highest-operating narrow-gauge railroad in Asia.

That was why Alina and the rest of the team were on this train. The data Kharlov and Vidya had collected had been analyzed by Moscow Center. One of the targets due to be hit by Chinese special forces was a short distance from this rail line. Not far from its highest point.

An anti-aircraft missile emplacement.

Approaching it on the single access road from below would have been difficult. But Moscow Center's planners believed no one had considered the rail line a possible access method. Particularly since the rail section closest to the facility was the one that had just been repaired.

That was another reason for Alina's foul mood. She thought the mission planners were far too optimistic.

But there had barely been enough time to get the team to Taiwan and then on this train. Alina was in no position to argue or suggest alternatives.

All she could do was share her misgivings with Evgeny and Neda Rhahbar, who were accompanying her on this mission.

Well, Alina thought, at least slipping off the train and into the surrounding forest unnoticed would be no problem. It was the weekend, and three trains a day were running. They wouldn't be the only ones who lingered at a stop along the way, presumably to resume their journey on another train later.

Though Alina was willing to bet they were the only ones with sniper rifles and very different outfits hidden at GPS coordinates near the train.

Then, Alina had to work hard to suppress another frown. The data accessed by Kharlov and Vidya had only a general time frame for the Chinese attack. On the one hand, that made sense.

Alina was certain assaults by special forces would be coordinated with the departure of the invasion fleet. Many variables, including weather, affected that departure. So, the timing of the attack on the anti-air missile emplacement could only be approximate.

But it left Alina wondering whether they had time to do proper reconnaissance when they reached the target area. Or whether they should rush pell-mell towards the missiles, hoping to save them from destruction at the last moment.

Alina found herself smiling despite herself. When she put it to herself that way, there was no choice.

Do it the right way, and trust to fate that they would arrive in time.

Chapter Twenty-Seven

Port of Taipei
Taiwan

Anatoly Grishkov looked at the familiar cases with disbelief. "Smyslov must be a magician! How could he possibly have had these transported from Russia in time?"

Mikhail Vasilyev shrugged and said in a low voice, "There can be only one answer. He foresaw that matters in Taiwan would require your special talents. Which you could only practice with the proper tools. So he had them put in place on this island. And now they are ready when needed."

Grishkov shook his head, bent down, and said just as quietly, "Well, I suppose that's how he became Director. I'll take the case with the Kornet. You get the one with the extra rounds."

Vasilyev nodded, knowing that Grishkov had given him the lighter load. Well, that was only fair since he already had a sniper rifle slung on his back and his jacket pockets stuffed with ammo.

The Kornet was a man-portable anti-tank missile launcher that, they hoped, would prove effective against metal shipping containers. Occupied by Chinese special forces and their weapons.

As Vasilyev lifted his case, he asked, "Any sign the crane we're going to use as the base for our attack is occupied?"

"At this hour?" Grishkov replied. "No, I've checked several times since we cut through the fence. Aside from the two guards we saw at the main gate, I haven't noticed movement anywhere. I think we'll be fine as long as we're quick and quiet."

Hunched over, they both moved toward the crane, which towered over the mass of containers at the port. Now and then, they spotted a surveillance camera. Each time, they both imagined it was pointed straight at them.

But they knew from experience that security guards were unlikely to be staring intently at every screen fed by those cameras. If, indeed, they were all in working order. Especially now, well after midnight.

At least, they hoped that was true.

As they reached the target crane, they both breathed a sigh of relief that, so far, it appeared they were still undetected. Now, though, came a real test of their luck.

There were multiple cranes scattered around the port. They had chosen one nearly as far from the main gate as possible.

It was also the one closest to the target Chinese ship, which they had spotted through a telescope that afternoon. And watched as its containers were quickly and efficiently unloaded.

That meant the crane should give them the best chance of spotting the three target containers. Out of the thousands stacked at the port.

It was also good news that they'd confirmed the cranes all had elevators in advance.

Climbing stairs with the Kornet and its extra rounds would have been more than a bit awkward.

But was there an alarm that would sound at the main gate if a crane's elevator was activated after hours? Or would the elevator make a racket that the guards couldn't ignore?

Only one way to find out.

The elevator was already at their level. Logical, Vasilyev thought since that's how the crane's last operator would have left.

Vasilyev pushed the only button and waved Grishkov forward. His total load might be a little heavier, but Grishkov's long case was definitely more awkward.

The doors slid open. There was only one button on the inside, too. That made sense. What point in stopping halfway?

This time, Grishkov pushed the button since he was closer. They both tensed as the doors closed, waiting for an alarm.

The elevator began its long climb upwards. No alarm. And their progress was marked by no mechanical noise they could hear.

Of course, that didn't mean a light wasn't blinking on a main gate console. Or that the oldest surveillance tool, a guard's Mark One eyeball, wasn't observing the elevator's ascent.

But until they saw someone moving toward them, there was no point in worrying about it.

The elevator doors opened next to the crane operator's cab. They were immediately struck by a biting wind, which served to hurry them into the cab.

That wasn't the only factor pushing them forward. There simply wasn't enough room to fire the Kornet in the small space between the elevator and the cab.

While Grishkov extracted the launcher from its case, Vasilyev took out the tool needed to make its use possible. A glass cutter.

But with the tool in his hand, Vasilyev remembered he needed to know something else first.

The direction Grishkov would point the Kornet.

That meant the first task was locating the target containers.

Vasilyev shook his head at his oversight as he put the cutting tool back in his jacket. *That had better be the last mistake I make tonight*, he thought.

Then he reached into his pack and pulled out the tool he needed. A pair of high-quality Zeiss binoculars.

Yes, they knew the ship that had brought the containers was near this crane. So logic said the containers should be near as well.

But now, seeing the size of the crane in person, Vasilyev realized that the containers could have been placed a considerable distance from the ship.

Not that the crane's operator would have done so deliberately. No, Vasilyev had read that they tried to minimize the distance a container traveled from a ship since every extra meter meant a greater chance of something going wrong.

Sometimes, though, the volume of containers already in place might leave a crane operator no choice.

Well, Vasilyev thought, I'll just start nearby and move out from there.

And tried hard to silence the internal voice saying they didn't have much time left until daybreak.

Minutes crawled by as Vasilyev looked through the binoculars at containers farther and farther away from the crane. Another now joined his first worry about the approaching dawn.

Were they in the right spot?

Grishkov, to his credit, said nothing. Instead, he spent his time thoroughly checking and rechecking the Kornet.

After all, Grishkov had yet to determine whether it had been adequately maintained. Or whether the Kornet had ever sustained damage.

But eventually, even he was satisfied.

Grishkov glanced curiously toward Vasilyev just in time to see a smile cross his face.

Still, Grishkov waited quietly.

Vasilyev's smile broadened.

Finally, he said in a low voice, "Positive IDs on two of the three containers. Another close by those two has most of a number visible matching the third container. As you might think, I'm certain it will be the most difficult shot. I suggest you save it for last."

With that, Vasilyev passed his binoculars to Grishkov and pointed to the three targets.

Grishkov took a long, slow look at the three containers. Vasilyev was right. The angle to one of the three could have been more comfortable.

But he could hit the first two in his sleep.

With the targets' direction established, Vasilyev had been using his glass-cutting tools well. He smiled as he recalled the several instruction sessions from Grishkov on what he called an "art."

Step 1- Firmly attach the suction cup that would keep the glass in Vasilyev's hand after it was cut. Instead of hurtling to the ground, where it would shatter with a noise likely to attract even the sleepiest guard.

Step 2- Carefully cut through the glass, applying consistent pressure along all the cut's dimensions. Otherwise, pieces of glass could detach, once again headed to a noisy finale.

Step 3- Slowly pull the cut piece of glass toward him. Avoid the edges, which would be sharp enough to cut through his gloves.

The first piece of glass was relatively the easiest. It only had to be large enough to allow the business end of the Kornet to emerge into the air.

Grishkov had stressed that it should be no larger. A more generous opening could allow the entry of that same biting wind they had experienced just minutes ago- directly in Grishkov's face.

That would not help his aim.

As soon as Vasilyev finished cutting the first piece, he moved on to the second on the opposite side of the cab.

The glass section to be removed there would be much more extensive and require several cutting operations.

This would be to allow the backblast from the Kornet's use to escape the cab. Instead of cooking them.

Vasilyev was now grateful for the hours of practice Grishkov had insisted on in Moscow. His hands moved automatically, and just minutes later, multiple glass sections were neatly stacked on the cab's floor, well away from Grishkov.

The whistling wind Vasilyev had feared mercifully stayed outside. It was blowing away from both new openings through sheer chance.

Vasilyev pulled out the first Kornet round to pass to Grishkov.

They were ready.

Grishkov had first used a Kornet during the war in Chechnya and many times since. He had drilled Vasilyev in the reload procedure and was confident he would do so quickly.

However, Grishkov's calculations were upset by the result of firing his first Kornet round.

The secondary explosions that followed were massive. Grishkov had apparently hit the container holding the heavy weapons and explosives the attackers had planned to use during their assault.

The crane swayed, making it impossible for Grishkov to aim the Kornet. Fortunately, the swaying lasted only seconds.

Long enough for soldiers to begin emerging from the other two containers.

Well, Grishkov thought as the crane settled, Vasilyev was right about that third container.

As he pressed the trigger on the reloaded Kornet.

Another hit. Most of the soldiers who had fled the first strike were now killed outright by shrapnel or the force of the Kornet's explosion.

But not all of them.

Glass nearby began to shatter as the survivors aimed at the source of the missiles striking them.

They ignored the incoming fire, and Grishkov fired their last Kornet round as soon as Vasilyev loaded it.

A hit but less dead-center than Grishkov would have liked. The secondary explosions had moved the last container even further from Grishkov's field of view.

Still, a quick look told them their mission had been a success. There were survivors.

But not enough to have any hope of holding the port.

Time to go.

They lunged from the operator cab to the nearby elevator, abandoning the now useless Kornet launcher and its case.

Grishkov mashed the elevator's sole button as hard as he could as if that could force its doors to open more quickly.

Fortunately, the doors opened without delay. Even though Grishkov had stopped firing, the surviving Chinese troops were still sending bullets in their direction with great enthusiasm.

Well, Grishkov thought as Vasilyev joined him in the elevator, that should stop as soon as they see the elevator beginning to move. Well-trained troops would realize the danger from the crane was now over, and their priorities would shift. To collecting their wounded, and moving on the front gate.

Certainly, the front gate guards must have already called for assistance. And after the fireworks display Grishkov had provided, surely a sizeable force was now on its way.

But as a soldier, Grishkov had always been told where there's life, there's hope. The hope of completing their mission might be unrealistic for the Chinese troops they had just hit. He was sure, though, that it would take priority.

Almost immediately, Grishkov realized he'd been wrong as the Chinese troops' fire shifted from the operator cab to the now-moving elevator. In seconds, most of the glass sides had been shattered.

Grishkov and Vasilyev were both on the floor, covered in glass and bleeding from numerous minor cuts.

"Are you hit?" Vasilyev asked.

"Not yet," Grishkov replied, then cursed as another glass shard barely missed his right eye.

I should have considered that even the best-trained troops can sometimes let their emotions get the better of them, Grishkov thought.

It could be summed up in one word. Payback.

"I hope that boat…" Vasilyev said, and then suddenly stopped talking as an enemy round finally found its mark.

The elevator came to a halt at ground level seconds later.

Fortunately, they were now protected from fire by dozens of intervening containers.

Not so fortunately, the crane could hardly be missed. Grishkov was certain Chinese troops were already on their way.

Grishkov dragged Vasilyev out of the elevator and far enough away that they were no longer visible from the crane. Only then did he bend over to check whether Vasilyev was still alive.

Yes. Still breathing. But unconscious.

No blood or wound Grishkov could see, except for the glass cuts on his face…

Wait.

There it was. A round was embedded in Vasilyev's ballistic vest.

Grishkov shook his head. "Bulletproof." Ha. Yes, such a vest could be counted on to stop most bullets from entering the body.

But they were not magic. A vest would dissipate some of a round's kinetic energy. Enough to save the user's life in most cases.

Plenty of energy remained, though, to cause shock and bruising. Or even internal bleeding.

They'd been told the boat that would pick them up wouldn't wait.

Grishkov doubted he could carry or drag Vasilyev fast enough to avoid that outcome.

Or evade the Chinese troops that he could now hear approaching.

That left just one option.

Grishkov reached into his vest and removed an ammonia capsule. Then, he snapped it open under Vasilyev's nose and held his breath.

Vasilyev coughed, and his eyes fluttered open. It only took a few seconds for them to focus on Grishkov.

"We've got company coming," Grishkov whispered. "Can you stand? We've got to get to the boat."

Vasilyev nodded, and Grishkov lifted him bodily to a standing position.

Yes, he was swaying, Grishkov thought. But at least he's still upright.

With one arm around Vasilyev's shoulders, Grishkov set off to where the boat was supposed to be waiting.

From what he could hear, the Chinese soldiers weren't far behind.

But they were moving cautiously. Probably, Grishkov thought with a grim smile, worried about a possible ambush.

Well, if I'd just been lit up by several Kornet rounds, I'd probably be careful too.

There. The maintenance dock where the boat was supposed to be waiting. At first, Grishkov could see nothing through the gloom.

And then, he could see nothing because a blinding light shone directly into his eyes.

In a fierce whisper, Grishkov said, "Get that light out of my eyes or shoot and get this over with."

A few seconds later, the light shut off.

Vasilyev slumped against him.

Perfect, Grishkov thought.

It took several more seconds for Grishkov's eyes to adjust.

The Chinese troops sounded much closer.

Now, Grishkov could see a low, black speedboat. One man was inside it, dressed in black.

He was holding a submachine gun, pointed directly at them.

The man wasn't smiling.

Chapter Twenty-Eight

Anti-Aircraft Missile Emplacement
Near Chiayi Air Base
Taiwan

Alina nodded appreciatively as she surveyed the scene through her night vision goggles. As expected, the anti-aircraft missiles were not only buried but well concealed.

However, Alina hadn't fully realized how effective the missiles were likely to be until seeing the emplacement. Any planes carrying bombs or occupying troops trying to reach Chiayi Air Base would receive a warm welcome. Missiles already perched thousands of meters above sea level would give their pilots minimal warning.

A pity that effective Chinese espionage now threatened to erase that advantage.

Unless, Alina said to herself with a fierce grin, they could give the attacking Chinese special forces troops an unpleasant surprise.

Alina turned to Evgeny and pointed to the opposite edge of the mountainside clearing. "If I were staging an assault on these missiles, I'd have a few soldiers go that way to protect my flank."

Evgeny nodded. "Agreed. I will make sure to give them a proper greeting."

Moments later, Evgeny had disappeared into the nearby brush and started toward his new position.

Alina then turned to Neda. "We have quite a bit to cover with only two rifles. Be sure of your first shot. Once they go to ground, they will be much harder to hit."

Neda, of course, knew that. And Alina knew she did. But it was still an important reminder, and Neda recognized it as such.

She quietly nodded and vanished just as quickly as Evgeny had moments before.

A Chinese attack on Taiwan was coming soon. But did "soon" mean tonight?

Well, at least they weren't late. The quiet that enveloped the clearing was undisturbed, except for a few insects.

One hour dragged after another. Just one more, Alina thought, and it will be too close to dawn for the assault to happen. The attackers must leave enough darkness for both the assault and the pursuit that would almost certainly follow.

There! Movement in the brush at the edge of the clearing. Neda's sector.

Clicks in Alina's earpiece told her that Neda and Evgeny had also spotted it.

One minute crawled agonizingly past another. No soldiers emerged into the clearing. Had it been an animal?

No. A soldier wearing night vision goggles much like hers strode confidently into the clearing, his gaze sweeping from side to side.

Alina froze as the soldier seemed to stare right at her.

But his survey continued past her position, and he was soon satisfied there was no danger.

Because he made a gesture that appeared to mean "follow me," since the other soldiers in the assault team quickly joined him.

They knew exactly where the missiles were located from their quick, intent pace.

As usual, Alina thought, Smyslov was right. Penetrated at the highest levels indeed.

While she'd been thinking, Alina's hands had been busy. Her night vision goggles were off, and her sniper rifle was trained on the soldier first entering the clearing.

Its scope, of course, included a night vision element.

The soldier might be a scout. But Alina didn't think so. No, everything about him said "leader" to her.

Her target selected, Alina waited patiently for Neda to do the same. They had agreed previously that Alina would choose the leader, and she was confident Neda would pick her target using the other agreed criteria.

The soldier carrying the heaviest load. With luck, that would be the one taking the explosive charges they would use to destroy the missiles.

Moments later, a single click in Alina's earpiece told her Neda was ready.

Now, one, two, three...

Alina and Neda's shots were so close together that they sounded like a single shot to Alina.

But two soldiers dropped to the ground like puppets with their strings cut.

Several soldiers immediately threw themselves to the ground. Those, Alina thought, would be soldiers who had seen combat before.

But that left several others still standing.

Two more nearly simultaneous shots later, four Chinese soldiers were lying dead on the grass.

Alina was confident that was so because she and Neda were doing only headshots. Chinese body armor might not stop the high-velocity rounds they were using.

But why take chances?

The surviving soldiers began to return fire. So far, wildly in their general direction.

But that would change the next time Alina and Neda fired.

Alina had made a guess before the mission, one she had shared with Neda and Evgeny. And suggested the best way to proceed.

She now followed her own advice and switched the night vision element in her scope off. Then, Alina slowly lowered her rifle and closed her eyes.

Was she right to guess that this unmanned, remotely controlled facility had humans monitoring its security, even at this hour?

Yes. Brilliant lights snapped on all around the clearing.

Two Chinese soldiers quickly discarded their night vision goggles.

The grass was fairly tall and provided reasonably good cover in the dark.

Now, though, it wasn't nearly good enough to conceal movement.

Alina's rifle sounded just a second before Neda's. Neither could be sure of a hit.

But there was no more movement from either soldier they had just targeted.

By Alina's count, there were at least two more soldiers left. What would they do?

Alina was already moving because she knew what she would do.

Sure enough, carefully aimed shots slammed into the position Alina had occupied just moments before.

Better visibility worked both ways.

Alina already had another position prepared, one further back in the brush. By the time she reached it, the fire from the Chinese soldiers had stopped.

Yes, Alina had a general idea of where they were. But unless one of them moved…

There. Alina spotted a small rock that would do. It would be awkward to throw it horizontally. But if she timed it just right…

Excellent! She struck a bush a few meters distant, just hard enough to make its branches sway.

One of the remaining soldiers took the bait.

Alina still couldn't see him. But she could make an educated guess from the movement of the grass where the soldier had just fired.

After she fired, Alina quickly moved on to the last of her prepared positions. But no shots followed.

Hmmm. Maybe Alina had hit the soldier who had last fired. And there was only one Chinese soldier left.

Perhaps he was weighing his chances between the unknown snipers who had wiped out the rest of his team. And surrendering to the Taiwanese troops who were surely on their way.

Or, Alina thought with a start, he could be awaiting the arrival of a flanking force. But she had heard no shots in Evgeny's direction.

That's right, a voice in her head said. But you know Evgeny uses a silenced pistol.

Alina tried to raise Evgeny on comms. Nothing.

I have to check on him.

But if I do, it will give that Chinese soldier waiting in the grass his chance.

Alina quickly made her choice. Evgeny had saved her life more times than she could count. It was finally her turn.

This wasn't Neda's first mission. Alina had to hope that she would have her back.

Time to move.

Gritting her teeth, Alina moved toward Evgeny's position, doing her best to keep what cover there was between her and the remaining Chinese soldier.

Rounds passed by so closely she could feel one tugging at her sleeve.

Then a single round went *craaak*. From Neda's position.

The rounds that had come so close suddenly stopped.

Just a few more minutes...there! A body. Not Evgeny's.

A second.

A third.

A fourth.

All Chinese soldiers.

Alina swore under her breath. Yes, even for Evgeny, this was impressive work. But where was he?

There. No, no...

Evgeny was lying next to a fifth, unmoving Chinese soldier.

But Evgeny's eyes were closed, too.

Was he still breathing?

Alina bent her head down to Evgeny's face and smiled. Yes, he was!

Just as she started to check him for injuries, Evgeny's eyes fluttered open.

"Ah, you came! I knew I could count on you," Evgeny said.

Alina's smile broadened. "Of course, you old goat! It is my turn, after all."

Evgeny chuckled and then coughed. "Just one favor to ask."

Alina shook her head. "Time for all that later. Now we have to get you out of here."

Evgeny smiled weakly and said, "Not this time."

Then Evgeny moved his left hand away from the knife hilt sticking from his side.

"That last soldier was tough. Still, though, five to one. Not a bad way to finish my FSB career, wouldn't you say?"

Alina looked at the knife's position and then at Evgeny's face.

He was right. The wound was mortal. There was nothing Alina could do to change that.

Alina felt tears filling her eyes and angrily brushed them away. There was no time.

"You asked for a favor," Alina said roughly.

Evgeny nodded toward his pistol, lying a short distance away. "I can't reach it, but I need it. You know why. Then, you need to use the thermite charges. If I trained you properly, I know you have some."

Alina did, and for precisely the reason Evgeny had in mind.

"But..." Alina said. She was immediately stopped by a glare from Evgeny.

"No time for sentimental foolishness. Local troops could arrive any minute. Do what needs to be done here, then take Neda and go to the extraction point. Now," Evgeny said, again nodding toward the pistol.

Alina bent down and handed Evgeny the pistol. "I'm sorry," she said.

Evgeny shook his head. "You have nothing to be sorry for. As a senior instructor, I grade our performance outstanding, you included. Now, turn around for a second."

Alina did. A few seconds later, she heard a single silenced shot.

Alina turned back and checked Evgeny's pulse to be sure he was dead. He was.

Then, she planted two thermite charges, one next to Evgeny's head and the other next to his hands.

There would be no way to identify the body. As specified in her orders.

Alina set the delay on the charges and turned to go.

But then something strange happened. Alina couldn't move. Even after the charges ignited behind her, and she could feel heat against her back.

Images crowded Alina's head of all the times she had been saved by Evgeny. Sometimes her career. Other times her life.

The occasional times they had been lovers. Always as Alina's way of thanking Evgeny when mere words weren't enough.

Strange. Someone was screaming. Who could it be? It didn't sound like Neda.

Then suddenly, Neda was standing in front of her. And shaking her.

Slowly, Alina realized that she was the one who had been screaming. And her eyes began to regain their focus.

"We have to go!" Neda hissed. "We will mourn him later. But you know Evgeny would insist that you complete this mission!"

Alina nodded. Yes. A lesson Evgeny had pounded into their heads as trainees. The mission isn't complete until all team members have reached safety.

Well, she thought bitterly, all surviving team members.

Pull yourself together, Alina told herself sternly. You're still responsible for Neda.

"Let's go," Alina said.

They could both hear a helicopter coming as they moved into the brush toward the extraction point. Without a doubt, carrying enemy troops.

Well, their priority would be securing the missiles, not pursuing fleeing survivors.

Hopefully.

Chapter Twenty-Nine

Port of Taipei
Taiwan

The man holding the submachine gun seemed to be waiting for something.

But what?

The way he was pointing the weapon at them made Grishkov wary of asking questions. Besides, from the noises he heard behind him, the Chinese troops looking for them could join the party at any moment.

Vasilyev was still slumped bonelessly against Grishkov. Now, though, Grishkov could hear him whisper, "Strobe."

Grishkov cursed. Not at Vasilyev. At himself. How had he forgotten?

Vasilyev was blameless. Not only was he semiconscious, but the bullet that had struck his vest had also destroyed the strobe light clipped there.

Grishkov had one, too.

Slowly, Grishkov lifted his free hand toward it.

The man watched and did nothing.

Grishkov's fingers finally found the activation switch.

The light flashed in a pattern that meant nothing to Grishkov. That was fine because he wasn't its intended audience.

The man holding the submachine gun looked at the light intently and was apparently satisfied. Because he lowered the gun and hissed, "Get on board! Hurry!"

It seemed the man had also heard the approach of the Chinese soldiers.

Just as Grishkov was able to put Vasilyev into the boat and sit down heavily beside him, rounds began to hit the boat.

Accompanied by a good deal of shouting.

The speedboat jumped forward so sharply that both Vasilyev and Grishkov were sent tumbling.

But they were still on board. Under the circumstances, Grishkov decided there could be no complaints.

Putting his arm around Vasilyev, Grishkov managed to lift him back into one of the boat's seats.

"How are you doing?" Grishkov asked.

"Are they still shooting at us?" Vasilyev asked, his eyes still closed.

Grishkov looked behind them. The dock had already faded from sight into the surrounding blackness.

Though the fires the Kornet had started when its rounds hit the Chinese soldiers' stores of weapons and ammunition were still visible.

"I think we're safe for the moment," Grishkov said.

"Good," Vasilyev said tiredly. "I'm going to rest now."

Well, Grishkov thought, he's certainly earned it.

Raising his voice, Grishkov asked the man holding the speedboat's wheel, "What is your name?"

The man kept his gaze firmly fixed forward but eventually answered.

"You may call me Kenzo," he said.

Grishkov was sure that had nothing to do with the man's real name. He was even more confident that Kenzo didn't care about the names of his passengers.

But, Grishkov had been told in FSB training that asking for a person's name helped to build rapport. Considering Vasilyev's state, Grishkov thought he would likely need all the goodwill he could get.

"Kenzo, how long until we reach land?" Grishkov asked.

"Not long," Kenzo said. "But that answer is misleading. This boat doesn't have the range to take you to the Japanese mainland. Our first destination is an island where a larger boat is waiting that will take you there."

Grishkov frowned. "Is medical care available on this island or the other boat?"

"The other boat probably has a better first aid kit than this one. But the island is uninhabited. What is wrong with your friend?" Kenzo asked.

"A bullet in his ballistic vest," Grishkov replied.

Kenzo nodded. "So, probably internal bleeding. The other boat has a radio. They can call ahead, so a clinic we use will be available. My boss says you are to be kept alive so you can be sure the clinic staff will do everything possible for your friend."

"I'd appreciate any help you can give him. Can this boat go any faster?" Grishkov asked.

"Not safely," Kenzo replied. "These waters are relatively calm, but this boat is so small that even a single errant wave could capsize us. It has happened before. That's why this is a new boat."

Grishkov knew Kenzo was telling the truth. What Grishkov thought of as "new car smell" had hit him as soon as he'd brought Vasilyev on board.

That wasn't all Grishkov had noticed. Kenzo's tattoos, as well as a missing finger.

Yakuza. Japanese organized crime.

Though Kenzo looked more Korean than Japanese.

Almost certainly a smuggler, Grishkov thought. Probably drugs.

Well, the FSB had to use whatever assets were available, criminal or not, Grishkov thought. And he'd heard that many Yakuza were ethnic

Koreans who had never been granted Japanese citizenship despite their families having lived in Japan for several generations.

Maybe not a surprise that some turned to crime, Grishkov thought.

Focus, Grishkov told himself sternly. All that mattered was that, for now, at least, they were willing and able to get Vasilyev to decent medical care.

Grishkov shook his head. It looked like Vasilyev was going to need it. Dawn hadn't yet arrived, but even in the moonlight, Grishkov could see that he was unconscious, not asleep.

Was he still breathing?

Grishkov bent his head closer to Vasilyev's.

No.

Cursing, Grishkov began to administer CPR to Vasilyev's lifeless form.

It took time, but eventually, Vasilyev breathed on his own again.

Grishkov had shifted Vasilyev's position, which he thought might have done just as much as the CPR to revive him.

Though Grishkov opened his mouth to speak, he almost immediately closed it.

Kenzo had already increased the boat's speed, and Grishkov realized he'd been right. The ride was noticeably less stable.

Well, that was OK. At least this way, Vasilyev would have a chance.

Chapter Thirty

Near Lotus Farm Ranch
Guanyin District, Taiwan

Lieutenant Xu looked down at the small tablet strapped to his left arm. According to the map shown in its dim illumination, they were only a few hundred meters away from their target. An underground Hsiung Feng III missile facility that could strike China's ships while they were still up to four hundred kilometers away.

Xu had trained with all the men who accompanied him on this mission. That was fortunate because they all needed to move quickly and quietly, with as little communication as possible.

It was hard to believe this rural area was so close to…well, everything. The airport where Xu had arrived in Taiwan was less than an hour's drive away. He'd passed through both New Taipei City and Taoyuan City on his way to the target.

While he traveled, Xu had noticed not one but two huge stores called "Costco." A friend had taken him to one near Shanghai in 2023, which he'd been told was the second to open in China. Xu found it comforting that even in this small detail, Taiwan and China were already not so different.

Though Xu had never understood why it took Americans to devise such a basic concept. Sell large quantities of goods to people who needed them. And had the space to store them. As an unmarried man who lived in a military barracks, neither applied to Xu.

And practically everything Costco sold in China, from the items in the food court to clothing to groceries to small appliances, was made or grown in China.

Xu grimaced. Time to focus.

As promised in his briefing, Xu saw no sign of sentries. No fences. All that had slowed them down so far was the soft, muddy ground irrigated for lotus production. They'd been able to skirt the worst of it, and the farm now lay behind them.

Though the smell of lotus flowers still persisted on the cool night air. Truly, it was hard to believe that office towers would be visible in the daytime not so far away.

It couldn't be this easy. Such a critical facility…wait! There was movement ahead. Not a person or his heat would have produced a bright return on Xu's night vision goggles.

What, then?

Xu held up his right fist, ordering his men to hold fast.

Then Xu increased his goggles' magnification and trained them on the source of the unexplained movement ahead. It quickly came into focus.

Xu nearly laughed aloud. It was one of those ridiculous robot dogs! A body suspended on four mobile stalks that served the same purpose as the legs of a dog.

There were differences, though. Metal and glass protruded upward from the robot's body at irregular intervals. For what purpose, Xu could only guess.

Sensors perhaps? Nothing looked like a weapon.

Xu thought he remembered that the Americans made these robots. Or were these locally made copies?

Either way, the robot was probably there to warn the Quick Reaction Force of intruders. And if Xu could see one, there were probably others.

Xu relayed what he had seen to the rest of his men in a few words.

Then Xu steadied his rifle and carefully aimed at the slowly moving robot. His long training as a sniper meant that this was far from the most challenging shot Xu had been required to make.

Except in one respect. Where should he seek to hit the robot?

It didn't really seem to have a "head."

Finally, Xu decided that center mass was the best choice. After all, it wouldn't do to miss!

Xu's shot did indeed hit precisely where he'd aimed. And the robot stopped dead in its tracks.

At the same time, the robot let out an ear-splitting sound that rose and fell in a way designed to draw attention from a distance.

Xu shot it again. And again. The sound continued.

Finally, the fourth shot silenced the siren. The robot remained standing upright, smoking and seemingly frozen in place.

But no lights came on. No troops appeared. No other robots were visible.

Yet Xu could swear he'd seen something else move. Reducing the magnification on his night vision goggles and scanning the area, though, did nothing to locate whatever it was.

If it wasn't just nerves, Xu thought ruefully.

Well, it seemed likely that the robot had sent a radio signal calling for human reinforcements after Xu's first shot.

But they had to wait for the impact of the first wave of missiles to strike the area around the missile installation, which should happen… Xu checked his tablet.

Any time now.

Xu flattened, waving his right hand for his men to follow his example.

They wasted no time doing so, which was fortunate.

Seconds later, the first missile flew overhead, scattering bomblets just as planned.

Xu had never ridden a horse but had read descriptions of some doing everything possible to throw off their rider.

This had struck Xu as perfectly reasonable. Why should a horse, or any other creature, welcome carrying around a heavy weight that occasionally jabbed metal spurs into its skin?

This image came to Xu's mind as the ground appeared determined to buck hard enough to send him skyward. Helped by his heavy pack, Xu remained in place.

Finally, the impacts from the bomblets dispersed by the first missile subsided. Xu remained aware, though, that another missile designed to deploy mines was already on its way from the mainland.

Time to move before it arrived.

Xu rose and waved his men forward. The soldier designated as scout for this mission led the way.

But not for long. Another robot had been hidden, crouching low in the grass. As the scout approached, it sprang up, and something flew from it.

Striking the scout in the neck.

The scout jerked, twitched, and fell. A taser!

Xu's rifle was back against his cheek without conscious thought. The second robot soon joined the first in smoking immobility.

How many of these cursed things were there? More important, how many had survived the bomblets?

Only one way to find out. Xu called another soldier forward to serve as scout.

Even though Xu would have preferred to do the job himself, his orders were clear. Xu had to acknowledge grudgingly that nobody else in his unit had actual combat experience. And that meant he was a resource that couldn't be wasted.

Xu glanced down again at the small tablet strapped to his arm.

They would have to hurry to reach the access point for the underground missile emplacement.

No sooner had the thought formed than there was another blur of motion in front of the scout. Another robot!

The aim of this one was just as good as the last. The taser dart struck the scout in the neck, and he fell, twitching and racked with spasms.

They'd had to leave the first soldier hit behind, alive and breathing but unconscious. This scout had fared no better.

Xu was no expert on tasers. But he thought that these were likely to have had their power increased quite a bit over ones commercially available.

And Xu realized it was no coincidence that both soldiers had been hit in the neck. It was the only area of exposed skin on the men in the unit.

These thoughts flashed through Xu's mind as his rifle sent this robot to the same frozen, smoking state as its fellows.

But they didn't have time to play this game. Not with the second missile arriving any minute to lay mines.

And if they were dispersed in a pattern that was off by even a fraction...

A high-pitched roar overhead told Xu he was about to find out.

Once again, Xu hugged the ground, gesturing at his remaining troops to do the same.

Two of his men, Xu thought grimly, needed no instruction.

Unlike the first missile, no explosions followed. Well, that's what was supposed to happen, Xu thought.

As he raised his head, Xu realized he had no idea how the mines' dispersal had been slowed on their way to the ground. Did they have little parachutes attached? Were they aerodynamically shaped?

Well, whatever the answer, Xu couldn't see anything now. Had any of the mines landed near them?

Xu grimaced. Only one way to be sure.

Xu waved another of his soldiers forward, pointing to the spot where the access hatch was supposed to be located.

The man nodded and, crouching low, moved forward.

No robot appeared. Still no quick reaction force.

The new scout was looking carefully ahead. As any sensible soldier would under the circumstances, Xu thought.

It didn't take long before the scout stopped and bent down. A few moments later, his right hand went up. With his thumb extended.

He'd found the access hatch.

Xu breathed a sigh of relief. Now, they had a chance to finish this mission before Taiwanese troops showed up.

As though to punish Xu for his momentary optimism, there was an explosion. Behind him.

Xu cursed. One of his men had set off a mine.

Not surprisingly, he was dead.

Almost as bad, another who had been within range of the blast had been badly injured. Two of his fellow soldiers did their best to bandage his wounds. They were able to stop the worst of the bleeding, but the look they exchanged told Xu all he needed to know.

The injured man wouldn't survive without real medical attention. And soon.

The scout waved Xu forward, and the reason quickly became clear.

The access hatch was now open. Everyone in the unit had been given the access code supplied by a facility employee, including the scout.

Before the mission, Xu had wondered whether that man had supplied the code for money. Or because he genuinely wanted Taiwan to be reunited with China. Or both.

Then Xu had realized it didn't matter. As long as the code worked, and the mission was successful.

Well, now they knew the code worked. All that remained was to set the explosive charges.

Fortunately, the few surviving and uninjured soldiers happened to include the one carrying the explosives.

The man Xu chose to think of as a Chinese patriot had said that at this hour, the facility would be unmanned. And they would only have to move a short distance within the underground launch operation to reach the missiles they needed to destroy.

The fact that much of the missiles' bulk consisted of fuel and explosives would simplify their task considerably. Correctly set charges could be counted on to set off sympathetic detonations that should destroy the entire facility despite the relatively small quantity of explosives they were carrying.

Per the mission plan, Xu stayed behind to stand watch as the rest of his unit went through the access hatch to plant the charges. The last man closed the hatch behind him.

Well, the plan had actually called for two of his men to stand watch with Xu. But Xu had fewer men left than anticipated.

So far, they still appeared to be on track to accomplish the mission. If the enemy's Quick Reaction Force just gave them another few minutes…

Movement.

Xu had been hoping the enemy forces would be foolish enough to arrive in trucks with headlights blazing. Apparently, they weren't quite that stupid.

Xu's night vision goggles let him observe several distant soldiers. Xu was flat on his stomach and behind a bush.

But Xu could see that the enemy soldiers also had night vision goggles.

Xu stayed as still as he could.

The enemy was advancing cautiously but, at their current pace, would undoubtedly reach the access hatch before his men could exit.

How long before one of the advancing soldiers tripped a mine?

It turned out the answer was – not long.

The closest enemy soldier was flung skyward by the force of the explosion, and after he hit the ground, he didn't move. The other soldiers froze in place.

Well, Xu thought, if I realized I was in the middle of a minefield, I'd do the same thing.

Barely moving, Xu sent his men a two-click signal that meant the enemy had arrived at their position. He received a single-click acknowledgment.

Xu looked intently through his goggles. No sign that he'd been spotted. None of the enemy soldiers were moving.

Wait. Was that movement behind them?

Whatever it was, Xu couldn't make it out yet.

His men should be exiting any minute.

Yes! Movement to his left that had to be the access hatch opening. And his men were well enough trained to have turned off the facility lights before exiting.

Would the enemy soldiers still spot the hatch opening?

Multiple flashes from silenced enemy rifles quickly told Xu the answer was yes. Xu returned fire and glanced to the side to see whether his men had been hit.

If any had been, their body armor had left them still able to fight. All of Xu's remaining men were prone and returning fire.

Xu was about to order withdrawal when a bright streak of light leaped toward the access hatch.

Where his men were still concentrated.

A rocket launcher!

The round's impact sent at least two of his men flying. Xu was far enough away that he was unhurt and continued to return fire.

From fire coming to his left, Xu could hear that at least one of his men was still in the fight.

Even better, from that soldier's high rate of fire, Xu knew he had one of their QJY-201 light machine guns. That might buy them more time.

Had the team set the charges correctly?

The answer to that question came in two forms. First, the ground Xu was currently hugging shook beneath him.

Much more dramatically, the access hatch lid flew off. That was accompanied by a gout of flame from the now open entry.

And repeated and intensified ground tremors from multiple explosions.

It was clear the underground missile facility was no longer operational.

But Xu had one more unanswered question.

Would all of these ground shocks affect the mines laid down by the second missile?

That question was answered even more quickly, as one mine and then another exploded in an intensifying pattern.

Fortunately, that pattern progressed away from his position.

Shouts and screams from that direction told Xu the mines were exacting a heavy toll on the enemy.

But then they started going off even more rapidly. And coming closer and closer.

Until, with a shout from his soldier nearby, one exploded to Xu's left.

There was no time, though, for Xu to worry about that man's fate.

Because there was another flash of light to Xu's right.

This one was even closer.

Xu felt as though he was flying.

And then blackness.

When he opened his eyes, Xu had no idea how long they had been closed. Or how long it took him to move his head far enough to take in his surroundings.

Probably not long. Because Xu saw movement neither near nor far.

No sirens. No enemy soldiers. At least none he could see.

But Xu was sure more would arrive soon.

Years ago, Xu had watched footage of an American boxer named Muhammad Ali fighting a man whose name he didn't remember. Xu would never forget, though, the beating that other man had taken from Ali. Until he finally dropped, and Ali had been declared the winner.

Xu now thought he understood how that man had felt. But as far as he could tell, Xu had no broken bones. Every step hurt, but he could move.

Xu wanted to check the many nearby unmoving bodies for some sign of life. To render first aid if he could find any such sign.

His orders, though, were explicit. Leave any soldier unable to move behind. Upon mission completion, Xu's first priority was to escape and report.

Well, at least it appeared the mission had been a success.

Xu shook his head while he moved away as fast as he could.

Success.

But at what a cost.

Chapter Thirty-One

Tactical Mobile Over-the-Horizon Radar
Angaur Island
Republic of Palau

Tom Burke hadn't been sleeping well for days. He knew the reason. But he wouldn't admit it.

Not even to himself.

His sleepless nights had started when the Chinese shot down that unarmed reconnaissance plane.

At first, Burke had tossed and turned, thinking about the obvious lesson from what the Chinese had done.

The Chinese didn't want anyone to know what they were doing. And they were willing to kill anyone who got in their way.

If they were willing to shoot down an American military aircraft, why not destroy the radar installation on Palau? Sure, it could cover a lot of ground – and water – besides just China.

But everyone knew China was why America spent so much money putting it in Palau.

After his first sleepless night, Burke had developed a new routine. His bunk was a short walk from TACMOR's receiving station and the Patriot battery that protected it. Both were manned day and night.

Last evening, Burke had visited TACMOR's night shift first. Tonight, he decided to make his first stop at the Patriot battery's engagement control station, a shelter mounted on the chassis of a five-ton cargo truck.

Either way, Burke thought with a smile, it's just as much walking before I go back to bed.

Burke was surprised his deputy Sam Holt was already there, talking with the Patriot battery commander, Captain Parker.

"Good evening to you both!" Burke said. "Sam, I see you couldn't resist the Captain's coffee either!"

Everyone laughed since Parker's coffee had only two virtues. It was hot and strong enough to keep everyone at the battery awake.

But it was not for delicate stomachs. And the less said about its taste, the better.

"Sam here was telling me he thinks this Taiwan business will blow over. At least until next year," Parker said.

"Is that so, Sam? What makes you think the Chinese will wait?" Burke asked.

"Well, we all know that the Chinese need good weather to launch an invasion," Holt said. "And it can't just be a fleet making a single landing. They'll need a sustained movement of troops, equipment, and supplies over at least a week to establish a solid beachhead. But the good weather period for this year…"

"Is just about up," Parker finished for him.

Burke shrugged. "Maybe. But I've looked today at the ten-day forecast, and there's nothing worse than a shower or two. No storm that the Chinese couldn't easily push through. In fact…"

The excited voice of one of the soldiers operating a Patriot console broke in at that moment.

"Contact! Multiple inbound missiles. Probable DF-26s based on data so far," the soldier said.

"Number of inbounds?" Parker asked calmly.

"Not yet clear, sir. Data so far is from TACMOR. We won't have a better read until they move into our radar coverage. So far, it looks like at least three DF-26s headed here and four to Babeldaob," the soldier said.

Babeldaob was Palau's largest island, and its TACMOR transmitter was over a hundred kilometers from the TACMOR receiving station on Angaur Island.

"And sir, TACMOR is also reporting other ballistic missiles launched at Okinawa and Guam. Both have been notified."

Now Burke remembered that the soldier speaking was Lieutenant Wills. Parker had introduced him as the Tactical Control Officer. Along with an assistant and a communications specialist, those three were the only ones required to operate the Patriot system in combat.

There were about a hundred men assigned to this Patriot battery.

Burke knew that all the other soldiers had jobs necessary for the battery to function. The ones who operated the radar. The ones who carried out repairs. And many others with tasks he knew nothing about.

Well, Burke supposed TACMOR would be just as great a mystery for most soldiers working at the Patriot battery.

"One more to Babeldaob," Parker said thoughtfully. "I wonder why?"

So did Burke. Both sites were equally important.

"Sir, one of the tracks is diverging," Wills said. "It's not going to the transmitter on Babeldaob."

Parker frowned. "Is it off course? Will it impact in the ocean?"

"No, sir," Wills replied. "It looks like it's headed for Koror."

A palpable sense of shock passed through everyone in the control station. At one time or another, they'd all been to Koror.

Palau's largest town with a population of about ten thousand, Koror probably had more people now at the height of the tourist season. Beachfront hotels and casinos catered to honeymooners and other vacationers from Japan, Korea, Taiwan, America, Canada, and Europe.

Before the COVID-19 pandemic, annual arrivals from China had peaked at about a hundred thousand. Burke had read that in 2022, the number of Chinese arrivals had been…fifty-seven. And had never gone above that in the years since.

Well, Burke thought bitterly, it looks like the Chinese knew something the rest of us didn't.

Burke could see that Holt was about to say something and stood up.

"Sam, we need to get to our work at TACMOR. These men have got a job to do," Burke said.

For a second, Burke thought Holt was going to object, but then he nodded.

They both left the control station, murmuring "Good lucks" that all the soldiers there knew they meant.

They hoped the incoming missiles had conventional warheads. Even so, Burke and Holt feared that if even one made it past the Patriot's missiles, it would wipe out TACMOR and the battery.

A siren howled, and most people were doing what they'd been trained to do.

Go to the nearest concrete shelter.

A half dozen shelters were scattered around TACMOR and the Patriot battery protecting it. All of them were buried underground, with a short series of steps leading to a heavy metal door. Every door they could see was still hanging open.

As they should be, Burke thought. The doors were supposed to be closed only after the siren changed from a long howl to a series of staccato beeps.

Because one or more missiles were about to strike. And anyone still outside a shelter would have missed their chance at relative safety.

Burke's comment about their "work at TACMOR" had been to get Holt out of the command post before he said something about how Parker and his men had to save Koror. Not least because there were sure to be dozens of American tourists there.

Burke thought they would try as hard as possible to do just that. But that might have meant after successfully defending the TACMOR facility nearby. The truth was, Burke didn't know what Parker's orders said about those priorities.

But Burke was certain that now wasn't the time to distract Parker and his men with such concerns.

Neither Burke nor Holt were trained to operate TACMOR equipment. They were managers. Going to TACMOR would just serve to distract the men collecting and relaying data to the Patriot battery. Data that might help keep them all alive.

As well as updates to the American bases on Guam and Okinawa about the missiles headed their way. That Burke hoped would also give the people there a better chance of survival.

So, the only work Burke and Holt had to do was to ensure that all personnel not actively involved in TACMOR's operation made it to a shelter. In practice, there was no time to do head counts. All they could do was hurry along stragglers.

At least, that's what Burke thought.

Until a man he recognized as a recent arrival walked up to him. A replacement, Burke remembered, for one of the men he'd fired for feeding the macaques.

"Hey, is this a drill or something? I was trying to get some sleep!" the man said.

Now Burke remembered the man's name.

Murphy.

Perfect.

"It's not a drill, Murphy," Burke said tersely. "Now, unless you want to get blown up by a Chinese missile, I suggest you get in that shelter right now."

Burke pointed at the nearest shelter, about a dozen yards away.

Murphy's face darkened, and he opened his mouth to say something. Then he closed it as Burke's words finally registered.

Very quickly, Burke and Holt were alone again.

They both looked in every direction. As far as they could see, everyone else had made it to a shelter without encouragement.

Time to join them.

Just as they turned to the nearest shelter, the siren's tone changed to staccato beeps.

Burke and Holt both started to run.

Too late. The door to the nearest shelter slammed shut.

And one after another, they could hear the sound of the other metal shelter doors as they closed with a metallic clang.

Where to? Well, any shelter had to be better than saying out in the open.

The rec center.

Luckily, Burke had the key.

Just as they reached the door, Burke could hear the sound of a Patriot missile firing.

And then another.

Then they were inside, hiding under a pool table.

Seconds passed, and they dared to hope the Patriot missiles had scored.

And then the floor seemed to lift. There was a flash of light and a sound like a freight train.

Then everything went black.

Chapter Thirty-Two

USS America
Between Taiwan and Japan

Captain Mercer sometimes thought that one of the greatest gaps between image and reality had to be ship captain. In every movie he'd seen growing up, the job seemed the definition of dashing action and adventure.

The reality was somewhat different.

Mercer considered putting the right person in the right job on his ship one of his most important responsibilities. Of course, he didn't personally pick every sailor and Marine aboard.

But Mercer did have an essential voice in the selection for all the key positions. And if someone turned out to be a poor fit, Mercer had full authority to take whatever corrective action was needed.

Including a new assignment somewhere else.

Then there was logistics. Did the over three thousand sailors and Marines onboard have everything they needed to do their jobs?

Because at sea, you fought with what you had. Not what you left behind at port and wished you'd remembered to bring on board.

Mercer didn't remember any of that in the movies.

Then there were Mercer's orders. In the movies, they were always simple.

Attack the enemy.

In Mercer's experience, though, orders weren't quite so straightforward. Yes, they always had details on what he should do. Sometimes, like now, orders also had details on what he should definitely not do.

Orders, though, could only anticipate some possible contingencies. Once fighting started, there would be little time to ask headquarters for clarification.

On top of that, there was an excellent chance the Chinese would try to interfere with their communications. Would they succeed?

Probably best to assume they would.

So, Mercer had called Commander Tyler to his office to discuss their orders. He respected Tyler or would never have approved his assignment as Executive Officer.

Time to see whether the thoughts rattling around in his head made sense when spoken aloud.

"Commander, I'd like to bounce a few thoughts off you regarding our orders. First, they specify that we're to remain in Japanese territorial waters. But that we should remain in 'proximity' to Taiwan. I've interpreted that as meaning within about five kilometers from the edge of the Japanese waters closest to Taiwan. I know you've been in regular contact with our Japanese escorts. Any issues so far?" Mercer asked.

Tyler shook his head. "No, sir. As you know, the Japanese aren't very forthcoming with how they feel about most matters. But the attack on Okinawa is different. They're mad. It's the first time Japanese military and civilian citizens have been killed by enemy action on Japanese soil since World War II. I think we could have counted on Japanese support in any case. But after Chinese missiles targeted Okinawa? They're with us all the way."

"Good," Mercer said. "That tracks with the conversations I've had. Any hint that one or more of our escorts will need to peel off soon or be replaced by another ship?"

"Not at all, sir. The three surface ships and the submarine all fought to get this assignment. They know that if the Chinese are going to defy their government's warning about another attack having 'grave consequences,' we're one of the most likely targets. Like I said, they're mad. If we get targeted by a Chinese ship, plane, or sub, they want to be the ones to take it out," Tyler replied.

Mercer nodded. "The Japanese have been ordered to stay in their waters. Any approach we can't detect with this task force is supposed to be covered by our subs, which are free to operate anywhere around Taiwan. As far as headquarters is concerned."

Tyler smiled. "Yes, sir. I'm sure the Chinese would disagree. But then, they seem to consider this half of the Pacific their exclusive property."

"Right," Mercer said. "Well, our point in being here is to remind them that it isn't. Now, on that subject, we're supposed to look like we might land the Marines onboard in Taiwan. How difficult or easy do you think that would be now?"

"Easy, sir," Tyler said. "All aircraft aboard are ready for deployment, except a single Seahawk down for maintenance. I've been told it will be back in service later today. That means we could get Marines on the Ospreys and their equipment on the King Stallions without delay. If they face no opposition, our Marines and their equipment could be in Taiwan quickly. We've updated our plans and have identified several points as the best landing locations. But we've been told plan, don't act. Is that still right, sir?"

"It is," Mercer replied. "I can't imagine headquarters sending our Marines to fight the Chinese in Taiwan. But I understand why they'd want the Chinese to worry about that option. At least as a distraction. At best, the Chinese may waste some resources on the possibility, ones that otherwise might have gone to better use."

"With the only downside, we become a pretty inviting Chinese target," Tyler said.

Mercer shrugged. "Well, yes. But this ship was built to be used in a crisis. And we have another mission. When you said 'all aircraft' are ready, that includes our F-35s, right?"

"Absolutely, sir," Tyler replied. "Ready in the unlikely event they need to cover the Marines while landing on Taiwan. And in the more likely event they're called on to support whatever actions headquarters decides are necessary after this Chinese attack."

"Good," Mercer said. "I have a feeling that support will be needed sooner rather than later. Now, we're due to get our first replenishment-at-sea tomorrow. That's still on track?"

"Yes, sir," Tyler replied. "It's still scheduled to be *Ranger*. Its primary cargo is aviation and ship fuel. Even though it hasn't been long since we refueled, topping off is still a good idea. Once the fighting starts, we'll need every drop."

Mercer grunted. "No argument there. What do you think about using *Ranger* for the job?"

Tyler did his best to conceal his surprise at the question. From the slight smile on Mercer's face, Tyler could see that his best hadn't been good enough.

"Well, sir, though *Ranger* is uncrewed, so far it's carried out its missions without incident. In the years since it and three other autonomous ships arrived at Yokosuka in 2023, they've all seen regular use. I understand that the Navy is planning to build more uncrewed ships, primarily for resupply missions like this one. Do you see a problem, sir?" Tyler asked.

"No, not really," Mercer said. "As you say, these uncrewed ships have done their jobs so far. But why do you think *Ranger* was picked to do this particular resupply mission?"

Tyler frowned and hesitated. Then his eyes widened, and Tyler nodded with understanding.

"Someone back at headquarters wants to say that uncrewed ships have been 'battle-tested.' Even though no shooting has started yet where we are now," Tyler said.

"Exactly," Mercer said, nodding. "So, as I said, I have no problem with using *Ranger*. We don't know if or when the Chinese will try to strike this task force. So, using an uncrewed supply ship will put fewer sailors at risk. That's a real plus. But I wanted to be sure you understood that's not the only reason we'll see *Ranger* tomorrow."

Tyler nodded. "Politics never stops, does it, sir?"

"Nope," Mercer said with a grin. "And that's how it's always been in every Navy. We just have to keep our eyes open, and be sure we understand why things are happening."

Chapter Thirty-Three

Zhongnanhai Compound
Beijing, China

President Gu waited impatiently for General Zhao's arrival. It wasn't that Zhao was late.

No. Instead, it was that Gu had many questions only the Air Force Commander could answer.

For just an instant, Gu thought back to their last meeting. When Gu had deliberately made Zhao cool his heels to remind him who was boss.

Since intervening in the Korean War in the 1950s, China had mainly used economic means and espionage to achieve its goals. Not war.

Was taking on the Americans a mistake?

Then, Gu thought about China's seemingly endless economic problems. Its massive debt. Youth unemployment. Aging and shrinking population. Capital fleeing for safer and more lucrative locations.

All problems that couldn't be quickly solved. Problems adding to the voices saying that China had lost its way.

That perhaps, letting the Party remain in charge was a mistake.

No, Gu thought to himself. We've spent billions on building up our military forces.

It's time to see some return on that investment.

No sooner had that last thought formed than Zhao stood at attention in front of his desk.

Right on time.

Deliberately putting his doubts aside, Gu said, "General, I have read your reports. It appears your plan to use obsolete J-7 aircraft as drones was a success. We inflicted significant damage on air bases in Taiwan without losing a single pilot. Our missiles destroyed the GPS satellites in our region that the Americans use for navigation and weapons targeting. Other missiles caused additional damage to air bases and missile installations on Taiwan. Yet more missiles eliminated planes and equipment at American bases in Guam and Okinawa. The American radar installation in Palau is no longer transmitting. So, do you believe the way has been cleared for reunification?"

Zhao's expression was impassive, and his tone flat as he replied.

"Sir, everything you have said is true. But there is much we still need to learn. For example, the Americans certainly have other means of navigation and weapons targeting that do not rely on GPS. Probably not as efficient. But maybe good enough. We penetrated Japan's military communications network as recently as 2023. But we can't be sure that we know the full capabilities of their radar installations. As for the Palau facility, we know it is damaged. But not whether it can soon be repaired. Finally, though we have landed heavy blows, Taiwan's military remains able to resist."

Zhao paused, and his expression shifted from impassive to resolute.

"My conclusion is that the Navy should be able to proceed. In the meantime, our planes and missiles will be used to the maximum extent possible to suppress enemy resistance."

Gu frowned. "General, your words don't exactly fill me with confidence. Wouldn't it be better to continue missile and bomber strikes against Taiwan before sending the invasion fleet? Wouldn't that reduce the risk our Navy will be taking?"

Zhao shook his head. "Our initial missile strikes were guided by intelligence sources, particularly patriots in Taiwan inside their military. Unfortunately, they have nearly all been uncovered after our successful strikes on some of their underground facilities. We will get no more help that way. Our bombers can and will continue to strike targets in Taiwan. But we will also pay a heavy price as long as their remaining underground anti-aircraft installations continue to be operational. But there is another even more important reason to move quickly."

Gu couldn't help himself, even though he knew Zhao was about to continue.

"Yes, General? What reason is that?"

Zhao shrugged. "The Americans, sir. Right now, I don't think they have the forces nearby necessary to stop us. But if we give their planes, ships, and submarines enough time to reach the waters around Taiwan, that could change."

Gu looked at Zhao in disbelief. "How is that possible? Won't we outnumber them in every respect, even if they send more forces?"

"Yes, sir, we will," Zhao replied. "But as we have briefed you, American military equipment is still superior to ours despite our best efforts. Just as important, their pilots and sailors have decades of experience using that equipment in combat. As a peace-loving nation, we do not."

Suddenly Zhao leaned forward and said in a low, intent voice, "But make no mistake, sir. We can and will succeed. All we need is for you to order the invasion fleet forward before the Americans can draw breath. My planes will fly in front of the fleet to ensure any enemy aircraft that dare to oppose us will go down in flames."

Gu had one critical political skill, which helped explain why he was now China's leader.

He knew when someone was telling him the truth.

Yes, the truth as he knows and believes it, a voice whispered in the back of his mind.

It was a voice that, this time, Gu chose to ignore.

"Very well, General. Prepare your pilots. I will give the order to Admiral Bai later today," Gu said.

Zhao stood, saluted, and quickly left.

Well, Gu thought, I've done all I can to ready us for the war ahead. It is finally time.

Within a matter of days, if all went as planned, Taiwan would again be reunified with the rest of China.

Chapter Thirty-Four

*The Oval Office, The White House
Washington, DC*

President Hernandez looked up from the file folder on his desk as General Robinson walked into the Oval Office.

"So, General, we're not quite as deaf, dumb, and blind as our Chinese friends may think," Hernandez said.

Robinson smiled. It was typical of Hernandez to come to the point in a crisis like this.

"That's right, sir. In fact, I'd like to discuss first the SpaceLink proposal to effectively replace the GPS satellites destroyed by the Chinese with his smaller but more numerous satellites."

Hernandez's expression made it clear he wasn't convinced. "I've read the proposal, General. It seems we'll have less than no time to test Eli Wade's theories before we risk the lives of pilots and sailors on his technology. Do you think that's a good gamble?"

"I do, sir. It's not a perfect option, but it's our best. It's also important to note that some of our top universities have been working on using SpaceLink satellites as a backup GPS for years. With no cooperation from SpaceLink. If the Chinese hadn't attacked us, I don't think that would have changed," Robinson said.

Hernandez grunted. "Yes, that's right. No love lost between Eli Wade and the Chinese, is there? Well, we're agreed on that much, at least."

Hernandez still wasn't happy. But finally, he shrugged.

"Fine, General. How much is this going to cost us?"

Now Robinson looked uncomfortable. "I asked Mr. Wade that question earlier today, sir, since none of his written proposals had any cost figures. I wrote down what he said."

Robinson opened the file folder he'd brought, extracted a single sheet of paper, and began to read.

"Tell the President that this cost me and my people real time and money. But we're at war, and I won't quibble about price. The software and access codes to as many SpaceLink satellites as you need is yours. If our solution works as well as I believe, you can decide later how much you want to pay to keep using both. I'm sure not expecting as much as it cost to build and launch the GPS satellites the Chinese just blasted out of orbit."

Hernandez winced. "Well, he's got a point there. I saw the preliminary estimate from the National Reconnaissance Office on how much replacing those GPS satellites will cost."

"Yes, sir," Robinson said. "We're still trying to get an estimate on how much GPS degradation will cost our transportation companies and the retail and other businesses that depend on them. There is just one bright spot there that I don't think the Chinese anticipated."

"Really, General? I'm interested in any good news I can get at this point," Hernandez said.

"Well, sir, quite a few European and Asian countries that had planned to sit out this conflict now see their interests threatened. Many of them rely on GPS access as well. Even though GPS was only blacked out over the area around China, it was degraded worldwide, including Europe," Robinson said, then paused.

"It's also becoming clear that the war won't end in a few days, as the Chinese have claimed. Taiwan shows no willingness to surrender. The longer the war, the greater the threat to trade and the world economy. I think we'll be able to pick up some new allies in this conflict, sir," Robinson said.

"Good," Hernandez said. "That may help with another idea I want to discuss. But first, let's talk about this unit's proposals."

Hernandez tapped on another folder liberally decorated with classification warnings.

Robinson nodded. "The one from the 75th Intelligence, Surveillance and Reconnaissance Squadron. Yes, sir. I thought that would interest you."

"That's one way of putting it," Hernandez said. "How haven't I heard more about these capabilities before? In fact, I'll bet I'm one of the few people who've ever heard this unit exists."

"Well, sir, their creation was publicly announced back in 2023. Along with a colorful unit patch. I think they were smart to keep a low profile after that," Robinson said.

"Right. I remember the patch. It's hard to forget one featuring the Grim Reaper. And if I'm to believe these proposals, they're ready to help quite a few of China's orbital assets shuffle off this mortal coil," Hernandez said.

Seeing Robinson's raised eyebrows, Hernandez couldn't help laughing.

"Didn't think the old man had a Shakespeare quote in him, huh? Well, how about it? Can these guys deliver or not?" Hernandez asked.

"I think, sir..." Robinson started to say carefully.

Hernandez shook his head. "None of that. You're going to tell me that this is a question the Space Force commander should be answering. Well, I already know what he'll say. Yes, because otherwise, this folder wouldn't be on my desk. It wasn't long ago that the Air Force did this work. And most of the staff at Space Force came right from your shop. So I'll ask again, can they do it?"

Robinson still looked unhappy, but finally, he nodded. "Yes, sir. You're right that a lot of the technology goes back to Air Force days. Much of the basic research was carried out as part of X-37B missions, dating back to 2010."

Hernandez frowned. "X-37B. That's the space plane that looks like a baby shuttle, right?"

Robinson smiled. "Yes, sir. Its missions were all classified, and now you know one of the reasons for that. Space Command thinks that a combination of small electromagnetic and laser weapons we've placed in orbit will succeed in disabling China's satellite navigation and reconnaissance assets. Based on what I've read, I think they're right."

"Both you and this folder used the word 'disable' not 'explode.' So, there's no chance of any Chinese satellite pieces falling on the heads of, say, Iowa voters?" Hernandez asked, without a trace of humor in his voice.

"Unlikely, sir. The power we can focus on any one satellite shouldn't be enough to ignite any fuel it carries to allow orbital maneuvers. But we don't have Chinese satellite blueprints, either, so we can't be certain. Even if one or two did explode, their orbits are high enough that any debris is unlikely to survive atmospheric reentry. Also, I saw from the proposal that most of the targeted satellites are over the Pacific and unlikely to impact land," Robinson said.

Hernandez grunted and was silent for several moments. Finally, he nodded.

"Very well. I'll approve the proposal. I hope you and all the bright folks at Space Force have realized that it won't take the Chinese long to figure out what we've done. And that soon they'll try to do the same thing to us," Hernandez said.

"Yes, sir," Robinson said. "For some time now, our satellites and planes have been hardened against the kind of attacks planned by Space Force. Of course, plenty of satellites in orbit predate that effort. Like some of the ones operated by SpaceLink, for example."

Hernandez shook his head. "The ones that Eli Wade has just been good enough to move to the top of China's target list. Well, let's hope this is all over before the Chinese can do anything about it."

Chapter Thirty-Five

UN Headquarters Building
New York, New York

Ambassador Jian did his best to appear composed. Nonthreatening.

The entire General Assembly was waiting to hear him speak.

The American Ambassador had just discussed China's attacks on American forces in Guam, Japan, and Palau. He had shown pictures of their consequences.

Jian had to admit that the ones showing the aftermath of a ballistic missile strike on Koror were particularly graphic.

The ones from Okinawa and Guam didn't help China's cause either.

Among those who cared about so-called innocent civilians, anyway. The ones the Americans liked to call "collateral damage" when they were firing the missiles.

Privately, Jian felt quite differently. After all the decades America had marched across the globe like an unstoppable colossus, her military had finally suffered a genuine blow.

And China had been the country to deliver it.

Jian coughed, peered over his glasses at his notes, and began.

"The American Ambassador has claimed that our strikes on their military facilities in the Pacific were acts of unprovoked aggression. Nothing could be further from the truth. We have warned America for many years that their interference in our internal affairs would not be tolerated. Yet, how did they respond?"

Jian looked down again at his notes. Though in truth, he didn't need them.

"They sent ships and planes practically within sight of our coastline to spy on us. Yes, to spy. They didn't even deny that's what they were doing. Their best stealth fighters and U.S. Marines were stationed in southern Japan. Long-range bombers and even more Marines were based in Guam. The Americans built a massive radar installation capable of spying deep into my country in Palau. But why? That is one thing the American Ambassador has not explained."

Jian paused. This time, simply for dramatic effect.

"Because the Americans intended to stop our reunification with Taiwan. Even though they have admitted in writing since the 1970s, it is part of China. That is not our guess. That is not our speculation. We have just posted to our mission's website pages and pages of verbatim quotes from American officials, including their Presidents, saying just that."

Jian slapped the table's surface next to him, and it sounded like a gunshot in the chamber's silence.

Jian had practiced the gesture on a similar surface at a conference table at his office and was now gratified to see so many Ambassadors jump.

"This was no unprovoked attack! China has been patient for many years. But no longer. We acted to prevent an American strike they told us was coming against our forces. We would have been fools to wait until the Americans had used their weapons against us, as they had promised so many times. Because today, ladies and gentlemen, China acts at long last to reunify its country. One that has been torn in two for almost a century. Reunification is China's right and its destiny."

Jian paused for the expected murmurs of agreement with his statement from China's allies, who were numerous in this building.

Protocol kept the larger number who disagreed with China's use of force silent. At least while Jian was still speaking.

"Now, the American Ambassador has warned you of the danger of what he calls 'unchecked Chinese territorial ambitions.' This from a country that has swallowed up lands near and far for centuries and invades sovereign nations whenever it pleases. But nothing could be further from the truth. China only seeks to reunify its people. China has no territorial demands to make against its neighbors in Asia or anywhere else. Unlike America and many other countries here, China has never possessed nor continues to hold so-called territories, possessions, or – let's be frank and call them what they are – colonies."

There was more murmuring among the other representatives but for very different reasons. The Indian and Vietnamese Ambassadors represented nations that had already lost soldiers in border disputes with China that still continued. Many other countries deeply resented China's insistence on claiming the South China Sea as its territorial waters, despite international law and their competing claims.

But Jian's remarks found more favor among Ambassadors from Africa and South America. France used its possession of islands in the Caribbean and the Pacific and Indian Oceans to claim vast swaths of ocean for its exclusive use. It even continued to hold territory on the South American mainland called French Guyana and used it to launch European rockets into space.

And America continued to hold territories in the Caribbean and the Pacific and Indian Oceans as well. One, Puerto Rico, had millions of American citizens who could not vote for President. Nor for representatives in Congress.

As far as many in the audience were concerned, there were only two reasons why that was so. Most in Puerto Rico spoke Spanish. Not English.

And most were brown-skinned.

Jian continued after the reaction to his last words had died down.

"No. The other countries here have nothing to fear from China. Unlike America, we do not send our ships and planes around the world carrying soldiers to invade any country we please. Reunification is all we seek. And I would ask America to remember one thing."

Jian paused again.

"The war where it lost more soldiers than any other was not World War I. Nor World War II. It was its Civil War, which it fought to remain a unified country. When other nations like the British tried to interfere, did the Americans meekly accept it? No, they did not. America, you should learn from your history. And realize that every nation is free to choose its destiny. I will conclude by saying to you all today that destiny can be summed up in one single word for China. Reunification."

Chapter Thirty-Six

Tactical Mobile Over-the-Horizon Radar
Angaur Island
Republic of Palau

Tom Burke opened his eyes slowly and almost immediately regretted it as a sharp pain lanced through his head.

"Take it easy, sir," a voice said to his side. "You took a bad hit to your head and probably got a concussion. I think that explains the pain I can see you're experiencing. I don't see any signs of a skull fracture, but we won't know until we get you a CT scan. It will be a little while before we can make that happen."

Burke didn't like the way the unknown voice said that last part. What was happening?

First things first.

"How is Sam?" Burke asked.

Now Burke could see he was on a gurney, still in the rec center. It looked like they'd been getting ready to wheel him out.

"I'm sorry, sir. He didn't make it," the voice said.

The medic walked into Burke's view. Army. Burke could see his name on a strip of cloth sewn to his uniform. Hutchins.

"A medevac flight is on its way here, sir. We'll get you to good care soon," Hutchins said.

"Hutchins. I need to speak with Captain Parker," Burke said, gritting his teeth against the pain in his head.

"Yes, sir. He said to let him know if you regained consciousness before the flight, so I'm pretty sure he wants to talk to you too," Hutchins said.

"Good. Thanks," Burke said.

A few minutes later, Burke saw Parker walking toward him.

"Captain. Thanks for seeing me. I know you must be busy," Burke said.

Parker gave him a crooked smile. "You could say that. How're you feeling?"

Burke shrugged. "Not so bad. I just need to get some aspirin and I'll be ready to pitch in."

"Huh," Parker said dubiously. "Didn't you just regain consciousness? And Hutchins says you're in obvious pain."

"Well, OK," Burke replied. "Maybe I'd prefer something a little stronger than aspirin. But you can't do without me. I'm told Sam is dead, and he's the only other person here who knew how to run TACMOR. What's our status?"

Parker gave him a long look and finally said, "TACMOR is down. We were able to intercept all but one of the missiles, and that one didn't hit TACMOR. But the debris from the missiles was bad enough. With ballistic missiles, sheer velocity is just as bad as explosives. We have multiple casualties to TACMOR and Patriot battery personnel on both islands. Both Patriot batteries are still operational in case the Chinese fire more missiles at us. But as long as TACMOR is down, I don't see why they'd bother. They have plenty of other targets for those missiles."

"So the missile you weren't able to stop. It was the one aimed at Koror?" Burke asked.

Parker nodded grimly. "We tried to intercept it. But we only had time to fire a single missile after destroying the ones targeting our base on Babeldaob. It missed. There's no casualty count yet, but first reports are that numbers are expected to be high."

Parker didn't say anything to Burke about prioritizing American military lives and property. He didn't have to since Burke had no trouble guessing Parker's orders.

"I need to look at the damage here and see the damage report from Babeldaob. Are we still in contact with them?" Burke asked.

Parker folded his arms and nodded. "We are. But I'm not convinced you're in any shape to take this on. Don't you have someone else who could do this job? Hutchins says you should get on that medevac flight."

"No," Burke said shortly. "Look, I'm no hero. But the other TAC-MOR personnel in Palau are all technicians, except for the deputy manager on Babeldaob. And he went on leave in Japan right before all this Taiwan business started. The techs are good people who will do their jobs. But they need someone who understands the big picture to set priorities, or this will all be over before we get TACMOR running again."

Parker gave him another long look but finally nodded. "I had two men killed here and one on Babeldaob. I hate to think the Chinese were able to take out what they died trying to protect. I'm sure you feel the same way about your men."

"Did I lose anyone else besides Sam?" Burke asked.

"No," Parker said. "Some injuries, but nothing serious."

Then he turned aside and called, "Hutchins! Bring your medkit!"

A few minutes later, Hutchins appeared holding a bag. "Yes, sir?" he asked.

"I want you to give Burke something to help with the pain without making him sleepy. I need him alert for at least the next few hours," Parker said.

A stubborn look came over Hutchins' face, and he said slowly, "Sir, I have to advise against that. This man has serious head trauma and should go on the medevac flight that's already inbound. If he doesn't get proper care, he could die."

"Corporal, that wasn't a suggestion. It was an order," Parker said.

"Yes, sir," Hutchins replied sullenly. He then reached into his bag and withdrew a small bottle of pills.

Handing them to Burke, Hutchins said, "Take one every six hours. Try to eat something when you take one, even if it's only a candy bar. If the pain gets worse, have someone find me. I need to get back to my other patients."

"Ones who will listen to me" wasn't said aloud by Hutchins.

Burke and Parker both heard it anyway.

Burke wasted no time swallowing one of the pills. Parker went behind the rec center counter. Then he nodded with satisfaction as he found what he sought.

Parker handed Burke a small water bottle and a granola bar.

"We'll try to get a real meal into you later. I'm betting, though, that right now you don't even want to think about food," Parker said.

Burke started to nod and then thought better of it. Instead, he just said, "You're right."

"OK," Parker said. "That pill's going to need some time to work. I'll stop by in about half an hour and see if you're in shape to look at the damage to TACMOR. And if you're feeling worse instead of better, speak up. There'll still be time to get you on that medevac flight."

"Understood," Burke said. Moments later, he was alone with his thoughts.

Burke was sure Parker was right about the pill needing time to work. Still, he already felt a little better.

Maybe psychological. But so is pain, at least in part, right?

Anyway, Burke was staying. As long as he could function at all.

Part of it was guilt over Sam Holt's death. Another part was anger over seeing years of hard work erased in seconds.

But mostly, it was fury and disgust over what had happened to the civilians in Koror. That missile strike had no military purpose. Instead, it was designed to send a purely political message to all of China's other neighbors in Asia and the Pacific.

If you dare to act against China, be ready to suffer the consequences.

Chapter Thirty-Seven

Chiayi Air Base
4th Tactical Fighter Wing, Taiwan

Captain Mike Han still sounded a little out of breath. First Lieutenant Jiro Kuo thought that wasn't too surprising.

After all, they'd had to run flat out to get to their F-16Vs in time.

"Comm check," Han said tersely.

"I read you five by five," Kuo replied.

Kuo's hands were a blur as he went through the checklist that ensured his F-16 was ready to fly. A bit faster than recommended.

Radar had reported ballistic missiles and enemy fighters were inbound. A coordinated Chinese attack.

Not an empty threat this time. China's invasion was underway.

Step one- establish air superiority.

Well, Kuo thought grimly, they were off to a good start. The J-7 drone conversions had caused little damage to Chiayi Air Base.

But they'd been forced to use quite a few of their scarce air-to-air missiles to shoot them down. They'd also had to sortie every available fighter to deal with the threat.

That meant fewer F-16s were available than usual to deal with this attack because many were undergoing maintenance.

Whoever was running China's air force knew what he was doing, Kuo thought bitterly.

This Chinese attack on Chiayi Air Base had materialized so suddenly that he and Han would be the only two F-16s responding. Against who knew how many Chinese fighters.

Yes, Kuo understood the logic. They could have tried to get more F-16s in the air from this base.

But some of them might have been caught on the runway. The other F-16s had a much better chance of survival if they stayed in their reinforced hangers instead.

Logical, maybe. None of that helped with the sinking feeling in the pit of Kuo's stomach, though.

They were going to be outnumbered. The only question was, by how much?

Well, at least they finally had AIM-120D air-to-air missiles. Though its reported range was one hundred sixty kilometers, this improved version of the AIM-120 could actually do a little better than that.

Unfortunately, their best intelligence said the PL-15 air-to-air missiles carried by most Chinese fighters had a range almost twice as great as the AIM-120D.

Well, Kuo thought, now we'll see which missile is better.

One bit of luck was that an E-2C Hawkeye was monitoring Chinese air activity and was giving all F-16s in the air constant reports. Though Taiwan purchased the E-2s in the 1990s, they had been heavily updated in a program completed in 2013. Improvements included the AN/APS-145 radar system, a new identification friend/foe system, the Joint Tactical Information Distribution System sending data to the F-16s, and a new global positioning system.

Taiwan launched an accelerated military drone program to great fanfare in 2023. So far, not much had come from it. One of the few products ready for deployment was supposed to be a drone that interfered with Chinese airborne radar.

Their briefing yesterday had said that two of these drones would be in the air at all times, ready to wreak havoc with any Chinese AWACS. Would that turn out to be true today?

Well, Kuo thought, we'll soon find out.

"You've received the E-2's vector?" Han asked over Kuo's headset.

"Roger," Kuo replied.

So far, the E-2C had only been able to point them in the general direction of the attacking Chinese fighters.

It stood to reason Kuo thought that the Chinese had electronic warfare capabilities, too.

After a couple of minutes, though, the data from the E-2C appeared on their radars. Solid radar returns showing that the attacking fighters were J-15Bs.

Eight of them.

Kuo's pulse started racing as the radar display showed missiles separating from the J-15Bs.

But not headed for them. These were air-to-surface missiles.

Four of the J-15Bs immediately turned around. Kuo nodded to himself. Those had been loaded entirely, or almost entirely, with missiles targeting his base.

The Chinese thought four J-15Bs would be enough to deal with two F-16Vs.

Well, Kuo thought, let's find out if they're right.

Chapter Thirty-Eight

Type 003 Aircraft Carrier Fujian
Somewhere Near the Taiwan Strait

Lieutenant Tan Sichun grinned as the catapult kicked her J-15B off the flight deck and into the air. With a bit of help from her jet's two Shenyang WS-10 engines.

Her mother kept asking her when she was going to get a grandchild. Including on her last leave.

Unless Tan found someone who could make her feel better than she did right now as her jet sped forward, it might be a long wait.

It was perfect flying weather, with unlimited visibility. Calm seas promised an easy landing upon their return.

To Tan's surprise, none of the pilots she now commanded had grumbled at her selection as flight leader. She'd even overheard one of them tell another pilot that he agreed with Tan's selection. Because she would give them their best chance of success.

It had been the best day since Tan's selection as a pilot.

Well, until today, she thought. Tan's grin grew even wider.

Yes, she had been given the honor of leading the first assault on Taiwan's Air Force. Just as they'd drilled it so many times.

The last few practice assaults, they'd turned away just minutes from Taiwan's coastline. Sure, they'd been shadowed by Taiwan's F-16s. Of course, they'd broadcast warnings.

But the F-16s had never fired on their planes. Or even locked radar.

Tan knew Taiwan's pilots were under orders to do nothing that might start a war. Talk about fighting with one hand tied behind your back!

Well, one thing would be different today. Before, they'd come in nice and high, so those F-16s had no trouble seeing their approach.

Not today. They'd be flying low enough to – with luck – avoid radar detection until it was too late to intercept them.

First, she had to get the other seven planes in her attack force into formation. That was going to be a little tricky.

Flying at such low altitude, some separation between the jets was necessary. That had to be balanced, though, with Tan's need to keep the attack force's radar return as low as possible.

Complicating matters was the reality that not all her pilots were equally skilled. Tan had ensured that the weakest pilots joined the formation last when it was already formed, and they only had to take up the rear.

That meant Tan and her best pilots were up front, ready to face whatever Taiwan's defenders managed to throw at them.

It wouldn't take long. Even at the slower speeds they had to maintain flying so low, it would take only minutes to reach the missile launch range of their target.

A Taiwanese F-16 air base.

The KD-88 missiles each J-15B carried had a one hundred sixty kilogram warhead with a maximum range of two hundred kilometers. Naturally, a bit closer would be better.

Two other missile attacks would follow theirs. One would be CJ-10 cruise missiles launched by Xian H-6 bombers. Like the American B-52s, H-6 production dated back to the 1950s.

Also like the B-52s, the H-6 continued to perform well, with numerous updates.

The CJ-10 had a range of 1,500 kilometers, though Tan doubted it would be launched from that distance. Instead, probably just far enough away to be out of range of any response from Taiwan.

As with any missile, unexpended fuel would add to the destructive force of the CJ-10's five-hundred-kilogram warhead.

The final wave would be land-based DF-16 ballistic missiles with a range of one thousand kilometers. Though shorter range than the CJ-10, the DF-16 carried a 1,500-kilogram warhead triple its size.

Most importantly, the DF-16's speed was supposed to be sufficient to defeat the American-made Patriot missile battery that guarded the F-16 base.

Tan had been surprised to receive all this information before their departure until the briefer explained its purpose. Their KD-88s had to be fired on time, exactly as ordered, or the attack could fail. Yes, they hoped their missiles, as well as the CJ-10 cruise missiles, would cause some damage to the target base.

But they were sure Taiwan's Patriot batteries had a finite number of missiles. And were unable to reload them instantly.

The attack planners believed that three waves of different missile types, arriving immediately, one after the other, would overwhelm the Taiwanese defenders.

Well, it all made sense to Tan. Now to see if theory worked in practice.

Tan checked her radar and gave thanks that unlike earlier types carried by the J-15B, it was the AESA version. AESA's main advantage was that it spread signal emissions across a more comprehensive frequency range. That made her radar more difficult to detect over background noise. As a bonus, it was also more challenging to jam.

So far, it seemed to be doing its job. There was still no sign of intercepting F-16s.

Moments later, Tan cursed as two flickering symbols appeared at the edge of her scope. F-16s. Headed straight for her attack force.

Would she have time to give the land missile launch order before they had to engage the enemy jets?

Well, there was that order for Taiwanese jets not to fire first, no matter what.

Even if Tan's force was coming in low in a blatant attempt to avoid detection?

Tan had only seconds to decide.

The mission came first.

There. Decision made.

It seemed like forever, but it was only a few minutes before they reached the launch coordinates. Within seconds of each other, all eight J-15Bs launched their KD-88s.

As planned, the four rear J-15Bs immediately turned back for the carrier. Tan had loaded those J-15Bs entirely with KD-88s, except for a single short-range air-to-air missile.

Only Tan and her three best pilots would go head-to-head with the F-16s. She'd been sure the Taiwanese wouldn't send more than a few interceptors. And she'd been right.

Now Tan ordered the remaining three J-15Bs to join her in firing their PL-15 air-to-air missiles at the approaching F-16s. They had a maximum range of three hundred kilometers, and from the steady lock shown on her instruments, Tan was sure they would score hits.

Tan thought the F-16s weren't yet within range to fire their AM-RAAMs. Though, if they had the AIM-120D with its reported range of one hundred sixty kilometers…

Apparently, they did because both F-16s fired missiles at Tan and her wingmen seconds later.

Tan's training kicked in, and her subsequent actions were automatic. The American AMRAAMs carried by the F-16s were radar-guided, so they should be subject to jamming.

Except that the AMRAAM targeting her appeared unfazed by the wall of electronic noise being put out by her plane.

It continued to head straight for her.

Yes! Both F-16 symbols disappeared from her scope. Hopefully, that meant both had been destroyed.

But the AMRAAMs they'd launched weren't affected. Tan and her wingmen were now all headed away from them at maximum speed, but the four AMRAAMs drew inexorably closer.

Tan shook her head as one of her wingmen deployed chaff. Too soon!

Then her entire world narrowed to the one small blip on her scope, seeking to merge with her jet.

Wait, wait...

Now!

Tan deployed chaff and made a bank so sharp she thought for a moment she would black out.

An explosion behind her.

Tan fought her way back from the edge of unconsciousness.

Three more explosions, one after the other.

No! I couldn't have lost all my wingmen!

Her scope was a mass of fuzz. It looked like all her wingmen had deployed chaff.

"Report in," Tan ordered.

The only answer from her radio was static.

No, Tan said to herself. Not all three.

Then, she started thinking logically. If any of her wingmen had survived, what would they do?

Since both the attacking F-16s had been destroyed, they'd return to the carrier.

One more bank, this time much more gentle, brought Tan to a course that would return her to *Fujian*.

There! Right at the edge of her vision. A dot that could only be one of her wingmen.

Tan frowned as the dot rapidly grew larger. Why was the other J-15B going so slowly?

The answer became clear as she carefully approached its wing, waving at the pilot in the other cockpit. He cheerfully waved back, giving Tan a thumbs up.

So, Lieutenant Zou wasn't injured. Too bad the same couldn't be said for his plane.

Smoke trailed from one of his engines. But Tan was relieved to see Zou had been able to shut it down. She could spot no flames, so it appeared safe for Zou to continue flying toward the carrier.

But landing would be out of the question. Zou's fuselage was peppered with holes, no doubt from an AMRAAM proximity hit.

The blast had probably taken out Zou's radio. Who knew what else had been damaged?

Well, their training covered this scenario.

Tan made the gesture for "Radio out." Zou nodded vigorously.

Right.

Next, Tan gestured for Zou to continue on his present course. More vigorous nodding in response.

Then Tan made the "next" gesture, followed by the "pull up" gesture for ejection.

That got her several seconds of silence, followed by a single, slow, and sullen nod from Zou.

Well, Tan didn't blame him. No pilot wanted to lose an aircraft. Or go on a dip in the chilly Pacific Ocean. Even if he'd be close enough to the carrier when he ejected, that rescue would be nearly certain.

Assuming Zou survived ejection. Tan had heard that at least once a J-15B canopy failed to separate properly during ejection.

But the rocket propelling the pilot's seat skyward performed flawlessly.

Zou had probably heard that story too.

Well, too bad. Only a miracle was keeping Zou's jet in the air. She wouldn't risk damaging *Fujian* on the slim chance that Zou could land it on the carrier.

Of course, if the single engine Zou had left failed, there'd be no point in worrying about it.

But the fates were smiling on Zou today. Progress was painfully slow, yes, but eventually, the carrier was in sight.

Tan had already radioed ahead that Zou would be ejecting within sight of *Fujian*. She saw with approval that the rescue helicopter was already in the air.

Carrier operations might be relatively new to the Chinese Navy. Plucking hapless sailors from the ocean was not.

As they came closer, Tan saw that *Fujian* was oriented almost perfectly for them to land.

Of course, Tan thought, they would have finished recovering the first four jets I sent back just minutes ago.

Then she saw Zou change course. Just slightly.

Toward the carrier.

A flush of anger came over Tan so quickly it surprised her. It was honestly not because Zou was defying her order.

It was simply that she couldn't imagine a pilot being so selfish and reckless.

Tan pulled her jet alongside Zou's and gestured for him to break off and eject.

Zou ignored her and stared straight ahead. Then he reached for a control.

Zou's landing gear lowered.

But to Tan's horror, his hook did not.

Zou's jet had zero chance of making a safe landing without a hook to catch the arrestor cables on the carrier's deck. Especially with only one engine.

Did Zou know his hook had failed to deploy? With all the damage his plane had sustained, did the caution lights even work?

Tan gestured furiously, trying to warn Zou.

Who continued to stare straight ahead.

The carrier landing officer's voice was coming over her headset, screaming at Zou to turn away.

What could Tan do?

One thing.

Tan quickly cut her speed down so far that she nearly stalled. But not quite.

She was almost immediately in position to fire her PL-10 short-range missile.

Tan locked it on Zou's jet. In seconds, it would be too late to fire without sending its burning wreckage onto the carrier.

The PL-10 was an infrared homing missile. Were Zou's IR warning sensors still functioning?

Apparently, the answer was yes. Because Zou ejected.

Well below the optimum altitude. But Zou's canopy separated cleanly, and his parachute deployed almost immediately.

Yes, Zou hit the water a bit too hard for comfort. Still, Tan could see Zou hit the quick-release button that freed his parachute.

The rescue helicopter picked Zou up a few minutes later.

He'll beat me to the carrier, Tan thought as she circled to line up her jet for landing.

And what version of events will he give to Commander Ge, Tan wondered.

She didn't have to think about that long.

One that put Zou in the best possible light.

Nobody could have seen the poor condition of Zou's jet from the carrier. Though obviously, the landing officer had spotted that Zou's hook had failed to deploy.

And now that the pieces of Zou's J-15B were on their way to the Pacific seabed, no one but Tan and Zou would ever know his plane had been full of holes.

But Tan had no doubt that everyone on *Fujian* knew she had targeted one of her wingmen.

That was the sort of news that had spread, seemingly by magic, since people had first ventured onto the ocean in rickety wooden ships.

The Commander didn't get to where he is by being stupid, Tan thought stoically. I'll tell the truth, and he'll believe me.

Tan wished she could sound more convincing, even to herself.

It's a good thing the seas are still calm, Tan thought. I'm so distracted that I might've done more damage to the carrier than Zou if he'd been allowed to continue his landing attempt.

But long hours of practice and her native ability kept Tan's hands moving and doing exactly what she needed to do.

Another textbook landing.

And there was the Commander, waiting for her.

The moment Tan's feet hit the deck, Ge's voice was in her ear.

Tan barely had time to see the holes in her fuselage.

She was lucky everything still worked.

"Report, Lieutenant," Ge said.

Report Tan did. She was surprised that it didn't take long to describe events that seemed so involved and complicated at the time.

Ge nodded. "You may not be surprised that your report does not match Lieutenant Zou's in every detail. Are you sure there are no changes you wish to make before you file your account in writing?"

"No changes, sir," Tan said.

Ge nodded again. "Good. Lieutenant Zou must recover before the doctors declare him fit for duty. Even after that, though, he will not immediately be available for missions. I have assigned him to other duties."

"Sir?" Tan blurted out, confused. If the Commander believed her, shouldn't Zou be standing trial?

"Lieutenant, how many sailors are serving on this ship?" Ge asked.

Tan replied, "About three thousand, sir."

"Correct," Ge said. "Now, how many toilets do you suppose are necessary for that many sailors?"

Tan had thought she was confused before. Her mind raced to find an answer that would make sense, but Ge spoke first.

"I don't know either. But Lieutenant Zou is going to find out for us," Ge said.

A sudden rush of understanding almost made Tan smile, but she was able to stop herself in time.

Zou would be put on a classic punishment detail after returning to duty.

Scrubbing toilets.

Still, Zou was getting off easy, she thought.

Ge had no trouble reading Tan's thoughts, even though she'd done her best to keep them off her face.

"So, you think I'm being too soft with Lieutenant Zou? Come, Lieutenant, you have my permission to speak freely," Ge said.

Tan hesitated but finally said, "Sir, Lieutenant Zou put one of our most important ships at risk at the worst possible time. I don't see how he can continue to serve as a pilot after that."

Ge nodded. "Ordinarily, I would agree with you. But consider this. Of the four planes that faced two F-16s, two have returned. Both damaged. One so badly that it could not safely land. Do you think every pilot in your group could have brought Lieutenant Zou's plane back within rescue range?"

That made Tan think.

She didn't have to think long, though.

"No, sir," Tan said reluctantly.

"And the two pilots who didn't return. Would you say they were good pilots?" Ge asked.

Tan quickly swallowed the resentment that question caused. Ge already knew the answer. He had approved her plan of putting the best four pilots up front to face the F-16s.

"Yes, sir," Tan answered immediately.

"Yet at least one of them released chaff too soon, you said. The other may have made no mistake at all. We have no experience against American air-to-air missiles. But they have shot down many other planes worldwide, as I think you know, Lieutenant," Ge said.

"Yes, sir," Tan replied.

"And consider this. Taiwan does not have access to the best American missiles. Or planes. Or pilots. Yet soon, I believe you will face all three," Ge said.

"Sir? Do you believe the Americans will intervene? Even in the face of our nuclear arsenal?" Tan asked.

"Yes. I do, Lieutenant," Ge replied. "We have struck American bases without first declaring war, including one on an American territory. Do you remember the last country to do that?"

Tan didn't have to think long.

"Japan, sir," Tan replied.

"That's right. And do you remember how that war ended for Japan?" Ge asked.

"Yes, sir," Tan said quietly.

Ge nodded. "There is, of course, one key difference. As you say, this time, both sides have nuclear weapons. I don't think either will fire them. But I believe the Americans will use everything they have left in this region to keep us from reunification. It's our job to use all we have to stop them. Now, would you like Lieutenant Zou to fly with you once I judge his punishment sufficient? Or should I send him back to base to stand trial?"

Once again, Tan strongly sensed this wasn't a real question. But instead, a test of whether she was worthy to continue as flight leader.

"Flying with me, sir," Tan said.

"Very well," Ge said. "One last question. Would you have fired your missile if Lieutenant Zou hadn't ejected?"

Tan could have claimed she had locked her missile on Zou as an empty threat. There would have been no way for anyone to prove otherwise.

"Yes, sir," Tan replied at once.

"Good," Ge said. "That answer shows me you have what I need most in a flight leader. Honesty. And common sense."

Chapter Thirty-Nine

Chiayi Air Base
4th Tactical Fighter Wing, Taiwan

First Lieutenant Jiro Kuo slowly opened his eyes.

He saw at once that he was in a bed in the base medical unit.

Not good.

Kuo looked down and saw that everything that was supposed to be there...was still there.

He experimentally tried to move each of his limbs. Everything worked.

Though he did feel some pain in his right side.

Kuo carefully lifted the sheet on that side, then peeled back the thin hospital gown he was wearing.

His efforts were rewarded with a view of the problem. A massive purple bruise.

Now Kuo remembered. He'd been forced to eject.

Kuo looked around the room. It was empty.

What about the Captain? He'd been trying to evade a missile when Kuo ejected. Had he succeeded?

Kuo looked around the bed for a call button. There was supposed to be one here somewhere...

"Good, you're awake."

The voice was familiar, but Kuo initially didn't recognize its source. Then, in a rush, he did.

"Sir, how is your son? Is he here, too?" Kuo asked.

Captain Han's father, retired Air Force Colonel Han, shook his head.

"No, Lieutenant. They say they're still looking for him. But if he did manage to eject, they haven't found him. No locator beacon ever activated, so it's more likely he went down with his plane," Han said sadly.

The Captain, gone?

For a moment, Kuo lay stunned, at a total loss for words.

Then he knew the ones he had to say.

"Sir, I'm very sorry for your loss. The Captain was a great man," Kuo said.

Han nodded. "Yes, he was. And the men who killed him are going to pay a price. One I'm going to help collect."

Kuo looked up, startled. "Sir, do you mean you're back on active duty?"

"That's just what I mean, Lieutenant. I'm your new commanding officer," Han said.

Kuo's eyes widened. But how in the world had this retired Colonel passed the flight physical?

Han nodded. "You're wondering how I passed the physical. Well, I never took it. Neither have the dozens of other pilots who have returned from retirement to fly F-16s. We've been flying F-16s since 1992, so there are a lot of us around."

"Understood, sir. You've been flying for EVA Air, right?" Kuo asked.

Taiwan's EVA Air had received an overall grade of five stars from rating organization SKYTRAX, and AirlineRatings had ranked it ninth in the world for attention to safety.

Kuo was willing to bet a big part of its success had been hiring retired Air Force pilots like Colonel Han to fly their planes.

"That's right. And once we've trained enough replacement pilots, I'll go back to them. But that's going to take a while. We've lost a lot of good pilots," Han said and looked sad again.

Well, of course, he does, Kuo thought.

Aloud, he said, "Sir, I hate to ask you for your help. But I know the people who run places like this. They won't let me out if I've still got as much as a hangnail. Could you use your influence to…"

Kuo stopped speaking as soon as Han started shaking his head.

"No, Lieutenant. I know you want to get back in the fight, and I admire you for it. But you need some time to heal. The good news is that the doctors tell me you'll be fine. But your body won't be able to handle the stress of combat maneuvers until after this war is over."

Seeing Kuo's reaction, Han shook his head again.

"I know it's not what you want to hear. But there is some good news. The Americans have joined us in the fight. And they're sending us F-16s faster than they're being shot down. I don't think the mainlanders realized how the Americans would react to an attack on Guam, their own territory. We're going to win this war. Oh, and one other thing, Lieutenant," Han said.

"Yes, sir?" Kuo asked.

Han smiled bitterly. "The AWACS monitoring your encounter with the Chinese jets confirms you and Han shot down two and, from its reduced airspeed, badly damaged a third. Outnumbered two to one, you both did well."

Kuo could think of only one reply. "Thank you, sir."

Han nodded sharply. "Now, obey the doctors and nurses here. That's an order, Lieutenant."

"Yes, sir," Kuo replied.

"And don't worry. You won't be able to recover in time to rejoin this fight. But after the Chinese lose this time, they'll be back," Han said.

Then he paused and added, "And if I'm still alive, so will I."

Chapter Forty

Tactical Mobile Over-the-Horizon Radar
Angaur Island
Republic of Palau

Tom Burke swallowed another white pill. On the one hand, they worked to keep the pain in his head at bay.

On the other, he had to take them more and more frequently.

So far, he'd resisted the temptation to double up on them. Mainly because he wasn't sure he'd get more if he asked.

If Captain Parker found out how many pills he'd already swallowed, he'd probably put him on the next medevac flight whether Burke liked it or not.

And that wouldn't do. Not while there was still work to do to get TACMOR operational again.

They were almost ready to run a full system test to see whether their numerous patch jobs would work.

The problem was every single one of them had to work. A failure at any of a dozen points would be enough to cause a systemwide outage.

Just as bad, even if every one of the jury-rigged repairs functioned, failure at some point was practically guaranteed. And could be caused by something as simple as heavy rain.

Captain Parker picked that moment to walk into Burke's office. Well, that spared Burke having to look for him. Because there was a question that only Parker could answer.

"So, Tom, how's the head?" Parker asked. The tone was light and casual.

The searching look that accompanied the question wasn't.

"Still attached," Burke responded in the same light tone.

Parker's answering grunt was the opposite of satisfied, but after a pause, he visibly decided to let that topic go.

"How are the repairs going?" Parker asked.

This time, his tone was eager. Parker had already told Burke that he didn't want the Chinese attack to have succeeded in its primary objective.

Burke believed him.

"We're almost ready to try a full system test. But you know what that will mean," Burke said.

Parker nodded. "The Chinese may detect it and decide to fire some more missiles at us. Well, we're ready. We've been fully resupplied, and I've had extra personnel arrive to replace our casualties."

Burke frowned. "Look, I know you'll do your best. But these repairs won't last, even if the Chinese don't fire anything at us. If they do, even the vibration from a near miss could be enough to shake a repair loose. Worse, if any repair fails, the whole TACMOR system will crash."

Parker slowly nodded. "I understand what you're saying. What can I do to help?"

Burke exhaled with relief. Exactly the right question.

"I need to know when the military needs TACMOR in operation. Right away? Or in connection with some specific event? Or when some other reconnaissance asset needs detail only we could provide?

Bearing in mind, that whatever coverage we can give may not last long. Especially if the Chinese hit us again," Burke said.

Parker had been furiously scribbling on a small notebook he always seemed to carry with him. Now he looked up.

"Got it," he replied. "I'll try to get you an answer later this afternoon."

Moments later, Parker was gone.

Burke thought that went about as well as he could have hoped.

Then Burke looked longingly at the bottle with the white pills. It had been less than half an hour since he'd taken the last one. But each one he took seemed to do less.

It didn't matter. He just had to hold on a bit longer.

Chapter Forty-One

The Oval Office, The White House
Washington, DC

This wasn't the first time General Robinson had seen a grim expression on President Hernandez's face.

Or an angry one.

Somehow, though, this time it was both.

"Sir, there are a few details we need to clarify on your No-Fly Zone order," Robinson said.

Hernandez nodded. "Go ahead, General."

"The Chinese are claiming that the Zone overlaps their claimed airspace. Of course, that extends quite a bit further than international law would recognize. But the Chinese claim does have support from some other countries," Robinson pointed out.

"I don't care," Hernandez replied.

Robinson just raised one eyebrow and waited.

"Fine, General," Hernandez said. "Let's do it this way. Our announced No-Fly Zone stays unchanged. But give orders to our planes not to fire on the Chinese until they exit their claimed airspace. Unless the Chinese fire before then. That way, we'll be able to prove the Chinese have no one to blame but themselves."

Robinson didn't bother pointing out that the Chinese would hardly agree. Hernandez knew that as well as he did.

Besides, after the American deaths and injuries caused by their sneak attack on Okinawa, Guam, and Palau, Robinson didn't care what the Chinese thought either.

As Hernandez's unofficial National Security Advisor, though, Robinson did care about support from other countries in the region.

"That should work, sir. Now, on handling commercial aircraft we intercept. The plan is to escort any violating the No-Fly Zone to Korea or Japan, depending on whether they are in the northern or southern half of the Zone. Korea should be no problem. However, I'm still concerned about Japan," Robinson said.

"I remember you saying that last time, General. I just talked to Prime Minister Kan. He understands that commercial flights violating the No-Fly Zone would probably be Chinese. With mostly or entirely Chinese passengers. He'll have extra security added at Japanese airports to protect those passengers until they can safely return to China," Hernandez said.

"That's good to hear, sir. Feelings against the Chinese are running pretty high in Japan at the moment," Robinson said.

They both knew that was an understatement. The Chinese had evacuated their consulate in Fukuoka in southern Japan. The one that covered Okinawa.

Just before a group too well organized to be called a "mob" had burned it to the ground.

The Japanese police had been conspicuous by their absence.

However, the Japanese government had expressed their "deep regret" over the incident.

Nobody believed them. Which appeared to concern Prime Minister Kan not at all.

"If that's all the questions you had General..." Hernandez said.

Robinson just nodded.

"Good," Hernandez said. "Now I'm going to give a more detailed answer to a question you posed this morning. You asked what our planes should do when Chinese warships, armed to the teeth with anti-aircraft weapons, violate the No-Fly Zone. As I said then, our planes dedicated to No-Fly Zone enforcement will not sink Chinese ships, either military or civilian. Unless, of course, those ships open fire on our aircraft."

This time, Robinson didn't even nod. He knew Hernandez well enough to be sure more was coming.

"Instead, I've now confirmed with the Navy that our submarines in the region can fire Tomahawk missiles at those Chinese warships. That we've sold similar missiles to Taiwan. And that nobody will be able to prove we fired them," Hernandez said.

"Yes, sir," Robinson said thoughtfully. "Of course, the Chinese will suspect us and probably point the finger at us publicly the first time one of their ships is hit by Tomahawk missile fire."

"I'm expecting them to do just that," Hernandez said.

His tone made it clear the prospect didn't worry him one bit.

"Sir, have you considered my proposal to use the 2,200-pound Joint Air-to-Surface Strike Missile, or JASSM?" Robinson asked. "In particular, I'm talking about the Long-Range Anti-Ship Missile version of JASSM. We have thousands of JASSMs in our inventory, including hundreds forward deployed to Japan."

"I have, General. In fact, you've saved me the trouble of bringing it up," Hernandez replied. "I know all about JASSM because I did read your proposal."

Hernandez opened one of the many folders from his desk, and started to read from the summary.

"Started in 2019 under the Air Force Research Laboratories' Rapid Dragon initiative. Two years later, in 2021, an MC-130 transport belonging to an Air Force special operation wing tested the system for the first time. Another test with the same plane type took place in

Qatar in 2023. Following many more tests, became operational last year."

"Yes, sir," Robinson said. "If I may, I'd like to go over a few details regarding the use of transport planes to deploy missiles from their cargo holds."

Hernandez nodded. This was an old routine with them. Robinson wanted to be sure that before the President made a particularly risky decision, he had the information needed to make a good one.

"The missiles, in this case, the Long-Range Anti-Ship Missile version of JASSM, are in racks fitted with parachutes. The crew first opens their rear cargo door to push out the racks. Then, the parachutes deploy, slowing the missiles in mid-air. A few seconds later, the missiles' rocket motors fire, and they fly free of their racks," Robinson said, then paused.

"We plan to have the cargo planes that will carry out this mission remain within Japanese airspace, and Japanese F-35s will escort them. However, we've had no time to refit these cargo aircraft with chaff or flares. We have installed electronic countermeasures, and we hope those will be sufficient if the Chinese target these aircraft," Robinson said.

Hernandez grunted. "It sounds like their best defense will be to land at the nearest Japanese airbase before the Chinese figure out what's happened."

"Yes, sir," Robinson replied. "The planes that will carry out this mission have been directed to do just that. The first time we use the Rapid Dragon procedure to launch Long-Range Anti-Ship Missiles, we'll have the element of surprise on our side. If we do it more than once, I expect the Chinese to target our cargo planes regardless of whether they're in Japanese airspace."

Hernandez shook his head. "If we do this, it's only going to happen once. We'll wait first to see how effective the submarine missile strikes have been. If the Chinese turn back at that point, then we hold off on Rapid Dragon. Unlike the Tomahawks, we won't be able to deny responsibility for firing the Long-Range Anti-Ship Missiles. Since we haven't yet sold those to anyone."

"Understood, sir," Robinson said. "You're also concerned about a possible Chinese nuclear strike if all we leave of their invasion fleet is floating debris?"

"That does worry me," Hernandez replied. "China has spent billions on building the world's largest Navy. Gu may not react rationally to seeing a large chunk of it disappear in an afternoon."

"Sir, while we're on the subject of the Navy, you asked me to plan air support for the Navy for the next move you plan to announce against the Chinese. I agree more than carrier air is needed. We'll be stretched thin because of the need to staff the No-Fly Zone, but I'm moving the necessary resources from our European and Central Commands. I think we'll be ready within the week..."

Chapter Forty-Two

Tactical Mobile Over-the-Horizon Radar
Angaur Island
Republic of Palau

Captain Parker did his best to suppress a frown as he greeted Tom Burke.

Burke's pallor made it obvious the man wasn't well. Of course, Parker already knew that.

Just as he knew from everyone he'd talked to, Burke was indispensable.

Now, though, Parker would finally be able to get Burke on a medevac flight.

"I just got the word from headquarters," Parker said. "They want us to operate TACMOR at full power or as close as possible with your temporary repairs. Our remaining reconnaissance assets strongly suggest the Chinese are planning a big push and need TACMOR to complete the picture."

"That's right now?" Burke asked.

Parker nodded. "As soon as you can get it done. Once it's operational, have your people let me know. Also, there's a medevac flight due to arrive this afternoon. You're going to be on it."

To Parker's surprise, Burke did not object. Instead, he just quietly said, "OK."

That worried Parker more than any other response he could imagine. But there was nothing to do but reply, "Good," and hurry back to his unit.

The Chinese had already attacked TACMOR once. Parker had done everything he could to prepare his Patriot batteries for a repeat attack.

Because he was sure the Chinese would detect TACMOR's reactivation. At a minimum, Parker thought they would launch an attack similar to the last one.

At worst, they could fire enough missiles to overwhelm any possible defense. But even the Chinese had a finite supply of missiles.

Right?

Word arrived quickly from Burke's staff that TACMOR was once again collecting and transmitting surveillance data. For now, all appeared stable.

Parker told himself again that he had done everything possible to prepare for another Chinese attack. And that his soldiers were on the highest alert possible.

It didn't help. Parker still had a feeling of dread he couldn't shake.

But minutes became hours, and still no Chinese attack came.

The medevac flight, though, did. Parker had nearly canceled it because of the heightened threat of a Chinese attack. Now, he was glad he hadn't.

Parker hurried over to Burke's office after one more check to confirm that no Chinese missiles were inbound.

"Hey, Tom, your ride's here!" Parker said as he opened the door.

When he saw Burke's head lying on his desk, Parker congratulated himself on making the short trip. Not a surprise that exhaustion had finally claimed him, Parker thought. But what a shame if he'd overslept the flight!

Then Parker noticed a trickle of blood from Burke's exposed ear.

Rushing to Burke's side, Parker checked his pulse.

He couldn't find one.

Parker called their only medic, Hutchins. He was there in under two minutes.

Hutchins needed only moments to confirm that Burke was dead.

"Internal bleeding, like you thought?" Parker asked quietly.

Hutchins shrugged. "That'd be my guess. But only an autopsy will be able to say for sure."

Parker could see Hutchins had more to say but was holding back because Parker was a superior officer.

"Say what's on your mind, Hutchins," Parker said.

"Sir, I don't blame you," Hutchins said, to Parker's considerable surprise. "Burke knew the risk he was taking, and you gave him every chance to leave for proper care. I just hope his sacrifice was worth it."

Parker found himself nodding. "So do I, Hutchins. So do I."

Chapter Forty-Three

Type 003 Aircraft Carrier Fujian
Somewhere Near the Taiwan Strait

Lieutenant Tan Sichun remembered how happy she'd been when she first took her J-15B into combat. Though only a couple of days had passed since then, it seemed like a lifetime ago.

And Tan was now anything but happy.

Taiwan's F-16 pilots and their AMRAAM missiles had continued to extract a toll on Tan's wingmen with every mission.

Yes, Commander Ge had described each mission as a success. Taiwan's Air Force bases were getting hammered. They lost F-16s daily, and not all their pilots could eject in time.

But F-16s continued to be launched, even from damaged bases. And even from highways. As a cadet, Tan learned that Taiwan had designed their major highways to be used as auxiliary runways. Ones stretching for hundreds of kilometers.

Bombing them all was impossible.

Commander Ge had never said they could afford to lose planes more easily than the Taiwanese. At first, Tan thought that showed his respect for his pilots' lives.

Maybe it did. But now Tan understood there was another reason. The Americans had announced that they were donating F-16s that would not only replace every one shot down so far.

But would give Taiwan enough extra planes to constitute another F-16 squadron.

Taiwan had already said that the new squadron would be piloted by retired Air Force pilots, who had volunteered to serve again during what Taiwan called the "current emergency."

That wasn't all. In reaction to China's attacks on Guam, Okinawa, and Palau the Americans had announced a "No-Fly Zone" around Taiwan.

Today would be the first time China challenged it.

Tan's force would not attack the Americans alone. Another eight J-15Bs would join her eight planes with a different attack force leader.

And what the briefer had called a "substantial number" of J-20s would attack simultaneously from air bases on China's coast.

On their previous missions, headquarters had decided against deploying Shaanxi KJ-500 airborne early warning and control aircraft. The large, lumbering planes with their top-mounted radars were the opposite of stealthy.

But now, China's planners had decided that the time for stealth and surprise was over.

Instead, it was time to use China's chief asset against Taiwan.

Overwhelming numbers.

This would be Lieutenant Zou's first mission under Tan since he had disgraced himself by trying to land on the carrier with a heavily damaged plane. Tan didn't know whether Zou had, in fact, cleaned every toilet on *Fujian*.

If not, though, it had been a substantial percentage.

The night before, Zou had approached Tan just after she'd finished giving the briefing to the other pilots for today's mission.

Zou had apologized for his error in attempting to land on the carrier. He'd said he had seen no warning light about his hook's failure to deploy and would never have tried to land if he had known.

Zou had also said that his motive was to save his aircraft. He'd said the distance it had flown on a single engine proved its worth.

Tan believed both statements were sincere.

Zou had acknowledged that his J-15B's value was nothing compared to *Fujian*'s importance to the invasion of Taiwan. And that he should never have substituted his judgment for Tan's.

Since she was flight leader.

Tan had replied that Zou would be the primary backup pilot for today's mission in case any of those already assigned needed to be replaced. She then thrust the briefing folder at Zou and told him to read it.

And thought no more about the matter.

Until the following morning, when Tan learned that one of her pilots had broken an ankle after tripping while descending one of the carrier's dozens of metal ladders.

Tan initially thought that perhaps Zou had been behind this accident, but no. She visited the pilot in the infirmary. As Tan arrived, she overheard him telling another visiting pilot that he had no one to blame but his clumsiness.

Well, Tan would at least give him credit for honesty.

Both China's land and carrier-based planes had given a good account of themselves against Taiwan's F-16s. By Tan's reckoning, they had shot down nearly as many enemy planes as they'd lost. Against surface-to-air missiles, though, the picture was more mixed.

Taiwan's Sky Bow II missile was fired from underground silos, had a range of 150 kilometers, a speed of Mach 4.5, and a ninety-kilogram warhead.

Its appearance on a Chinese jet's radar screen was the last thing many pilots ever saw.

Tan had been briefed that Chinese commandos had destroyed

many Sky Bow II missiles before a single plane had launched from *Fujian*. She was sure that was true.

The briefing had also said that many of the underground silos housing Sky Bow II missiles had been struck by ballistic missiles. One was believed to have been completely demolished.

Tan was sure that was true as well.

So far, though, Taiwan seemed to have plenty of Sky Bow II missiles left.

And now they would be facing American F-22s and F-35s. So-called "stealth aircraft."

Briefings from headquarters had insisted since Tan had first trained as a pilot that China's ground-based radar and KJ-500 airborne early warning and control aircraft could detect the American planes.

Maybe so.

But briefers had never said that the radar in any Chinese fighter could detect F-22s and F-35s.

And could ground radar feed Tan's plane data she could use to strike the American stealth fighters? Could the KJ-500?

Yes, knowing the American planes were "somewhere ahead" would be better than nothing. But without information Tan could use to target her missiles, how much better?

Well, Tan was about to find out.

Sky Bow II missiles were the first to strike. From their number and bearings, Tan knew immediately that both attack groups from *Fujian* and the J-20s were being targeted.

These J-20s were supposed to be the best stealth fighters China had. Today was the first time they would be deployed in this operation.

Well, Tan thought uneasily, maybe the Sky Bow IIs only have the J-20s' approximate bearing. The missiles may ultimately fail to hit them.

Then Tan was too busy to spare any more thought to what might happen to the J-20s. She was too occupied with the survival of her attack group.

Tan had mercilessly drummed into every pilot's head the need to wait until the last moment to deploy chaff. Since like the American AMRAAM missile, the Sky Bow II used radar to home in on its target. And to couple chaff deployment with aggressive maneuvering.

That approach had worked for Tan over the past several missions. And it worked this time, too.

For Tan, anyway. Two of Tan's J-15Bs were missing from her radar display. Another three were gone from the second attack group.

There was no answer to repeated calls to the missing planes. No signal indicating a pilot had successfully ejected. Nobody had seen a chute.

There were also two J-20s missing. So, stealthy or not, missiles could target them. Even at long range.

"American aircraft directly ahead on your present bearing, distance approximately one hundred fifty kilometers. At least two dozen enemy aircraft. Targeting data will be provided as soon as it is available."

The transmission from the KJ-500 ended just as abruptly as it had begun.

So, the Americans weren't all talk and intended to enforce their so-called No-Fly Zone.

Good to know.

The American fighters still weren't on the radar display in Tan's J-15B. At first, that didn't concern her. After all, the whole point of the KJ-500 was to provide early warning with its much larger and more powerful airborne radar.

But as more and more seconds passed, Tan became increasingly uneasy.

Where was that targeting data from the KJ-500? Why wasn't anything at all showing on her radar?

Then suddenly, there were many contacts visible on Tan's radar. Too many to count.

Not planes. Missiles.

How could they possibly avoid them all?

Tan quickly decided that her top priority would not be survival. It would be firing on at least one American jet.

She pushed her plane to its top speed. If I get close enough, Tan thought, my radar should be able to get a lock no matter how good their stealth technology may be.

Movement to her left caught Tan's attention. To her surprise, it was Lieutenant Zou flying in formation next to her. Close enough that she could see his thumbs-up gesture.

So, Zou was going on this suicide run, Tan thought. It seems Commander Ge was right about him.

But it didn't take Tan long to realize her gamble wouldn't work. There was still no sign on radar of the American fighters.

Which, Tan now realized, could have headed back to base as soon as they fired their missiles.

Missiles that would be on both of them in seconds.

Snarling a curse, Tan keyed her radio and ordered Zou to break formation and evade.

This order, Zou had no trouble obeying.

Tan did what she had done several times before. Wait until the last possible moment, deploy chaff, and make a maneuver that she believed the missile would be unable to follow.

And it worked.

With the first missile.

Tan, busy desperately pulling her jet away from the missile she had seen, never saw the one that exploded off her right side.

Not quite close enough to destroy Tan's J-15B outright. But the shrapnel that sliced through her right engine immediately shut it down.

And started a fire.

And threatened to send her jet spinning out of control.

Tan immediately realized that keeping her plane in the air would be impossible. All she could do was stabilize her plane enough to allow her to eject safely.

For several agonizing moments, Tan thought even that would prove too difficult.

Then, almost by sheer force of will, Tan was able to get her jet flying straight and level.

She didn't hesitate. Tan pulled the ejection lever.

Tan had thought that being catapulted from a carrier deck had prepared her for ejecting from a jet.

It had not.

When her eyes regained focus, and she could again breathe, Tan realized her parachute had deployed. And she had survived ejection without serious injury.

Tan could see her plane hitting the water even before she did. Far enough away that she was in no danger of being injured.

But still too close for comfort. One of her instructors had called a plane hitting the water a "shark dinner bell."

Tan had no idea whether that was true or not. But as she hit the water as well, Tan had more immediate problems.

Like getting rid of her parachute. And finding the life raft that was supposed to be strapped to her seat. That so far seemed not to be there.

Very quickly, though, another task took priority. Detaching herself from the seat before it dragged her underwater.

In a matter of seconds, Tan was free of both the seat and her parachute. But she had never found the raft.

Not the fault of the Chinese ejection seat manufacturer. A piece of missile shrapnel had shredded the raft, and its fragments had not survived ejection.

Fortunately, the seas were calm in this area, and Tan's life jacket had automatically inflated on contact with the water.

So, Tan's head was above water, and her only injuries were a few bruises.

Her locater beacon was supposed to have initiated automatically when she ejected. Had it?

Where was Zou? Had he survived?

Tan had no way to know the answer to the first question about her beacon.

But it was no. Thanks to another small piece of shrapnel. In fact, it was sheer luck that none of them had struck Tan.

Tan thought she might know the answer to the second question as a J-15B roared overhead. Too fast for her to see the tail markings.

Was it Zou?

Then Tan saw the jet gently rock back and forth before it sped off for the carrier.

Yes. It was Zou. Presumably, he had radioed Tan's position to *Fujian*, and a rescue helicopter would soon be on its way.

Until then, all Tan had to do was keep her head above water.

And, she thought darkly, remain uneaten.

Tan slowly turned in a complete circle, taking care to make as little noise as possible. The instructor who'd made the "dinner bell" comment had said that noises, particularly splashing in the water, were likely to attract sharks.

Well, Tan was sure her ejection seat hitting the water had made plenty of noise. Though she'd thought little about it, being busy at the time.

Perhaps the instructor had been right, though, and the much louder sound of her plane hitting the water would have drawn off whatever sharks were in the area. And the plane's impact was at least two kilometers away, Tan thought.

Maybe three.

No sharks she could see. With luck, Tan thought, I'm worried about nothing.

Sharks. The only time Tan had thought about them recently was reading a story about the number of sharks killed for their fins.

Over seventy million annually.

To make shark fin soup. Consumed mainly in China.

The fins didn't grow back. And the sharks needed them to swim.

So after their fins were removed and they were dumped back in the ocean, death was a certainty.

When she read the story, Tan had been revolted by the cruelty of the practice. And embarrassed to see that China was one of the few countries that had not banned "finning" by its fishermen.

Well, Tan had never eaten shark fin soup and resolved after reading that story that she never would.

Now Tan was ashamed to admit to herself that she was glad so many sharks were killed each year. Because it would improve her odds of survival.

Wouldn't it?

Movement to the right, at the edge of Tan's vision. Slowly, she turned her head. At first, she saw nothing.

Then Tan turned her head a bit further. Yes. A dorsal fin.

Was it alone?

No. Tan saw a second fin. And then a third.

What could she do?

Tan thought furiously.

She had found the flare gun attached to the ejection seat. If a shark swam next to her and close to the surface, she might be able to defend herself.

But the flare gun had only one round.

And Tan had read that sharks often struck from below. She might never see her attacker.

Would the rescue helicopter arrive before that happened?

So far, there was no sign of it.

Tan looked at the fins slicing through the water more closely. Two seemed closer to her than the third. But all three were swimming in circles around her.

Now she remembered reading that most sharks found humans unfamiliar prey. So, they would often start with observation.

Tan also recalled that sharks, after a single bite, sometimes moved on. Because that taste let them confirm that the human was not worth consuming.

But sometimes not. It depended, in part, on how hungry the shark happened to be.

Of course, a single bite would probably be enough to kill Tan. Either at once from shock or more slowly from blood loss.

Tan found herself struck by both fear and frustration. None of this speculation was getting her anywhere.

There had to be something she could do!

Besides clutching the flare gun as tightly as possible, though, nothing came to mind.

Minutes passed. Tan wasn't sure, but the sharks seemed to be circling closer.

Why could she only see two now?

Tan felt something bump her right leg.

Or had it been a bump? Tan had read that shark bite victims sometimes felt no pain due to shock.

Well, if she had been bitten, Tan thought blood in the water would have drawn in the other two sharks.

Then Tan chided herself as she looked around and saw three dorsal fins again. Had she imagined feeling something?

Tan grimaced as she realized there could easily be another explanation. No law said sharks had to advertise their presence by swimming near the surface.

There could easily be a fourth shark. One swimming at, well, let's call it leg depth, Tan thought bitterly.

Then Tan's eyes, which had been fixed on the ocean surface, finally registered a new and very welcome sight. A dot that was rapidly growing into a recognizable helicopter.

Rescue was finally on its way!

Almost as if the sharks could see the helicopter, too, they started to circle more closely. For some reason, the third shark continued to maintain a greater distance.

The helicopter kept moving in her direction. Not in a straight line, though.

Tan didn't hesitate. A single flare gun round would do her little good against multiple sharks.

She fired the flare straight up.

Now the helicopter was flying right for her. And it seemed to be picking up speed.

It only took a couple of minutes for the helicopter to come overhead. But it seemed much longer.

Because now the sharks weren't just distant dorsal fins. The two closest were long, dark shapes that were becoming easier to make out with each passing second.

They were both well over two meters long. Maybe closer to three.

Why wasn't the helicopter lowering a harness for her?

Instead, Tan could see...a rifle sticking out of the helicopter.

Oh no, was it Americans coming to finish her off before the sharks could?

No. She knew what the rescue helicopter on *Fujian* looked like. Exactly what was flying overhead.

There was no way the Americans flew one that looked just like it.

Then suddenly Tan realized they were trying to save her from the circling sharks!

Tan really hoped whoever was holding the rifle was a good shot. Because at this range from a moving platform, it would be very easy to hit her rather than one of the sharks.

A shot rang out.

Well, it hadn't hit her. And it hadn't hit one of the two sharks. A clean miss!

Suddenly, the two sharks circling so close to Tan disappeared.

And a harness attached to a cable was quickly lowered to Tan.

She wasted no time attaching herself to the harness and waved vigorously at the crew above. Tan was lifted with a speed that at first surprised her. Until she remembered observing a mechanical winch inside the helicopter when she had seen it on *Fujian*.

Once she was out of the water, the first thing Tan did was look down. A wave of relief washed over her as she saw both legs were still attached and none the worse for wear.

Then, movement on the water's surface not far away caught her eye. What was causing it?

Seconds later, Tan was brought on board the rescue helicopter.

"Welcome aboard, Flight Leader! Glad you made it in one piece!" the nearest crewman said with a broad grin.

"Thanks to all of you," Tan said with all the sincerity she could muster through her exhaustion. After a breath, she added, "And I'm going to tell Commander Ge about your performance as well."

"Ah, we're just doing our job," another crewman said. "But Chin here, he made a shot for the record books! If you're going to tell the Commander something, tell him about that!"

Then, the crewman pounded another one on the back. That crewman was still holding a rifle.

Tan thought, well, that must be Chin. But what shot was the crewman talking about? Neither shark near her had been hit.

Chin grinned sheepishly, clearly embarrassed.

Seeing Tan's confusion, the crewman laughed and continued. "You see, Chin saw two sharks near you. He knew that even if he managed to shoot one without hitting you, blood in the water would make both you and the shark he hit likely targets for the remaining sharks. So, he aimed at the shark furthest away. Honestly, I didn't think Chin could make the shot, even though these guys were doing their best to hold this beast steady."

The crewman jerked his thumb toward the two pilots at the front of the helicopter.

Tan's eyes widened with realization. "So, Chin shot that shark to draw away the two close to me! That must be what I saw making all that movement in the water as you pulled me up!"

The crewman grinned and nodded. "Yes, we saw it too. No loyalty among sharks! If Chin's shot didn't finish him, his buddies sure did."

Tan nodded thoughtfully. "Well, all that will go in my report. What I'm seeing here is more than just a crew doing its job. I'm putting you all up for commendations."

Then Chin spoke for the first time. "Lieutenant Zou said you would do that. Said you're one of the good ones and to bring you back in one piece."

Tan smiled. "He did, did he? Well, I'll have to be sure to thank him too."

To Tan's surprise, the unmistakable bulk of *Fujian* was already visible near the horizon. Some of that might be flying away from Taiwan's coast as they sought to escape the missiles but...

Chin saw her surprise and correctly guessed its cause. "We heard the order to make top speed for your location as soon as Lieutenant Zou radioed your position. I also heard an officer say every second could count, especially if you were injured. And that we couldn't afford to lose any more flight leaders."

Tan nodded and was barely able not to wince.

Yes. They'd already lost many flight leaders over the past several days. And it sounded like more had died today.

Had they shot down any of the American planes?

Chapter Forty-Four

No-Fly Zone
Near Taiwan

Lieutenant Colonel Dave Fitzpatrick, the commander of the F-35s that made up the 44th Fighter Squadron, was surprised.

Not by the procedures that had been announced by headquarters for No-Fly Zone operations. No, those made perfect sense to Fitzpatrick.

American and Japanese AWACS would detect any planes nearing the No-Fly Zone. Both countries' AWACS would fly well within Japanese air space and be escorted by Japanese F-35s.

Warnings would then be broadcast from the AWACS in Chinese, Japanese, and English to any planes violating the Zone.

If the intruders were identified as military aircraft and continued to fly toward the No-Fly Zone, interceptors would be vectored by the AWACS to destroy them.

These procedures met with Fitzpatrick's complete approval. The 44th Fighter Squadron was kept out of the warning process, which could have given enemy planes a way to locate his F-35s.

Fitzpatrick's surprise came from the reaction of the commander of the F-22s, Lieutenant Colonel Frank Drake, who led the 67th Fighter

Squadron. As long as he could remember, Drake had always objected to some aspect of every new procedure.

It would have been even more annoying if Drake had just objected to be contrary. But no. Fitzpatrick had to acknowledge that Drake sometimes had a point.

Even if he didn't always agree with Drake's observations.

But not this time. Instead, after Fitzpatrick had briefed Drake on the procedures for the new No-Fly Zone, Drake's reaction had consisted of a single word.

"Good."

It was odd. Fitzpatrick could hardly complain that Drake was satisfied.

The closest comparison Fitzpatrick could think of was pushing against a door you were sure was stuck. Only to find out it wasn't. And nearly tumbling through the door as a result.

Well, it was good that they were both on the same page. Because they were up against some of the best enemy aircraft in the world. The Chinese J-20, in particular, was a near-match to the F-22 and F-35 in many respects.

A formidable ground and air-based radar collection capability also backed up the Chinese planes.

The number of planes America was sending to enforce the No-Fly Zone was substantial. Fitzpatrick had no doubt the Chinese would be able to see them.

But see them well enough to provide the Chinese fighters with missile targeting data? Fitzpatrick didn't know and didn't think anyone else did either.

A better question was, "Could Chinese radar provide their fighters with missile targeting data before they came under missile attack themselves?"

Japanese ground radar coverage of the No-Fly Zone existed but was less robust than China's. On the other hand, American and Japanese AWACS were more capable than their Chinese counterparts.

They thought. In truth, data on Chinese military capabilities was sketchy at best.

Fitzpatrick smiled to himself. If they accomplished nothing else, this conflict would surely be a military intelligence gold mine.

Helping with that task would be several EC-37Bs, which had just replaced the EC-130H. Their primary mission was jamming, spoofing, and disrupting command communications and other vital electronic systems. The EC-37Bs aimed to disable enemy air assets and command and control systems.

The EC-37Bs were smaller and lighter than the EC-130Hs they had replaced. However, the electronics they carried were more sophisticated. As a bonus, the EC-37Bs could fly higher, faster, and longer.

Though their primary mission was offensive, the EC-37Bs would also record data on Chinese electronic warfare defensive capabilities for later analysis.

The plan was for the EC-37Bs to fly just within Japanese airspace, escorted by Japanese F-35s. Even if the Chinese decided to risk firing on targets within Japanese airspace, the EC-37B's robust electronic warfare capabilities gave them some chance of surviving a missile attack.

Now to see if the most important data point would be, "American planes and pilots are better than their Chinese counterparts."

Because one fact was indisputable. The Chinese had far more planes available here than America, Japan, and Korea put together.

With that thought in mind, it was a relief when Drake's voice came over Fitzpatrick's headset.

They were both on their way to the No-Fly Zone, in command of what was left of their squadrons after the Chinese ballistic missile attack on Okinawa.

More planes were left than the Chinese probably realized. Empty decoy hangers had been built at Kadena Air Base starting in 2022. The Patriot batteries protecting Kadena had also been able to shoot down some of the attacking Chinese missiles.

But many American planes had still been destroyed on the ground in Okinawa.

And American pilots killed.

"I heard just before we left that our friend made it back OK," Drake said.

Drake knew Fitzpatrick would understand that "our friend" was Colonel Kim, the commander of Korea's 38th Fighter Group. The Korean F-16s had arrived at Kadena with zero fanfare as soon as the base had resumed operations after the Chinese missile strike.

Neither pilot envied Kim his mission.

Go up against Chinese jets that were as good as Kim's F-16s. Or, in the case of J-20s, better.

Keep communication to a minimum to keep the Chinese in the dark that they were facing Korean F-16s. Not the dozens of F-16s America had sold to Taiwan.

Kim's F-16s had to refuel midair before going on patrol, just like Fitzpatrick and Drake. For the same reason. They had to stick to Kadena rather than fly out of a base in Taiwan.

Though defending Taiwan was the mission.

Fitzpatrick sighed. Politics. It always made accomplishing the mission so much harder.

Well, there was one plus for all of them. Once American or Korean planes crossed back into Japanese airspace, they were relatively safe. Japan's F-35s and surface-to-air missile batteries saw to that.

Or, anyway, safer than they would have been in Taiwan. But still farther from the fight than Fitzpatrick liked.

"Good to hear," Fitzpatrick replied. And he meant it. Kim's F-16s were giving Taiwan's fighters sorely needed time for repairs and crew rest.

Not to mention the arrival of replacement F-16s. The President had decided to transfer F-16s from Air National Guard units to Taiwan on the understanding that they would be replaced as soon as more could be manufactured.

Politically, the move would have been impossible. If China hadn't killed hundreds of American service members and civilians in a sneak attack.

A number that was still rising. They were still digging out bodies of American tourists killed in Palau and American service members and civilians who had died at bases in Guam, Fitzpatrick thought.

Colonel Kim might have made it back this time. Fitzpatrick and Drake knew that many of his fellow Korean F-16 pilots hadn't been so lucky.

Speaking of luck, it was fortunate that TACMOR had returned online just in time to warn them of Chinese fighters headed in their direction. As well as their approximate number.

With TACMOR's help, they had at least a chance to give the Chinese an unpleasant surprise.

"Multiple contacts approaching the No-Fly Zone. Identified as J-15Bs and J-20s. Data being transferred to all task force pilots now."

The AWACS transmission was followed at once by symbols appearing on Fitzpatrick and Drake's display. As well as the displays on all of the other F-35s and F-22s under their command.

Fitzpatrick and Drake both frowned for the same reason.

"Screen's telling me data is good enough for missile lock on the J-15Bs. But all I've got is an approximate location showing for the J-20s. Same for you?" Fitzpatrick asked.

"Yes," Drake said shortly. "I suggest we take on the J-15Bs now and then see if we can get a lock on the J-20s once our range closes."

Fitzpatrick nodded, knowing that Drake couldn't see it. It was the only logical approach.

"Agreed. We're heavily outnumbered, so attacking the J-15Bs will make it more like a fair fight. They're just coming within AIM-120D range now. Every plane in both our squadrons will fire one missile at each J-15B. That will be two for each enemy aircraft, which should be enough to keep them busy while we deal with the J-20s," Fitzpatrick said.

"Copy," Drake replied, relaying the order to the other F-22 pilots while Fitzpatrick did the same for the pilots in his squadron's F-35s.

Less than a minute later, a volley of AIM-120D missiles was on its way to the J-15Bs. So far, there had been no answering missile fire.

The EC-37Bs and MALD jammers were both proving effective.

"Task Force, we are closing range to improve target resolution. Stand by."

Gutsy, Fitzpatrick thought. He imagined the AWACS transmission meant they were pushing right up to the edge of Japanese airspace.

Fitzpatrick also imagined the AWACS' Japanese F-35 escorts wouldn't like that one bit.

Another minute passed as the distance rapidly closed between the American fighters and the J-20s.

Then suddenly, a tone told Fitzpatrick that missile lock was available. He immediately contacted Drake, but before he could say anything, he heard, "We've got them too."

"Same as before, one apiece," Fitzpatrick replied.

"Copy," Drake said.

Seconds later, another missile volley erupted from the American fighters.

It took time, but from the J-20s, there was an answer.

Or at least an attempt at one.

"I count four PL-15 launches so far," Fitzpatrick said.

"Me too," Drake replied. "The rest look too busy evading our missiles to fire."

"We should do the same. See you back at base," Fitzpatrick said.

It turned out that neither Fitzpatrick nor Drake's jets were among the four planes targeted by the Chinese missiles.

Three PL-15s failed due to effective jamming and chaff.

The fourth American pilot, flying an F-22, was not so lucky. His plane was badly damaged by a PL-15's proximity explosion, and he was forced to eject. However, he was quickly rescued with only minor injuries.

F-35s flying from *USS America* took over patrolling the No-Fly Zone behind them. So far, though, the Chinese had no appetite to test the Zone further.

For now, anyway.

When Drake arrived back at Kadena Air Base, his first action was to get out of his rank flight suit and shower. He knew that many of his fellow pilots considered him fussy and precise. But he honestly couldn't understand how anyone could stand themselves after hours of high stress strapped into a fighter cockpit seat.

Especially in combat.

But Drake knew from experience where he would find Fitzpatrick once he was clean and had on a fresh flight suit. The briefing room.

Not that Fitzpatrick expected any of his pilots to be ready for a briefing yet. No, just his fellow squadron leader.

At least, Drake also knew that Fitzpatrick would be short and to the point.

"As far as AWACS tracking could tell, we took out seven J-15Bs and five J-20s. Based on observed airspeed, it looks like two J-15Bs and four J-20s sustained damage," Fitzpatrick said.

Drake nodded but said, "I'd take those damaged numbers with a grain of salt. Damaged planes may have been accompanied back to base by ones that slowed down to keep an eye on it. In case the pilot later needed to eject."

"Agreed," Fitzpatrick said. "That would neatly account for the even numbers."

Drake nodded again, but this time with respect. They made a pretty good team, he thought reluctantly.

"So, what's next?" Drake asked. "Even larger numbers of Chinese fighters? More ballistic missile attacks?"

Fitzpatrick shrugged. "Maybe both. The Chinese have plenty of fighters and missiles. Next time, though, I hope we'll get more support from Taiwan's surface-to-air missile batteries."

"I wondered about that," Drake said. "What was the problem there?"

"What wasn't," Fitzpatrick said with a grimace. "They've already fired most of the missiles they had on-site, and it's taking them longer than expected to get more from storage to the launch sites. Making matters worse is that the sites are underground, increasing resupply time even after more missiles arrive. But that's just the first problem."

Drake groaned. "And?"

"Chinese commandos took out two launch sites. A ballistic missile took another out with a hit so precise it looks like someone on the inside fed the Chinese exact GPS coordinates," Fitzpatrick said.

Drake shook his head. "Either spies or traitors. Maybe both. Bad news for our side."

Then Drake paused. "Can we do anything to help with the resupply issue?"

"No," Fitzpatrick said. "All Taiwan's surface-to-air missiles are made in-country. Except for ones fired from ships, but they're keeping those in reserve for when the Chinese Navy makes a landing attempt."

"I notice you said 'when' and not 'if' on that landing. Are you sure the Chinese will try it, even though the war hasn't gone well for them so far?" Drake asked.

"I am," Fitzpatrick replied. "I think the Chinese have already invested so much in this operation that they feel they can't turn back now. The only question is whether we can hurt them badly enough that they see it's impossible."

"Or," Drake said thoughtfully, "something happens away from this immediate theater of operations that makes the Chinese recalculate their position."

Fitzpatrick cocked his head, genuinely curious. "Like what?"

Drake shrugged. "I have no idea," he replied. "Admirals, generals, and politicians get paid to make those calls. I hope one of them is smart enough to find the right move. One that will make the Chinese sit up and take notice. Without making them escalate to nuclear weapons."

Chapter Forty-Five

USS Silversides
Off the Japanese Coast

Captain Jim Cartwright sat down heavily in the chair that faced the small desk in his cabin.

For the third, or maybe fourth time, Cartwright read his latest orders. Proceed to rendezvous with two other *Virginia* class submarines. Further details on the Japanese Self-Defense Force naval escort will follow.

Cartwright ran his right hand through his close-cut, prematurely gray hair. His wife would have known that meant he was thinking hard.

Silversides was a Block V version of the *Virginia* class submarine. A bit different than the Block IV that Cartwright had commanded on his last several missions.

The Block V version had increased in length from one hundred fifteen meters to one hundred forty meters. Its displacement had risen from 7,800 tons to 10,200 tons. Most of that had been to accommodate the Virginia Payload Module (VPM). The VPM added twenty-eight Tomahawk BGM-109 missiles to the twelve already carried by the Block IV version.

Even better was that they were all the Maritime Strike Tomahawk (MST) introduced in 2021. The MST's improvements allowed the missile to engage a moving target at sea. In 2023, work had started on incorporating advanced seeker technology in the MST, and that project had been completed in 2026.

And that meant *Silversides* didn't have to close to within torpedo range to attack a surface ship.

Cartwright's orders also specified he was to use MSTs to attack the Chinese fleet that was shortly expected to set out for the invasion of Taiwan.

A soft knock announced someone was at Cartwright's cabin door.

"Enter," Cartwright said.

Lieutenant Commander Fischer poked his head in. Short and thin with sandy hair, Cartwright once again thought that Fischer looked like a much better fit for submarines than an officer like him, who stood over two meters tall without shoes.

"Sir, new orders," Fischer said, glancing at the folder he was carrying.

Cartwright gestured towards the only other chair in his cabin. "Have a seat, Commander. Give me the gist," Cartwright said.

Fischer nodded and sat.

"Sir, headquarters reports that the Chinese invasion fleet is preparing to get underway. We've just established contact with the two other submarines assigned to this mission and our Japanese surface escort," Fischer said.

"I'm guessing that escort includes a *Kongo* class destroyer?" Cartwright asked.

"Yes, sir," Fischer replied. "Carrying a SH-60L anti-submarine helicopter. That's their newest version with upgraded sonar and comms. The destroyer has also just had MSTs installed as well."

Cartwright nodded. "Good to see the Japanese sent one of their best surface ships. We're being screened by two *Taigei* class submarines, right?"

"That's right, sir," Fischer said. "Brand new with a much larger quantity of lithium-ion batteries than the old *Soryu* class subs. Part of why they weigh a hundred tons more. But they're quieter and faster, too. I'm betting that we still have better sonar gear than the Chinese. And even we have trouble detecting the *Taigei* class subs. I'm certain the Japanese will detect any Chinese attack sub before it gets close to us or has any idea the *Taigei* class subs are there. Assuming, of course, that the Chinese risk sending their subs into Japanese waters."

"It's a lot more likely than the Chinese sending surface ships. But it's a big ocean. Plus, it would take a brave Chinese sub captain to come so close to a *Kongo*-class destroyer. Or a foolish one," Cartwright said.

"Yes, sir," Fischer replied. "The bottom line is we're ready to execute the mission as soon as we receive missile attack coordinates from headquarters."

Cartwright nodded thoughtfully. "If this goes the way it has in our most recent exercises, we can expect firing instructions as well."

"I think that's likely, sir," Fischer said. "With the goal of having missiles from all three of our submarines strike the Chinese fleet simultaneously. Or, as close to simultaneously as possible."

"Without the missiles striking each other on the way," Cartwright added.

"Yes, sir," Fischer said. "Those exercises made it clear we need help from computer calculations to achieve that result."

Cartwright nodded. "All MSTs are loaded and ready to fire?"

"They are, sir," Fischer replied. "There's nothing more for us to do but wait for word from headquarters."

"Very well," Cartwright said. "So, with forty MSTs apiece, we'll be firing one hundred twenty MSTs from the three submarines. Each carrying a warhead with about four hundred fifty kilograms of high explosive. If this goes how it has in exercises, at least a few MSTs will malfunction on the way to the target. The Chinese will certainly manage to shoot some of them down. Maybe eighty to a hundred will strike one of the Chinese ships."

Fischer nodded. "And a single hit might disable a warship, but unless their damage control is poor shouldn't sink it. I'm sure the Chinese are sending their best ships and crew."

"I agree," Cartwright said. "This missile strike will damage many ships in the Chinese invasion fleet. It might even sink a few that get hit multiple times. But it certainly won't destroy the fleet."

Fischer nodded thoughtfully. "But it will send a message. We see what you're doing, and we can hurt you if you don't turn back. Do you think the Chinese will listen?"

Cartwright shook his head. "No, I don't. They've built the world's largest Navy. Only one immediate goal justifies that expense. What the PRC calls reunification. What Taiwan calls a hostile invasion. I don't think the Chinese invasion fleet will stop until they're hurt so badly they can't carry out their mission."

"But our orders say nothing about next steps. There's nothing more we could do, anyway, until we're resupplied with MSTs. By then, the Chinese fleet could have reached Taiwan," Fischer said.

"Correct," Cartwright replied. "I think that leaves an air strike. With the Long-Range Anti-Ship Missile."

Fischer looked up, startled. "Sir, they've never been used before in battle. If enough of those missiles are fired, they won't leave much of the Chinese fleet. And I understand we've stockpiled hundreds of them at our bases in Japan. Do you think it will come to that?"

"I expect the decision to go all the way to the President," Cartwright said. "But yes, now that the Chinese have struck American territory and military bases, I don't think he'll have any choice. If the MSTs we're about to fire don't convince them to turn back, I think Hernandez will authorize whatever steps are necessary to stop the Chinese from conquering Taiwan."

Chapter Forty-Six

Chinese Invasion Fleet
En Route to Taiwan

Senior Captain Ding had argued against the decision to proceed with the invasion despite failing to achieve air superiority. Admiral Bai had agreed with him.

Air and submarine attacks had indeed decimated Taiwan's surface Navy. In particular, every one of Taiwan's surface ships capable of launching either Standard or Harpoon missiles had been severely damaged or sunk.

However, the whereabouts of Taiwan's first *Hai Kun*-class submarine was still unknown.

Launched in 2023, *Hai Kun* carried the UGM-84L Harpoon Block II, the same model used by Japan since 2015. Compared with earlier Harpoon versions, it had greater range, more resistance to electronic countermeasures, and better targeting.

The Harpoon's two hundred twenty kilogram warhead's impact would be enhanced by the fact that it was a sea-skimming cruise missile. Detonation was likely to happen near the waterline.

Every sailor knew that would be bad news for damage control teams.

The only good news was that even with the Harpoon Block II's improved range, they wouldn't encounter any fired by *Hai Kun* for a while yet.

So, they lacked air superiority and *Hai Kun* was still out there somewhere.

But President Gu had insisted that the invasion proceed. And once the Party gave the order, the Chinese military had only one option.

Obey.

The result was that Ding was now on the bridge of the cruiser *Lhasa*. Looking at a radar plot next to Captain Song.

A plot that showed dozens of incoming missiles. They had been identified as American-made Tomahawk missiles. A variant designed to attack ships.

China's intelligence agents had never discovered these particular missiles in Taiwan's possession. Only the land attack Tomahawk version.

That meant the missiles weren't just made in America. They had probably been fired by Americans, too.

Well, Ding thought, after we attacked their military bases in Guam and Okinawa, that doesn't come as a great surprise.

Song was issuing a stream of orders, all with one purpose. Minimize the damage caused by missile hits.

The crews on all the ships in the fleet were already trained in using their weapons to intercept enemy missiles. And in damage control to deal with impacts from any they missed.

All Song could do now was to alter the position of some of his ships relative to the oncoming missiles. Even there, the few minutes remaining until the missiles arrived limited Song's options.

And then the Tomahawks arrived.

Damage reports streamed from one ship after another to *Lhasa*.

Ding did his best not to be obvious about it. But he was watching Song closely for his reaction to the reports.

Especially after *Lhasa* was rocked by first one, and then two Tomahawk strikes.

Song ignored the hits to *Lhasa*. As fleet commander, he had already delegated *Lhasa*'s damage control responsibility to the ship's executive officer.

Ding was pleased to see that Song remained focused on the fleet's condition as a whole. Even as smoke from fires onboard *Lhasa* could be smelled on the bridge.

It quickly became apparent that several ships were too badly damaged to save. Song ordered the evacuation of all crew from those vessels. In one case, despite the objections of the ship's Captain, who stubbornly insisted it could still be salvaged.

Song had that Captain arrested on the spot and turned to Ding, who was still silently watching.

"I'm not going to sacrifice good sailors to one officer's foolish pride," Song said. "And you may tell Admiral Bai I said so."

Ding nodded. "This may surprise you, but I'm certain the Admiral will agree."

From Song's expression, Ding could see he was indeed surprised.

Ding added, "The Admiral sees the fleet and everyone in it as resources sent to serve the Chinese nation. 'Going down with the ship' or refusing to recognize realities like a sinking vessel wastes those resources. You are right not to tolerate such nonsense."

A lieutenant's voice drew their attention back to the radar plot.

"Sir, multiple additional missiles inbound. The type is...HF-3s. Number detected is climbing...now appear to be at least one hundred incoming."

Song immediately issued a coded order to every fleet frigate, destroyer, and cruiser. They were to begin transmitting a prerecorded signal on a specific frequency, which had already been programmed on each ship's communications console.

It didn't take long before the same lieutenant returned with another report.

"Sir, some of the incoming missiles have disappeared from our scopes. Others are veering off in different directions."

Song nodded. "Excellent, Lieutenant. Keep me updated if any of the HF-3s continue toward the fleet."

Without bothering to wait for an acknowledgment, Song turned to Ding.

"Once this ends, you'll have to tell me how we managed that."

Ding smiled and nodded.

The truth was, Ding hadn't been sure it would work.

In 2022, Taiwan's National Institute of Science and Technology had sent equipment used in the development and testing of the HF-3 to its Swiss manufacturer for repair and maintenance. Without informing Taiwan, the Swiss company sent the equipment to a subcontractor to do the work.

A Chinese company. Located, of course, in China.

Once Taiwan finally received the equipment back and discovered what had happened, their technicians thoroughly examined every component. They found nothing wrong.

Because the Chinese technicians who had dismantled, examined, and then reassembled the equipment had changed nothing.

However, China had learned a great deal about the HF-3. And Taiwan's technicians informed their military that this would be the likely result of the equipment's inadvertent stay in the PRC.

However, Taiwan's military did not realize China had obtained information that would help them achieve an important goal. To allow the use of precisely targeted electromagnetic transmissions to disable the HF-3's guidance system. So that HF-3s targeted at Chinese ships would either crash into the ocean or fly off in random directions.

That failure was understandable. Taiwan had security precautions in place to prevent such an attack on the HF-3's guidance system. Knowing its internal schematics was not enough. China would also have to know the exact frequency used when a particular missile attack was launched.

A frequency that was changed daily. Only the Taiwanese technicians entrusted with programming HF-3s had that information.

Until one of those technicians was offered the equivalent of over one million American dollars by a Chinese agent to send him that information every day.

The technician was promised an additional two million dollars if a particular frequency allowed China to avert an HF-3 attack.

The man eagerly accepted the money and the promise of more to come. He had been sending frequencies every day like clockwork.

Today, Ding mused, that one million dollar investment had paid off handsomely.

His thoughts were interrupted by the same Lieutenant, once again addressing Song.

"Sir, many more missiles are approaching the fleet! Dozens of them!"

Song nodded. "More HF-3s? More Tomahawks?"

"No, sir," the Lieutenant said. "The computer identifies these as Long-Range Anti-Ship Missiles."

Song nodded again, doing his best to appear unconcerned.

"Ensure that all ships in the fleet are aware of the threat," Song ordered.

Ding, standing next to Song, hoped his face was as impassive as Song's.

It wasn't easy.

The Long-Range Anti-Ship Missile was the latest such missile the Americans had deployed. Though it carried the same roughly five hundred kilogram warhead as the Tomahawk, its guidance system was supposed to be superior.

Also worrying was that after the first wave of attacks by the Tomahawks, their anti-missile defenses had been depleted.

And on many ships, some crewmen who would have been manning those defenses were busy with damage control. Especially fighting fires.

Would they be redeployed in time?

Ding noticed movement outside the bridge's windows, and his blood ran cold.

Sailors who had been fighting fires on *Lhasa*'s deck were dropping hoses and running. Was it toward anti-missile defenses or for some other reason?

It was Ding's last thought before one of the missiles struck *Lhasa*.

Damage from the two Tomahawk hits had been largely contained, though not all the fires they had started had been completely extinguished.

This third missile strike, though, hit the aviation fuel storage for *Lhasa*'s two medium-lift helicopters.

Lhasa rocked with the impact, sending both Ding and Song crashing to the deck. In moments, multiple hands were helping both of them up.

Just in time to feel the ship rock again from another explosion.

This one, though, was more distant.

Ding shortly heard the news he had feared most.

One of the *Fuchi*-class replenishment ships had been sunk. The explosion of the fuel it carried had been so powerful that several other nearby ships had also been damaged.

As the missile strikes finally stopped, damage reports from ship after ship flooded into *Lhasa*'s bridge. Where Song listened and issued a steady stream of orders.

Ding knew Song was doing all he could. As was every sailor in the invasion fleet.

But Song had to order ship after ship evacuated due to heavy damage that couldn't be repaired in time. Ding knew Song would have to come to the same conclusion he had already reached.

There wasn't enough left of the fleet to mount a successful invasion.

Ding was wrong.

To his horror, Ding heard Song give a series of orders to move all undamaged and lightly damaged ships on to Taiwan.

As well as one heavily damaged ship. *Lhasa*.

"Captain, have we reported the extent of the damage the fleet has sustained to Admiral Bai?" Ding asked.

Ding already knew the answer to that question was "No." Song had been entirely and correctly focused on responding to the latest attack.

But Ding had been sure that his question would remind Song of the need to involve headquarters in the decision to proceed.

Ding was wrong again.

Song shook his head. "No, and I see no need to do so. The damaged ships we're leaving behind will make reports to headquarters as soon as possible. Of course, they must concentrate on extinguishing fires and critical repairs first. In the meantime, I have my orders and intend to carry them out."

Ding lowered his voice and gestured to the billowing smoke visible from the bridge's windows.

"But Captain, this ship has taken heavy damage. If we report, reinforcements could be sent quickly to make up our losses, including *Lhasa*."

Song stiffened, and he lowered his voice to match Ding's.

"*Lhasa* has not been lost. The fires are serious but under control. Most important, there is no damage to our engines. We will continue to lead this fleet to victory."

Then Song paused and looked at Ding directly. His voice dropped even lower.

"I know you represent Admiral Bai. But I command this fleet. It is time for you to choose. I intend to bring every ship still capable to Taiwan. Are you with me?"

Ding quickly realized he had no choice. Ding knew what Song would do if he tried to insist on contacting Admiral Bai or raised further objections.

He would have Ding arrested and thrown in the ship's brig for mutiny.

Ding might still be able to make a difference on the bridge.

"I'm with you all the way, Captain," Ding said, trying to inject some enthusiasm into his voice.

From Song's expression, Ding guessed he hadn't done a very good job.

But apparently, good enough.

"Very well," Song said. "I do plan to report to Admiral Bai, you know."

Ding's eyebrows flew up. Had he reached Song after all?

"When we get to Taiwan. And that won't be long now," Song said.

Ding looked at the chart and saw it was true. The waves of missile attacks had slowed the fleet but not completely stopped it.

Song was right. They might still make it to Taiwan. But would the remaining troops and equipment still carried by the fleet be enough to force a landing?

Well, it seemed they were about to find out.

For nearly an hour, the fleet continued its progress toward Taiwan. Ding started to think that Song had been right all along and he had been too cautious.

Then the same Lieutenant who had warned them about the last two missile attacks appeared.

Ding thought that he should have learned the man's name by now.

"Captain, multiple missiles inbound! Dozens of them! They appear to be a mix of Standard and Harpoon missiles, sir."

Song nodded and replied, "Inform the fleet."

So, the reports are accurate, Ding thought. The Americans had first developed the Standard as a surface-to-air missile fired from ships during the Vietnam War. Later, anti-ship and land attack versions had been developed.

Their agents had advised that Taiwan had upgraded old Standards purchased from the Americans. They had improved its rocket engine and added an active seeker.

And based at least some of them underground.

One disadvantage of the Standard was its limited range, effective only to about one hundred fifty kilometers.

A line the fleet had crossed about fifteen minutes ago, Ding thought.

Another disadvantage was that the Standard's warhead was much smaller than the other missiles used against them so far. Only about sixty-five kilograms.

But the missile and its fuel weighed about fifteen hundred kilograms.

And unlike all the missiles the fleet had faced so far, the Standard was supersonic, flying at about Mach 3.5.

The sheer kinetic energy released by the Standard on impact would more than make up for its smaller warhead, Ding thought.

And its speed would give the Standard a better chance of evading the fleet's anti-missile defenses. Those that remained.

The Harpoons came as less of a surprise. *Hai Kun* had no doubt fired every Harpoon it carried.

Not enough to threaten the fleet seriously on their own. But those Harpoons coordinated with the Standards...

I must give the Taiwanese Navy credit, Ding thought. It couldn't have been easy to match the arrival times of two missile groups with such different speeds, fired from separate locations.

It was Ding's last thought before Standards and Harpoons began hitting ships in the fleet.

Almost immediately, another massive explosion rocked *Lhasa*. Another of the *Fuchi*-class replenishment ships had been sunk.

This time, though, no other ships were damaged. Experience had taught the other ships in the fleet to give the supply ships a wide berth.

Damage reports poured in from ships in the fleet as one missile after another found its target.

We're not going to make it to Taiwan, Ding thought numbly.

Ding never saw or felt the Standard that struck *Lhasa* only a few meters below its bridge.

Just a bright light, and then darkness.

Chapter Forty-Seven

Type 003 Aircraft Carrier Fujian
Somewhere Near the Taiwan Strait

Lieutenant Tan Sichun had been sure that bobbing helplessly in the ocean, surrounded by circling sharks, would stand forever as her least favorite experience.

All right, Tan thought with a sigh. I must guard against exaggeration and self-pity.

Yes, that "least favorite" record still stood.

But being confined to a bed in the carrier's medical unit was, for Tan, a close second.

To be fair, she understood Commander Ge's order sending her to the unit in the first place. Tan would admit that she felt cold, though she thought the doctor's diagnosis of hypothermia an exaggeration.

And his other diagnosis of shock was ridiculous.

The doctor's decision to force her to lay passively in bed while endless tests were run for no purpose she could see?

Outrageous.

Adding insult to injury was the parade of well-wishers, starting with Lieutenant Zou. They all piously wished her a speedy recovery. And told her how much they admired her courage.

What courage? All she'd done was float helplessly while waiting for a sea creature to make a meal of her.

The one and only good thing the doctor had done was put an end to the stream of visitors.

Though his reason for doing so, that "The Lieutenant needs her rest," made Tan grit her teeth in frustration.

After the doctor issued that order, however, it was true that Tan had fallen asleep almost immediately.

Tan had no idea how long she'd slept when she woke up. But she thought it had been quite a while.

Maybe, she acknowledged to herself grudgingly, because I feel quite a bit better. Though still a bit groggy.

Fine. So maybe this doctor isn't the complete fool I thought he was earlier.

But now, I have to get back on duty.

That turned out to be easier said than done. There was nobody in sight.

How could that be? Every space on the carrier except the flight deck always had plenty of people.

Wait. What was that sound? It kept repeating.

It was the general quarters alarm!

Tan threw off her covers and sat up.

The room started spinning and stubbornly refused to settle down.

The doctor picked that moment to return. And he wasn't alone. Sailors were carrying men on stretchers. Tan couldn't see how many.

"You, lay back down in that bed!" the doctor shouted to Tan. "I don't have time to deal with you right now."

Tan caught a glimpse of one of the injured men as he was lifted onto a bed. There was blood. Quite a bit of it.

Well, the least I can do is get out of this bed for someone who needs it more, Tan thought.

As though Tan had summoned him with that thought, a sailor pushing a wheelchair appeared next to her bed. Tan saw that the name stitched on his uniform was "Zhuang."

"Climb in," Zhuang said. "I saw you sit up, and the doctor says he needs this bed."

Tan didn't argue. Moments later, they were out of the medical unit. To her relief, Tan saw they were headed for the flight deck.

"Finally!" Tan said, "A return to sanity! I'm going back on duty!"

Zhuang shook his head. "No. You're on the next flight back to base. All wounded who can be moved will be on board."

"There's been a mistake!" Tan said indignantly. "I'm not wounded!"

Zhuang sighed. "Wounded. Hurt. Unfit for duty. Look, the doctor said to get you on the helicopter. I follow orders, just like you."

That brought Tan up short. Well, yes. Like it or not, you had to follow orders. Otherwise, there'd be chaos.

Wham!

"What was that?" Tan asked, not expecting Zhuang to know.

But he did. "Right, you were unconscious. We're under missile attack. Our escorts are knocking down most of them, but a few are getting through."

To his credit, Zhuang delivered that news in the same tone Tan had heard a restaurant worker use once to explain why her takeout order was late.

It's just how it was. Nothing to be done about it.

"I can't leave while we're under attack! It's desertion!" Tan exclaimed.

Zhuang shrugged. "The commanders want everyone not fit for duty off the carrier. You have your orders, just like I do."

With that, Zhuang pointed at the helicopter at the other end of the deck.

"You're the last passenger I was told to put onboard. So at least you won't have long to wait," Zhuang said.

No sooner were the words out of Zhuang's mouth than a blinding flash of light and a massive explosion sent Tan flying out of the wheelchair.

Tan returned to consciousness slowly. Several unmoving bodies were in her field of view.

One looked like Zhuang.

The helicopter had been reduced to flaming debris. It was apparent nobody aboard could have survived.

I was just moments away from being among them, Tan thought dully.

I have to move. Am I injured?

With some effort, Tan sat up.

Her ears were ringing. It was hard to focus. Her head hurt, but not too severely.

Tan's left cheek was scratched and bleeding. But she couldn't find any other injuries.

I have to stand. And help my crewmates.

The deck seemed to be spinning at first, but Tan could stay standing after a few deep breaths.

She'd been right about Zhuang being nearby. Tan checked for a pulse.

None.

The same was true for everyone else nearby she checked.

Until Tan spotted someone lying face-first near a ladder leading from the command center. It was a senior officer!

Tan rushed to his side and gently turned him over. The amount of blood pooled around the man made her fear that, once again, she was too late.

It was Commander Ge! And he was alive!

Tan could see the injury at once that was causing the bleeding.

I need something to stop it!

Tan was still wearing the light gown put on her in the medical unit. Grasping the gown's hem firmly with both hands and pulling, she tore off a long strip of cloth.

Moments later, Tan had managed to stop Ge's bleeding.

Where are the medics? There was so much smoke it was hard to see anything.

There they were! Tan had finally caught a glimpse of three men in medical uniform leaning over the bodies that covered the deck not far away.

"Hey!" Tan shouted. "I've checked those sailors already! None survived. But Commander Ge is with me, and he still has a chance!"

The medics turned in Tan's direction, but the smoke shifted again at that moment.

Tan couldn't see the medics anymore.

"Follow my voice!" Tan called. "I'm at the ladder leading to the command center!"

Tan could hear stumbling and cursing as the medics approached her through the smoke. Still, it wasn't long until they were by her side.

And they were carrying a stretcher.

Tan mentally retracted every unkind thing she'd thought about the carrier's medical contingent since her involuntary confinement.

The three medics worked quickly. One of them grunted as he examined the bandage Tan had applied to Ge's wound.

"You did this?" he asked Tan.

"Yes," Tan replied shortly.

The medic nodded. "Good work. Gives us a chance, anyway."

Then he ordered the other two medics to use their stretcher to get Ge to the medical unit.

Tan looked more closely at his uniform and saw that he was the senior of the three.

Quickly, they were alone.

"Do you have underwear beneath that gown?" the medic asked.

Tan was so astonished by the question that she nearly failed to respond. But finally said, "Yes."

The medic nodded. "Good. Now, if you're going to help me, you can't wear a torn gown."

Then he reached into his bag and pulled out a medical uniform.

"It should fit well enough," the medic said. "I'd have sent you with the others back to the medical unit, but I remember what a fuss you made there. You may not be well enough to fly, but you know how to tie a bandage. Now change, and help me save some lives."

With that, he handed the medical uniform to Tan and turned his back on her.

As she changed, Tan thought she finally had her wish. She was back on duty. Doing work that was needed right now.

But how long would it be before she could fly again?

And pay the Americans back for everything they'd done?

Chapter Forty-Eight

Zhongnanhai Compound
Beijing, China

President Gu could see that General Zhao was agitated as soon as he laid eyes on him. Even from across his sizable office, as Gu's aide was escorting him inside.

Not that a Westerner would have noticed. But part of climbing to the Presidency was being able to read a person's state of mind, their emotions.

Even ones they thought they'd successfully suppressed.

The Air Force Commander didn't like his latest orders? Well, Gu hadn't enjoyed giving them.

Zhao saluted and stood at attention. Gu waved him to the chair in front of his desk.

"You asked to see me, General. Please make what you have to say brief. I must soon speak with the Americans," Gu said.

"Of course, sir. I just wanted a better understanding of your plans for the invasion of Taiwan. You ordered all air operations to stop immediately. When do you wish them to resume?" Zhao asked.

Well, there it is, Gu thought. Zhao is no fool. He knows the war is over.

But Zhao simply couldn't believe we were giving up. He wants to know why.

"There will be no resumption. I am about to speak to the Americans to discuss terms for ending this conflict," Gu said.

"But sir, we have succeeded in destroying much of Taiwan's Air Force, as well as its bases. Surely, continued air operations could force Taiwan's surrender. We could bomb Taiwan's ports, its power plants, and…"

Gu shook his head, and Zhao was smart enough to stop talking.

"We started this war thinking we could blind the Americans, disable their communications, and interfere with their navigation. Thanks to technology we didn't know they possessed and multiple satellite launches within a couple of days, none of that turned out to be true. Instead, they succeeded in attacking many of our most critical satellites. How, we're still not sure," Gu said.

Gu paused, but Zhao still knew better than to interrupt.

"General, given more time, I have no doubt your planes could lay waste to Taiwan," Gu said. "For that matter, we could press a few buttons and render Taiwan a glowing, radioactive hellscape unfit for human habitation. But that was never the goal of this war, was it?"

There was only one answer to that, and Zhao quickly gave it.

"No, sir."

"You have indeed inflicted great damage on Taiwan's Air Force. But the Americans keep sending more F-16s to replace the ones you've shot down. And even if you destroyed them all, planes cannot control the country they fly above. We need soldiers on the ground. You have read the reports on the fate of our invasion fleet?" Gu asked.

Now Zhao didn't even try to hide his emotions. "A terrible tragedy. We must make the Americans pay a heavy price for all the brave sailors they killed without mercy."

"How do you propose we do that, General? Are we ready for nuclear war with the Americans?" Gu asked.

Zhao knew the answer to that, of course. China's nuclear arsenal had grown tremendously in recent years.

It was still nowhere close to matching America's numbers.

"No, sir," Zhao replied.

"I know you objected to my decision to respect Japan's borders during this conflict after our initial strike on Okinawa," Gu said. "But consider this. Japan has over thirty nuclear reactors, though not all are currently operating. How long would it take them to produce the nuclear material needed to produce weapons? For their scientists and technicians to produce nuclear bombs and missiles?"

"Not long," Zhao said, nodding thoughtfully.

"That's right," Gu said. "If this war were to continue, I would have to allow your planes to strike targets within Japan. Your latest report said that many missiles that hit our ships were fired from Japanese airspace, correct? By American planes under Japanese escort?"

"Correct, sir," Zhao replied.

"Well, I may not be a General. But even I know we can't win a war when our enemy can attack us with complete safety. And the only way to challenge that safety would be to widen the war. Your planes have done well against Taiwan's F-16s. Not so well against the American F-35s. Isn't that the same plane the Japanese fly?" Gu asked.

Though he knew the answer.

"Yes, it is, sir," Zhao said.

Gu had to admire the man's self-control. There was a lot more he wanted to say.

But Zhao was smart enough to know that saying any of it would cost him his job.

"So, perhaps now you understand better why I have decided to end this war. We have made some miscalculations. Especially we underestimated America's willingness to fight to protect Taiwan. And their anger at our attacks on Okinawa, Guam, and Palau," Gu said.

Zhao nodded glumly but said nothing. He had made the same mistakes and couldn't deny it.

"Also, the Americans have just closed the Straits of Malacca to all sea traffic. A step I never imagined they would dare to take. As you know, most of the oil we import passes through those straits. They must be reopened, or our economy will collapse," Gu said, then paused.

"But make no mistake, General. Our history is measured in thousands of years. The Americans, a few hundred. They may have stopped us for now."

Gu looked Zhao in the eye.

"But in the end, our flag will fly over Taipei. And the Americans will regret their attempt to prevent our reunification."

Chapter Forty-Nine

The Situation Room, The White House
Washington, DC

At President Hernandez's insistence, General Robinson had sat in on several poker games between him and some of his wealthy friends. Who also happened to be some of his campaign's chief financial backers.

Hernandez had been blunt. He wanted Robinson's assessment of the others around the table. Which Robinson had been happy to provide.

While playing as conservatively as possible. A General's salary was substantial. But nothing compared to the money earned on interest alone by the other players.

Robinson folded a lot.

But to his surprise, Robinson had also learned something about Hernandez. Yes, Robinson already knew Hernandez could bluff. But now he saw Hernandez was sometimes ready to take chances that bordered on reckless.

The stakes in the White House often dwarfed those at any poker table, even with players as rich as Hernandez's friends. As a politician, so far, Hernandez had generally been quite conservative.

Not today, though.

Hernandez and Robinson could see that President Gu was upset, even before either side said a word. And despite the mediocre quality of the video conference display.

"Mr. President," Hernandez said carefully, "I would like to request that we both clear the room of our interpreters and have just one other person remain on each side. Here, that will be General Robinson, the Air Force Chief of Staff. I understand your English is excellent, so I hope this will not be inconvenient."

Gu muted the connection at his end but left the video feed active. Hernandez and Robinson could see him speaking rapidly, and in moments, only one person was left with Gu.

Just as quickly, Hernandez and Robinson were alone.

"General Zhao, our Air Force Commander, will assist on this side. His English is also excellent," Gu said and then paused.

"I have requested this meeting to ask that you reconsider your decision to close the Straits of Malacca to all sea traffic. Ninety percent of our trade goes by sea, and a large percentage goes through those straits. Eighty percent of our oil imports come to us by sea, mostly through the Straits of Malacca. Our economy will be devastated if your closure continues. Is that your intention?" Gu asked.

"Not at all," Hernandez replied. "As we have stated publicly, though recent hostilities have centered on Taiwan, many other countries have been affected. Like Palau, Japan, and the United States. We are ensuring that innocent civilian vessels don't become targets."

"That is absurd!" Gu snapped. "Why would we fire on our own ships?"

"Mistakes happen," Hernandez replied with a shrug. "For example, your government has said the missile that struck Palau's capital went off course and hit it by mistake. Not to punish its government for allowing the construction of an American radar installation on Palau's territory. That is what happened, right, Mr. President?"

Gu opened his mouth to speak but then visibly reconsidered and closed it. Finally, he ground out, "Yes, that is what happened."

Hernandez nodded. "Good, then we understand each other. All we want is to avoid any more unfortunate, unintentional mistakes."

Gu looked up sharply, but Hernandez's voice had no trace of sarcasm. There was no hint of a smile on his face.

Gu understood that Hernandez didn't believe a word of China's explanation for the missile that had killed hundreds in Koror. Either directly from the initial explosion or the many fires that swept through any buildings left standing.

But Gu also realized that Hernandez planned to stand by his explanation.

"And what about the countries that, by treaty, are responsible for the administration of the Straits of Malacca? None of them have said they agree with your actions," Gu said.

Hernandez didn't react at all. Instead, he calmly said, "That is true. But neither have Malaysia, Singapore, nor Indonesia objected to our actions in closing the Straits. Either publicly or privately. Meanwhile, many other countries in the region have expressed support for our steps. I'm afraid that on this issue, Mr. President, China stands alone."

Gu was seething but, for a moment, said nothing. Yes, countries throughout Asia had many reasons to resent and fear China. Vietnam, India, and Japan over territorial disputes. Vietnam, Japan, Malaysia, Indonesia, and the Philippines over Chinese claims to the entire South China Sea. Even to waters much closer to those other countries. Sri Lanka, Pakistan, and the Maldives over predatory loans from China.

Yes, there were good reasons China had never been able to secure a permanent base in Asia outside of China's territory. In contrast, America had dozens of bases in East Asia alone.

"Very well," Gu said. "We both know we will never accept what the other is saying. There is only one question worth asking. What will it take for your Navy and Air Force to end this closure?"

"It could not be simpler, Mr. President. Withdraw all of your forces currently attacking Taiwan. Once we verify that has been done, we will reopen the Straits," Hernandez said.

"And what about your so-called No-Fly Zone? Will that end as well?" Gu asked.

"Once we are satisfied your efforts to take Taiwan by force have ceased, we will reduce the area covered by the Zone to allow most commercial air traffic in the area to resume. Including traffic from China. However, our Air Force will remain in the skies near Taiwan to ensure regional peace," Hernandez said.

"Peace," Gu repeated bitterly. "You mean the end of our hope of reuniting our people. Who, make no mistake about it, are just as Chinese as I am."

Hernandez shook his head. "That is not our intention, and it never was. We only stand against the seizure of any territory by force. We did when Iraq attempted to annex Kuwait. And again, when Russia tried to conquer Ukraine. But if Taiwan ever decides of its own free will to unite with China, we will do nothing to prevent it."

Gu looked directly into the video monitor; his suspicion was evident even through the blurry video feed.

"So you say. But tell me this- why would Taiwan ever agree to unite with China now, after all that has happened?" Gu asked.

Robinson had to struggle to keep his expression neutral. Yes, indeed. Why would Taiwan ever agree to unite with a country that had killed thousands of its citizens and left chunks of its largest cities smoking rubble?

Hernandez, though, had been expecting the question. "The people of Taiwan want peace and prosperity above all else. Convince them that their best chance to achieve this lies with unification. Yes, it will take some time for the bitter feelings stirred by this conflict to fade.

But fade they will. After all, Germany and Japan took less than a generation to change from our mortal enemies to our most reliable allies."

"And what if we decide to weather the closure of the Straits? The flow of goods works both ways. Do you think our trading partners won't soon feel the lack of Chinese goods?" Gu asked.

"I'm sure they will," Hernandez replied. "But China produces little that other countries don't sell as well. Perhaps at a slightly higher price. But the economies of other countries will continue to function. Is the same true of China's economy without foreign oil and gas?"

"I have already said it is not," Gu said tiredly.

"But there is an alternative path forward. One that will set China's future toward an economy that Taiwan may someday wish to join. The path of cooperation, not confrontation," Hernandez said.

"Fine words. But will they be backed by concrete actions?" Gu asked.

Hernandez spread his hands wide. "First, the fighting must end. But when it does, I can promise you this. For many years, my predecessors have increased tariffs on goods from China. Instead, I will reduce them. If peace continues, I may eliminate them by the end of my term."

Gu shook his head. "I am no expert on your politics. But even I know your opponents will fight any move to reduce tariffs on goods from a country it has been fighting with just moments before."

"You're right," Hernandez replied. "But I can raise or lower tariffs no matter what my political opponents think. Changing that would take passing a new law. Which I would veto. My opponents lack the strength to overcome my veto. I think your experts on our political system will confirm that is true. But that is not all I mean by cooperation."

"Yes? And what else?" Gu asked warily.

"There are many areas where we could work together. For example, in 2023, India rejected your proposed multibillion-dollar investment in electric car production. No other country has accepted it. What if we did?" Hernandez asked.

Gu's eyes narrowed suspiciously. "You have your own companies producing electric cars. Why would you welcome a competitor?"

"For the same reason you welcomed Tesla to Shanghai. Whether one believes in manmade global warming or not, nobody favors air pollution. Electric cars are the best way to cut it down. Chinese production in America will help us reach that goal faster. And competition will be good for our companies. I say this as an unapologetic capitalist," Hernandez said with a smile.

Gu grunted. "Yes, I am familiar with your background in business. So that much I can believe."

"That's just the start of what we could accomplish together. Why not cooperate in space rather than knocking each other's satellites out of orbit? If we had our scientists meet, I'm sure they could find projects where we could pool our knowledge and resources. We'd probably cut years off the completion time of many projects," Hernandez said.

Gu shook his head. "I'm afraid suspicion will run too deep on both sides to make such joint projects practical."

"Maybe you're right," Hernandez said with a shrug. "But remember that Apollo–Soyuz was the first crewed international space mission, carried out jointly by my country and the Soviet Union in 1975. I think it's fair to say that suspicion also ran quite deeply between the U.S. and the USSR. Still, we found a way to work together."

"An interesting example," Gu said, nodding reluctantly. "But your political opponents are not interested in cooperation. Instead, they demand that China compensate your country, Taiwan, Japan, and Palau for damage caused during this conflict. Of course, we have suffered losses as well."

"I'm sure you have," Hernandez said neutrally. "But I think we can simplify this matter considerably. We both accept that there will be no compensation for the loss of military lives or equipment on either side. Compensation will be expected, though, for American civilian casualties and property damage."

Gu nodded but said nothing.

Hernandez continued. "Claims from other countries will be a matter for direct negotiation between China and the governments of Japan, Taiwan, and Palau. Of course, those political opponents you mentioned will watch closely to see that those settlements are made promptly and for fair amounts. I am sincere in wanting to change from a path of confrontation to one of cooperation. But I cannot do it if my opponents are united by anger against China. I hope you will help me avoid such an outcome."

Gu nodded again. "You have given me much to consider. I will discuss our talk with others in my government and contact you soon with our decision. In the meantime, I have ordered our forces to suspend all offensive operations."

General Zhao's expression didn't change, and he remained silent, as he had throughout the entire exchange between Gu and Hernandez.

However, Robinson and Hernandez had the same thought at that moment.

If it were up to General Zhao, the war would still be underway.

"That is a welcome step, Mr. President," Hernandez said gravely. "I look forward to hearing your decision on my proposals."

Gu made a sharp gesture, and the screen went dark.

A technician had been monitoring the stability of the video connection from an adjoining room. Moments later, he announced through a recessed speaker, "We're clear."

Hernandez looked at Robinson and sighed. "So, do you think he'll go for it?"

"My best guess, sir? I think he will. Technology gave us the edge over numbers in the conflict, and there's no way in the short term China can overcome that," Robinson replied.

"Maybe," Hernandez said. "I'm worried about the Chinese military's reaction, though. They've taken a real hit, especially their Air Force and Navy."

Robinson started to speak, but Hernandez waved him to silence. "I've read the briefings. I know the planes and ships will be quickly replaced. And the pilots and sailors killed and injured were less than one percent of their personnel."

Hernandez paused and lifted one finger. "But. The point isn't how many planes and ships we destroyed. It's how easily we did it. And how few we lost in return. Even more, how poorly even the best Chinese equipment performed. Finally, I'm betting that many Chinese casualties, especially their pilots, represented the best they had."

Robinson nodded thoughtfully. "I agree with all that, sir. Especially the blow they took with their pilots. Replacing them won't be quick or easy. Plus, their reputation as an elite service with some of the world's best equipment also suffered. Recruiting replacements may not be so easy."

"I think we both know Chinese nationalism will take care of that, General," Hernandez said, grimacing. "That's why I offered cooperation in some areas. China is a rising power with real and growing capabilities. If they don't have a constructive outlet, we'll get...well, what we just got."

"Yes, sir," Robinson said. "Frankly, I don't envy you the task of selling that approach to your opponents. Or the American electorate."

"It won't be easy," Hernandez admitted. "It may even turn out to be impossible. But I have to try. I know it's the right approach if we're going to avoid another shooting war. That next time might escalate to a nuclear exchange. Besides, there is some good news."

Robinson looked puzzled. "What's that, sir?"

Hernandez grinned. "I've already been reelected. I'll never face the voters again, thanks to the 22nd Amendment. If they decide to reject my proposal to find areas of cooperation with the Chinese, so be it. That's what democracy is all about, General. Sometimes leaders can get voters to go along with what they think is right."

"Yes, sir," Robinson frowned. "And sometimes they can't."

Hernandez's grin widened. "Exactly."

Chapter Fifty

Presidential Office Building
Taipei, Taiwan

President Cheng looked up from reading yet another report as National Security Bureau Director-General Yan walked into his office.

Cheng waved Yan to one of the chairs in front of his desk and gestured toward the stack of reports he still had to read.

"Here's my summary, in advance of reading them all- we'll live to fight another day," Cheng said.

A rare smile appeared on Yan's face. It looked like it actually hurt the man to do it, and it didn't last long.

"Yes, sir. The Americans are resupplying our foreign munitions stocks as quickly as possible. Also, we now have more F-16s than at the war's outset. Clearing debris from missile attacks on our cities is almost complete. Of course, rebuilding both civilian and military structures will take some time. However, I expect the work to proceed quickly," Yan said.

Cheng nodded. "And what about our domestic munitions, particularly drones, but also anti-air and anti-ship missiles?"

"Their performance in this conflict was outstanding. Your approval of my proposed spending increase in this area was vital. Production staff in all areas has been increased. The Ukrainian technicians' assistance was especially valuable. They agreed to stay once their salary was raised by fifty percent," Yan replied.

"The Americans seem to believe that the PRC has accepted their proposal to begin so-called 'cooperation rather than confrontation.' What do your sources on the mainland have to say about that?" Cheng asked.

Yan shrugged. "It is now the official Party line. They failed to conquer us. So, they're telling the populace that they forced the Americans to adopt this new policy. And that this 'victory' justifies the ships, planes, and men they lost. Of course, it helps that the average PRC citizen believes official figures for those losses, which are much lower than the real ones. Also, that no bombs or missiles fell on the mainland."

"Good," Cheng said. "Now, one question I had isn't addressed in any report I've read. About our mysterious benefactors in stopping two attacks. What about my guess that they were American special forces?"

Yan shook his head. "No, sir. I agree that the Americans would have had reason to deny involvement. President Hernandez has been saying from the start that there would be no 'boots on the ground' in Taiwan. Their involvement in stopping those two attacks would have been quite awkward as a domestic political matter. But I'm sure it wasn't them."

"Really?" Cheng said doubtfully. "How can you be so certain?"

"Sir, all the bodies we recovered from the attacks were those of PRC special forces. Ethnicity, equipment, weapons – everything tracked. Except for one. That body was destroyed by two thermite grenades. So little was left of the remains that we couldn't draw any conclusions. Not even whether the person was male or female. Not even enough undamaged material for DNA analysis," Yan said.

Cheng grunted. "I see your point. Not how the Americans would have handled the death of one of their soldiers. Even in a covert operation."

"Yes, sir. More like how, say, the Russians would have dealt with the problem," Yan said.

Cheng's eyebrows flew upwards, and for a moment, he was at a loss for words.

Then he laughed. Slowly at first, but then so hard tears streamed down his face.

It didn't take long for Yan's laughter to join Cheng's.

A few moments later, they both regained control of themselves and shook their heads.

"Thank you. I needed that," Cheng said. "Obviously, the Russians are the last people who would help us. Well, not every mystery has to be solved. I'm sure you have plenty of other problems to keep you occupied."

Yan nodded and said, "Yes, sir. I certainly do."

Chapter Fifty-One

The Kremlin
Moscow, Russia

FSB Director Smyslov made every effort to stand ramrod-straight as he was ushered into the President's office. Partly habit, partly pride. No matter how poor his health had become, a voice in his head insisted that appearances were still necessary.

Even if another voice reminded him that slouching might fit better with the purpose of this visit.

Without even thinking about it, that was a voice he chose to ignore.

The President rushed forward to meet him, a broad smile on his face. "Ah, Director! As always, a pleasure to see you! Come, let us sit."

This was the President's working office, where Smyslov had met him many times. The long, comfortable couch was a familiar sight, as was the set of chairs opposite a handsome table.

No sooner had the President waved Smyslov to the couch than a man entered the office pushing a cart groaning with the weight of food, tea, and vodka bottles.

"Who else is coming?" Smyslov asked.

The President laughed. "Just us. I've heard you've been a bit under the weather and can see you've lost some weight. I've decided to apply the most effective traditional Russian cure- good food and drink. I know you have something to discuss. But whatever it is can wait until we've done justice to the efforts of my best cooks. And as you know, that is saying something!"

It was true. His official salary might be laughable. Despite it, the President might be rumored to be the wealthiest man in Russia. Nobody but the President himself knew if that was true.

But the power of his office meant that nobody could outbid the Russian President when it came to getting what or who he wanted.

As usual, the President was right. Smyslov had thought the food he'd eaten before as the President's guest had been excellent. But this was another level altogether.

Why?

Once they had finished eating and drinking strong black tea, the President reached for one of the vodka bottles. Its label was one Smyslov had never seen before.

As he poured shots for each of them, the President said, "I'd like to save you some time, my dear friend. I think I know why you've come to see me."

Smyslov's eyebrows flew upward. He had said nothing to anyone. How could the President possibly know?

"I said earlier that you were a bit under the weather. You've made no secret of that but have worked harder than ever. Exactly what I would expect of the man I picked to replace me as FSB Director," the President said with a smile.

Smyslov did his best to return the smile, but it wasn't easy. His murmured thanks broadened the President's smile.

"But we are all human. We all have limits. You feel you have reached yours. And so, you are here to give me your letter of resignation," the President said.

Even though the letter weighed next to nothing, Smyslov now felt like he was carrying a large stone in his jacket pocket.

It was exactly as the President had said.

But Smyslov had typed the letter at home, using an old mechanical typewriter, just before coming to see the President. He always locked the typewriter ribbon in a safe with a combination he had picked. The safe was supposed to be impossible to open without an explosive charge strong enough to destroy any of its contents.

Was there a hidden camera in his home that he and his trusted technicians had somehow missed?

Looking at the President's smile, Smyslov realized the answer was much more straightforward. They had known each other for a long time.

Like any good agent – or former agent – the President had deduced what Smyslov would do in his current situation.

Taking Smyslov's silence as acknowledgment, the President continued.

"Now, I applaud you for hiring private doctors outside Moscow for your care. Good security practice. After all, our enemies can be counted on to keep tabs on the FSB Director. You will be happy to hear that none of them, as far as I can tell, have any idea how serious your health problems have become. That includes the Americans," the President said.

Smyslov was pleased. He'd gone to a lot of trouble and expense to keep his medical issues private.

But he should have known that no secrets like this could be kept from the President.

"Now, was that the only matter you wished to discuss, or was there something else?" the President asked.

"Just one favor to ask," Smyslov said.

"Very well, but it will have to be a small one. You do remember that you used the big one on your agent Grishkov just a short time ago," the President replied with a smile.

"That is true," Smyslov said, returning the smile. "But this is more in the way of redeeming a promise, one made long ago. Do you recall what I asked when you appointed me as FSB Director?"

The President frowned and sat back. "When I appointed you," he slowly repeated. "I don't think..."

Then his eyes widened. "Do you really intend to hold me to that?"

Smyslov shrugged and said, "Let me tell you who I propose as my replacement and the logic behind it. Then, of course, as President, it is always your decision."

"Fair enough," the President said, curiosity evident in his voice.

"First, we must eliminate all female agents from consideration. A pity since that rules out Alina, who I thought otherwise would have made an excellent candidate," Smyslov said.

"Agreed, on both counts," the President said, nodding. "Women are almost always too emotional and unreliable. And the men won't follow a female agent, not even one as good as Alina."

Smyslov nodded as well, but inside, he was groaning. This was one of the many reasons Russia had failed to reach its true potential. Women had advanced further and faster in law, science, education, and medicine than in almost any other country during the Soviet days.

But government? No.

And after the USSR's collapse, Russian attitudes toward women in the workplace had also started to slide backward in other areas. Now, the government favored women having children and staying home to raise them.

Never mind that few women listened, and Russia's population continued to decline.

"Next, I think we both agree that the Director must have served as a field agent. More, that his reputation for mission success must be outstanding," Smyslov said.

The President nodded vigorously. "Agreed again. That led the long list of reasons I selected you, after all."

Smyslov lowered his head to acknowledge the compliment and continued.

"There are many capable agents who are either themselves or by their parents from former Soviet republics. But for the Director, only a full-blooded, native-born Russian will do," Smyslov said.

The President's eyebrows arched upward in surprise. "Agreed most emphatically. I must say, though, I didn't know you felt that way about our ex-Soviet cousins."

Smyslov shrugged and said, "They're fine for almost any job. Especially for missions in those former Soviet republics, they're often indispensable. But they cannot become Director."

This had nothing to do with how Smyslov actually felt. But he was headed toward a goal, and the process of elimination was the easiest way to get there.

"Very well," the President said. "Is that all?"

Smyslov shook his head. "One more qualification. The Director must be experienced, but not too old. You need someone mature but vigorous enough to stand up to the stress of the job. Especially, you don't want to be faced with appointing another Director within a year or two of naming my successor."

"All very sensible criteria," the President said. "I can see you have drastically limited the number of candidates. As a result of your lead team's last mission, Evgeny is dead, and though Vasilyev survived, he will need months of physical therapy. Neda Rhahbar and Vidya Kapoor are both foreign-born and women. Alina is not only female; I doubt in her current state she'd want the job."

Smyslov nodded. "Alina took Evgeny's death hard. I've been to see Alina twice since her return and think she'll eventually return to duty. Even then, though, I agree she wouldn't want such a high-stress position."

"I've already approved Anatoly Grishkov's retirement. Thinking through the record of your other teams, few members have the outstanding performance record you rightly seek. So, who is left?" the President asked.

"Kharlov," Smyslov said.

If Smyslov had seen the President surprised before, now a better word would be "astonished."

"Seriously? A Spetsnaz deserter who then became a warlord in pre-invasion Ukraine? Yes, he does meet all the other criteria you laid out. But surely his years pre-FSB disqualify him from consideration!" the President exclaimed.

Smyslov shook his head. "Not if you explain to the other FSB agents that Kharlov was a deep-cover agent acting at your direction. The files already document that Kharlov fed us information and carried out small tasks for us while in Ukraine. And that he saved the life of an FSB agent in Ukraine at considerable risk to his own. Like most successful lies, this one will have an element of truth."

The President frowned and then sank into deep thought for several moments.

Smyslov knew him well enough to remain completely still.

Then the President looked up. "Very well. I will speak with him. If Kharlov answers my questions correctly, you may get your wish."

The President rose, quickly followed by Smyslov.

Then the President walked Smyslov out of his office, draping his arm around Smyslov's shoulders.

"I'm sorry to see you go, my old friend. May I still call on you in the future when I need your wise counsel?" the President asked.

"Of course," Smyslov said with a smile.

Inside, though, his heart sank. Smyslov had hoped to be completely free of the stress of leading the FSB.

Well, if his doctors were to be believed, at least Smyslov wouldn't have to deal with that stress much longer.

Chapter Fifty-Two

Six Months Later
Saint Paul de Vence, France

Arisha stood near Grishkov. Her hands were on her hips in a pose that had become familiar to Grishkov since his retirement to this small village just north of Nice.

"So, you have the list I gave you yesterday?" Arisha asked.

"Yes, dear," Grishkov replied, fighting to keep any trace of emotion out of his response.

Apparently, he hadn't done a very good job because Arisha scowled immediately.

"When do you plan to start?" Arisha asked.

"Right away," Grishkov said, leaving as fast as he could through the front door.

Heavily armed foreign terrorists. Rogue nuclear weapons. Grishkov had never fled from any of those threats.

But his wife, irate at Grishkov's failure to do his gardening chores as quickly as she wished?

Full reverse, he thought with a small smile.

Of course, Grishkov still loved Arisha very much. But retirement life had been...an adjustment.

Grishkov looked around at the front garden in full springtime bloom. Arisha handled all the delicate work of keeping everything growing and ready for display.

But there was plenty that required brute force, not a green thumb. Weed pulling. Leaf collection. The list went on.

And on.

The garage door was open. Inside, Grishkov knew he would find a collection of garden tools with which he had become very familiar.

Grishkov was willing to do the work. He was certainly able.

No, it was just so...boring.

Grishkov knew better than to suggest paying someone to take his place. First, no matter how much they had in the bank now – and they had plenty – Arisha would see it as an unforgivable waste of money.

More importantly, Grishkov knew that Arisha wanted him to do the work for two other reasons. To give him something useful to do. And to get him out of the house and out of her hair.

Well, Grishkov sighed, I've had enough excitement to last two lifetimes. Time to start on the list.

Grishkov was halfway on the short walk to the garage when he saw the man. With the practiced eye of an ex-policeman, he drew several conclusions almost at once.

The man was French. Grishkov could not say how he was so sure. But after six months living in France, Grishkov thought he could tell.

He was not one of the criminals to be found in even the smallest villages. And though it was not large, Saint Paul de Vence was far from the smallest.

The man was middle-aged, and his pallor said he probably spent most of his time at a desk.

But he was remarkably fit despite that fact. Maybe someone who had led a more active life until recently?

Grishkov could see no sign that the man was hiding a gun or other weapon in his clothing. Still, many weapons were small enough to conceal from even the most practiced eye.

So Grishkov was still wary as the man walked up the driveway to his house.

"Monsieur Grishkov, I believe?" the man asked in lightly accented English. In a pleasant voice.

Grishkov nodded. "And you are?" he asked in a tone that, while not hostile, was not particularly welcoming.

The man smiled. "Please call me Jacques. Here is my identification."

With that, Jacques handed Grishkov a slim leather case enclosing a laminated ID card. It had been issued by the Direction générale de la Sécurité extérieure, or DGSE.

Even if Grishkov hadn't heard of it before, he would have had no trouble using his knowledge of English to translate that to General Directorate for External Security.

The French version of the FSB. Or, more accurately, the CIA.

Not just because the DGSE was a Western intelligence agency. But, because the FSB had responsibilities both inside and outside Russia.

The DGSE, like the CIA, was supposed to operate only in foreign countries.

"Should that mean something to me?" Grishkov said, handing Jacques back his ID.

Jacques' smile broadened. "Come, Monsieur Grishkov, let's not waste time. I know that you are a former homicide detective who went on to perform many impressive missions for the FSB. You are now retired and living here with your wife. Your two sons are going to university in Paris. Where their grades so far have been excellent."

Grishkov's face darkened. "I'll thank you for not speaking about my family since I don't know you or anything about you. Your information is incorrect. I am a retired Russian police officer, nothing more. All I know about the FSB is what I've seen in movies. So, if you want something from me, please say it and then be on your way."

Jacques softly clapped his hands. Hands, Grishkov noticed, not as soft and manicured as he would have expected from a bureaucrat.

Yes, his earlier impression had been correct. This man had spent most of his life as a field agent.

"Very good," Jacques said. "If you had admitted to being a former FSB agent, our conversation would have been over. As it is, I will make my proposal short and to the point. The French government requires your assistance with a matter of national security."

"Why me?" Grishkov asked.

"For several reasons, you have been identified as a necessary team member in stopping a planned attack on a French city," Jacques replied. "If you agree, your role will be explained in more detail. Of course, you will be well compensated for your time."

"And if I don't agree?" Grishkov asked with a scowl.

Jacques shrugged. "Are you familiar with the story of the so-called 'ghost train' in Paris?"

Grishkov shook his head.

"A new Parisian subway line was built in 1998, requiring no driver to operate the trains. Very expensive, and not at all necessary. Except that the transit union's strikes had annoyed the government. The ghost train was a message. Stop annoying us, or suffer the consequences," Jacques said.

"Did the transit unions listen?" Grishkov asked.

"No, not really," Jacques replied. "Perhaps as a result, more driverless trains have been introduced. Soon, the conversion of the entire Paris metro system to driverless will be complete."

"So, if I refuse, the French government will find a way to make me regret it," Grishkov said.

Jacques shrugged again. "First, please believe that I don't like to make threats. I am merely informing you of certain realities that apply to you in this situation, as I have been instructed to do. However, in one respect, I have decided to disobey my instructions. Because you strike me as a man who will respond poorly to threats."

Grishkov frowned. "Disobey your instructions? What do you mean?"

"I am supposed to tell you no details of the threat until you agree to join us in trying to stop it," Jacques replied. "But, I have decided to ask you a related question. Which city do you think a terrorist would pick to attack France?"

"Paris," Grishkov replied immediately.

And then let his breath out with a hiss.

"Where both of my sons are attending university," Grishkov said bitterly.

Both men were quiet for a moment.

"A weapon of mass destruction, I suppose?" Grishkov asked.

"Given your mission background, that would be a reasonable assumption for why we might be interested in you," Jacques said.

Grishkov shook his head with resignation. "You understand that I must clear this with Russian authorities," he said.

"But of course," Jacques said. "FSB Director Kharlov is awaiting your call."

"How long do I have to make that call and explain all this to my wife?" Grishkov asked.

"All afternoon," Jacques replied. "A military transport is on standby to transport you to the mission location. I can give you no more details while we stand in your garden. I can say, though, that the flight will take only a few hours."

Either North Africa or Eastern Europe, Grishkov thought to himself.

Aloud, he said, "And when I am ready to go?"

Jacques smiled. "Just walk outside your door. Within moments, I will be there to pick you up. And give you some more details before you board your flight."

Grishkov nodded, turned around, and walked back into his house without a backward glance. He was, for the moment, not concerned about the danger of working for a foreign intelligence agency that was completely unfamiliar.

Or yet another mission featuring powerful weapons of some sort. Doubtless guarded by men unwilling to part with them peacefully.

No, Grishkov first had to face a danger greater than all that put together.

Justifying his return to the field to Arisha.

Only the fact that their sons were at risk might give him a chance of success.

Hopefully.

First, thank you very much for reading my book! If you have any questions or comments, please get in touch with me through my blog at https://thesecondkoreanwar.wordpress.com/

I've noted before that this novel is set in a fictional near future like all the others in this series. It's one where Vladimir Putin is no longer the President of Russia.

I've given that fact and the main characters' awareness that the Russian regime they serve is far from perfect as justification for continuing the Russian Agents series even after Putin invaded Ukraine.

But no more. As you have probably guessed if you've read this far, this is the end of the Russian Agents series.

I'm holding over Grishkov, my favorite character, for the new French Agents series. But the – not yet introduced – French characters will take center stage.

My main goal remains the same. To entertain readers while exposing them to something different than the usual American or British viewpoint that dominates English language thrillers.

In part because I find the same perspective all the time boring. But also because I think it's useful to broaden one's point of view. That doesn't mean agreeing with the differing (Russian, French etc.) viewpoint or adopting it as your own.

However, seeing things from a different perspective has many benefits. Better ability to cooperate effectively with an ally. A better chance of success in deterring or defeating an enemy.

Finally, I know many readers will think the victory over Chinese forces achieved in this book is too easy. I urge you to research the impact of Rapid Dragon on forces like China's that will have no effective counter. Many previous wargames featuring Taiwan have ended with either Chinese victory or American victory at a terrible cost.

Not once Rapid Dragon is included.

A more debatable point is whether China would avoid violating Japanese territory on sea and air after what I think are likely strikes on American forces in Okinawa.

In the end, though, I think it's a wash. Either America gets a haven for its forces, as in the book. Or China keeps striking targets within Japan.

And Japanese forces join us in pushing Chinese naval and air assets back to the mainland.

Japan already possesses one of the world's largest and most technically advanced military forces. Consider what a few years of accelerated military spending will mean for Japanese forces.

Again, this book is set in the near future.

Then, decide whether China would be willing to risk fighting Japan, America, and Taiwan.

Thanks again for reading my book, and I hope you will enjoy the next one in 2024!

Cast of Characters

Alphabetical Order by Nationality
Most Important Characters in Bold

Chinese Citizens
Admiral Bai, the Navy Commander
Colonel Chang, officer assigning Sergeant Xu to mission in Taiwan
Senior Captain Ding, Admiral Bai's representative on the invasion fleet
President Gu
Ambassador Jian, United Nations Headquarters, New York City
General Shi, the Army Commander
Captain Song, invasion fleet commander
Lieutenant Tan, flight leader, Aircraft Carrier *Fujian*
Lieutenant Xu, sniper assigned to mission in Taiwan
General Zhao, the Air Force Commander

Taiwanese Citizens
President Cheng
Captain Mike Han, Commander, 4th Tactical Fighter Wing
First Lieutenant Jiro Kuo, Han's wingman
National Security Bureau Director-General Yan

Russian Citizens
Alina, FSB Senior Field Agent
Evgeny, FSB Field Director
Anatoly Grishkov, FSB agent, former Vladivostok homicide detective
Vidya Kapoor, FSB Agent, former Indian citizen
Boris Kharlov, FSB agent, ex-separatist Ukrainian warlord
Neda Rhahbar, FSB agent, former Iranian citizen
Sergei, Rosoboronexport agent in Myanmar, former employee of **Kharlov**
FSB Director Smyslov
Mikhail Vasilyev, FSB agent

Japanese Citizens
Haruto Takahashi, JSDF Crewman
Kaito Watanabe, JSDF AWACS Commander
Prime Minister Kan
Former Prime Minister Yoshida

Korean Citizens
Colonel Kim, 38th Fighter Group commander

American Citizens
Tom Burke, TACMOR Director, Palau
Captain Jim Cartwright, commanding submarine *USS Silversides*
Captain Dobbins, commanding submarine *USS Reno*
Lieutenant Colonel Frank Drake, commanding 67th Fighter Squadron, Kadena Air Base, Japan
Lieutenant Commander Fischer, Executive Officer, *USS Silversides*
Lieutenant Colonel Dave Fitzpatrick, commanding 44th Fighter Squadron, Kadena Air Base, Japan
President Hernandez
Sam Holt, TACMOR Deputy Director, Palau
Captain Mercer, commanding *USS America*
Captain Parker, Patriot battery commander, Palau
General Robinson, Air Force Chief of Staff
Mark Rooter, SpaceLink project manager
Captain Mark Ross, commanding RC-135U flight off the Chinese coast
Commander Tyler, Executive Officer, *USS America*
Eli Wade, SpaceLink CEO

Printed in Great Britain
by Amazon